TEMPTATION
the aftermath

A NOVEL

Victoria Christopher Murray

BROWN GIRLS BOOKS

Houston, Texas * Washington, D.C.

Temptation: The Aftermath
© 2017 by Victoria Christopher Murray
Brown Girls Publishing, LLC

www.BrownGirlsBooks.com

ISBN: 978–1–944359–58–4 (Digital)
978–1–944359–59–1 (Paperback)

First Brown Girls Publishing LLC trade printing

Manufactured and Printed in the United States of America

chapter 1

Jasmine Cox Larson Bush

The coffee pot slipped from my hand, crashed to the floor, but made no sound. I didn't hear anything because the image on the television screen was louder than any noise.

"Jasmine!"

I heard Hosea's shout and I even comprehended that he'd called my name, but there was no way I could respond. The shock kept me silent.

"Darlin'!" Now, my husband stood in front of me. "What's going on?"

It was only when his hand touched my shoulder that I was able to step out of my fog. But I did it only with movements, because still, I had no words. I lifted my arm and pointed to the television that was perched on the kitchen counter.

Hosea picked up the remote and aimed it at the TV, increasing the volume.

"The perpetrators of this, what's come to be known as a flash rob, are still at large," the NBC reporter holding the mic spoke to the camera. She was standing in front of Harlem Hospital and a 'Breaking News' banner was across the bottom of the screen. "But the police chief said that while there were dozens of teens who entered the store, they have no doubt they will find the shooter and the others and bring them to justice."

The television screen switched shots, this time moving to an image of New York's police commissioner, Ted Hardwood, standing in front of a podium and facing a gaggle of reporters.

"We want to insure the citizens of New York and all visitors that our city is safe. Crime, especially violent crime is way down, and it is unfortunate that this happened during the American Medical Association convention, one of the largest conventions to come to New York. We also want to let the family of Doctor Jefferson Blake know that we will use all of our resources to find the shooter and everyone involved. And we're sending Doctor Blake's family our thoughts and prayers."

Now, Hosea stood as still as I was as the screen switched back to the news anchor.

"There is one last thing, Kristen," the reporter spoke to the anchor in the newsroom. "This morning, the police are reporting that they're looking for a potential witness who may be able to identify the shooter. The manager of the bodega said that Doctor Blake came into the store with a woman and the police are searching for her to get more information about ...."

The sound faded as Hosea, once again, used the remote and this time, quieted the television. He set the remote on the table, then turned to me. I knew that he wanted an explanation. His questions weren't verbal, though; he interrogated me with his eyes.

Finally, I was able to squeak out, "I know him." I paused to give my brain time to compute. "I know Doctor Blake." Another pause. "Jefferson Blake." And then another. "Jefferson."

"Really?" Hosea said. "Wow! I saw the news I guess just minutes after it happened."

I tilted my head. "You saw it? When?" My voice was still shaky.

"Last night. It was a breaking story."

"Why didn't you say anything?"

"First, it was after midnight and you were asleep and second, I had no idea you knew this dude." He paused and glanced at the TV once again. "So, you know him? Like know-know him or just know *of* him?"

The way Hosea asked that question brought back a flood of

memories. Of that time with Dr. Jefferson Blake. Of that time when I knew this man in the truest sense, the biblical sense. Of that time when I slept with my best friend's husband.

Hosea was giving me that look again, that glance that was filled with questions. "I ... know ... know him." That was my way of telling the truth, I guess, without actually telling the truth. I took a breath. "Yes, I know him. I know him ... well."

There were more questions in his eyes as I grabbed the remote, then clicked off the television. Then sinking down onto one of the kitchen chairs, I fixed my elbows to the table and held my head in my hands.

"Jefferson was shot." That wasn't a question, just a statement. That wasn't for Hosea, just for me.

Hosea crouched down, picked up the coffee pot and returned it to the counter before he sat next to me. "Who is he?"

"He was ... I mean, he is ... married to a woman who used to be my best friend. He's married to Kyla."

The mention of her name brought a new shock to my mind. "Oh, my God." I looked up and into Hosea's eyes. "Kyla was with him. Maybe the guy who shot Jefferson kidnapped Kyla. Oh, my God." I jumped up.

"Darlin' wait. Slow down. Don't make up a story in your head."

"But you heard them." I pointed to the television. "They said that he was with a woman. The only woman that he would have been with that late at night is his wife."

"Last night, the news said he was from California here for a convention."

I nodded and spoke as fast as I paced. "He's a doctor, a pulmonary specialist. One of the best in his field. But Kyla must have come to New York with him."

"Kyla." He said her name, blinked a few times, then paused. "Well, if she was with him, she would have stayed with him, right?"

"That's my point." I stopped moving. "Kyla was with him, but now she's not. That must mean ...." I pressed my hands to my lips. "Oh, my God. She's been kidnapped."

Hosea stood and pressed his hands on my shoulders. "Jasmine, you've made a big leap to this conclusion."

"But you heard the police."

"I did. So, let's find out for sure. Why don't you call Kyla?"

I nodded. "Okay." I moved toward the kitchen's entrance, already planning the next move in my mind. But I'd only taken a couple of steps before I slowed, then stopped, then turned back.

He frowned.

"I don't have her number." Those words, that thought made me sad. Even though I had spoken to Kyla only once in almost twenty years, she was still the one person on this earth that I'd known longer than anyone with the exception of my sister. Meeting in kindergarten back in Los Angeles made it so.

But then, there were the twenty years of silence that had come between us because of my transgression. My sin with her husband. When I'd done all that I could to get her husband to take me to bed. And when I'd succeeded at that, I'd done all that I could to take over her life. Before I had my own.

The memory of who I used to be made me shudder. "I don't think …."

"What?"

"That I have her number … anymore." Then, I added with surety, "I don't have her number." I *was* sure of that. The last time I'd had her number, we were using flip phones that had no screens. And once I'd moved from Los Angeles to Pensacola in 1997, I'd deleted her number, knowing that I'd never want to speak to her again since she had ruined my life by not giving up hers.

But, I wanted to speak to her now.

Hosea nodded, and I was surprised he didn't ask me more — like why didn't I have her number if I once called her a best friend? But all he said was, "Well, let's do a search. On the Internet. Maybe her number will be there."

In an instant, my husband took over. As he moved from the kitchen into the hallway, he said, "Kyla and Jefferson Blake." He stated their names as if he knew them; still, I told him he was correct.

I followed him up the stairs and into the office where, with determination and deliberation, he sat behind the desk, clicked a few keys, grunted a few times, then scrolled through a few pages.

Behind him, I paced, willing myself to keep the images of Kyla tied up in some long ago forgotten warehouse from my mind. But I couldn't stop myself. I closed my eyes and my mental pictures became even clearer. I saw Kyla bound and gagged, maybe even beaten. By the time my husband finally said something, I was ready to run to the bank and withdraw all that we had to pay the ransom.

Hosea said, "The only thing that I found is the African American Complete Wellness Medical Center."

My husband's words dragged me away from the story in my mind. "Yes! That's it," I said, as new memories rushed through my mental banks. In that moment, another flash from the past: the two-story futuristic-looking building with its all-white interior.

"I have a number, but," he glanced down at his watch, "it's just after three in the morning in LA."

I shook my head and he shrugged. Thank you, God. Once again, I was grateful that Hosea hadn't asked me the next logical question: if Kyla Jefferson was my best friend, why didn't I have her number?

"Well," he began, "all we can do is wait until the clinic opens."

"No." I paused, feeling helpless, feeling almost now, like I was about to cry. "I just have a really bad feeling, Hosea. I have a feeling that Kyla is in trouble and we may be the only ones who can help her."

He nodded. "All right. Look, let's do this first. Let's get up to Harlem Hospital and see what we can find out. Maybe Kyla is there. Or maybe there'll be someone there who can give us some information. Then, we can go to the police."

"All right." We stood together and I wrapped my arms around my husband. "Thank you," I said.

"I'm going to schedule an Uber. How long will you be?"

"Give me twenty minutes. Can you check on the kids and tell Mrs. Sloss that we're leaving?"

"Definitely."

I dashed from the office and down the stairs into our bedroom suite. I had shed my bathrobe before I even hit the heated floor of our master bath. Inside the shower, I turned the water to full blast and as I stood under the shower's rain, my thoughts traveled through my years of friendship with Kyla. It was more than friendship really; we'd been sisters. Closer even sometimes than me and Serena since Kyla and I were the same age. Second to Mae Frances, there was no one who I had loved more dearly who didn't share my DNA.

The years had separated me from what I'd done, though the time that had passed had done little to assuage my guilt. But maybe I could make up for all that I'd done then, by saving Kyla's life now. And with that thought, I jumped out of the shower.

chapter 2

Kyla Blake

"Okay, sweetheart, I promise," I said to my daughter in a tone that was much steadier than I felt.

"Mom."

Her soft, but shaky voice almost broke me. I pressed the tips of my fingers to my lips, praying that move alone would hold back the sobs that threatened to force their way forward. It took a moment for me to be able to say, "I know, sweetheart. You're scared. And so am I."

"I just wish that I could be there with you," she cried.

"I know." It took all that I had to hold myself together. I wanted to fall apart, right here on this airplane. But I had to stay strong — first for Nicole. "But you'll get here when you can. And I'll call you the moment I land in New York. The moment … I see your dad."

"Is he going to be all right?" She sounded like she was five instead of thirty.

"Yes," I said with the same kind of surety that I used to give my daughter when Jefferson and I would go into her room every night to make sure there were no monsters hiding under her bed. This morning, though, I needed those same assurances. I needed someone to tell me that this monster of a nightmare wasn't real.

"Okay." Nicole's voice was stronger now than it'd been in each of my three calls to her since last night. It was as if my words became her gospel — something in which she could believe. "You're right. Dad will fight for us. But Mom, what about you? Are you going to be okay?"

"Sweetheart, nothing can happen to me. I'm on the airplane, I'll catch a cab as soon as I land and I'll be at the hospital the whole time. I'll be fine."

"Don't take a cab. Uber over. They can track you."

I chuckled for the first time since I'd received the call about Jefferson. "Okay," I told my daughter. At any other time, this would have turned into a good-natured battle. *You think you're the boss of me?* I would have asked.

But now, I acquiesced because Nicole needed to be in charge of something. She needed to take care of me so that I could take care of her dad.

"And send me your map from Uber when you get in the car."

"You're in Beijing, what are you going to do if the driver decides to kidnap me?"

"Mom, just do it, okay?" There was no patience in her tone.

"Okay, sweetheart."

"I just hate that you're going to be alone."

I hated that part, too. But there were few choices when quick decisions had to be made. "Not alone. I'll be with your dad."

In her next words, I heard her smile. "You're right. Even unconscious, he's going to take care of you. The way he always has."

Now, I smiled through the tears in my eyes. "Yes, we're going to take care of each other."

The flight attendant's voice interrupted my conversation. Told me that the plane's doors had been closed. "I have to turn off my phone."

"Okay, Mom."

"Try to get some sleep," I said, used to the time difference now. Her Tuesday was ending as mine was beginning.

"Are you kidding me?"

"Just try."

Then, together we said, "I love you," and added, "Me, too," in chorus as well.

I clicked off my phone, closed my eyes and pressed the phone to my chest, feeling just a bit closer to my daughter with that move.

Then, I leaned back, but I didn't do what I always did as the plane edged away from the gate, then cruised down the runway. I didn't close my eyes. I wanted to be awake because my prayer was that somehow my conscience would connect with Jefferson's. Through some kind of mental telepathy or osmosis that came with the love we shared, I had to let him know that I was on my way.

So, though I leaned against the leather headrest, I kept my eyes opened and focused my thoughts, praying they would travel the three thousand miles to Jefferson.

"Hang in there, baby," I whispered.

As the plane rounded the tarmac and the hotels on Century Boulevard came into my view, I sent a special thank you to the Lord for finally being on this flight. It had been too many hours since I got that call. Too many hours since I'd heard: "Kyla, it's Jefferson … he's been hurt …."

As I remembered Travis's call now, what I couldn't remember was when had my heart started pounding? Was it when I heard the shaking in Travis's voice? Or had my heart already been pounding before I even answered just because the phone rang at 1:11 in the morning?

"He's been hurt. Jefferson was shot. Tonight. At a store. In Washington Heights."

Really, I was surprised that I remembered that many words. Because after I'd heard — Jefferson was shot — my mind could focus on only one thought:

Please God. Please let Jefferson be alive. Please God.

He was alive, Travis told me. Alive, but already in surgery.

My husband was in surgery because he'd been shot in the head inside a store in Washington Heights — wherever that was.

It was difficult for me to make sense of those words.

Please God. Please let Jefferson be alive. Please God.

That had been my prayer for the five hours since I'd spoken to Travis. That had been my prayer when I jumped out of the bed, my prayer when I got on my knees, then, my prayer as I searched the Internet for the first flight that would take me to my husband.

That h ad b een m y p rayer w hen I c alled N icole (for t he fi rst time) and then, reached out to the person who'd always been my strength.

Not even twenty minutes had passed from the moment I dialed and then sobbed into the phone, "Alexis, I need you," before she and Brian were busting through my front door with the key we'd given them for emergencies:

"*Kyla!*"

I heard the tears in Alexis's voice before I rounded the corner from the kitchen. But by the time I stood in front of my best friend, there was no sign of sorrow, just her signature strength.

She grabbed me in a hug that let me know she would always be there, just like she'd been for more than thirty years. Then, she stepped back and with her hands on my shoulders, she said, "Jefferson is going to be all right."

That was a command for me to believe. And I gave a nod to my friend before Brian pulled me into his arms for a hug.

He said, "I really wish you'd let one of us go with you to New York."

Before the last word was out of his mouth, I shook my head. "No, I'll be all right. I really need you here." Turning to Alexis, I said, "I'm so grateful that you'll stay with Mom."

"Of course. She's my mom, too."

That made me pause for just a moment. That was something that Jefferson always said.

I faced Brian again. "Jefferson will really need you at the clinic because we don't know …." I had to pause for air. "We don't know how long he'll be away."

He gave me a long stare, then a short nod, as if he knew that I was right, but he still didn't agree. "I hate it because Travis won't even be there when you land."

I nodded. "He wanted to cancel his trip to Guatemala, but Jefferson wouldn't want that. You guys do such good work down there, and there's nothing that Travis can do for Jefferson in New York."

It didn't seem like I was moving Brian at all.

So, I added, "And I won't be alone for long; Nicole will fly in as soon as she can."

"You spoke to her?" Alexis asked as she took my hand and led me into the living room.

"I did," I said right before I sat on the sofa. Alexis dropped down next to me. "I was just glad that I didn't have to wake her in the middle of the night. She was just about to leave the embassy. Which helped a little .... I think." I shook my head. "I'd rather call her at work than have to wake her in the middle of the night when she's six thousand miles away."

"All right, then," Alexis began. "So, what do you need me to do?" She didn't take a breath. "You have your flight arrangements; did you pack?" She spoke in a chop-chop kind of tone, taking over like she always did.

"I didn't even think about packing. I don't know what ...."

Before I could finish, Alexis jumped up and as if she were pass-ing me off, Brian sat down. Alexis was on the staircase headed to my bedroom before I could even gather the words to stop her. Not that she would have listened.

Once Alexis was out of sight, Brian took my hand. "Jefferson is going to be all right," he said.

I wasn't quite sure that his words were for me, but I said, "I know," just in case.

He asked, "What about your mom? Did you wake her? Tell her?" I shook my head. "She's going to be so worried and I don't want to put that stress on her heart."

"You can't keep this from her."

"I know. I just didn't want to wake her when there's nothing that she can do. I know this is going to ...." I swallowed back my fear.

Brian squeezed my hand. "Don't worry. Alex and I will tell her in the morning. And she'll be in good hands. Remember, I'm a doctor."

That almost made me smile.

He chuckled. "I mean ophthalmologists are good for something."

*"You're good for everything." The little bit of the smile I felt inside faded and in its place, were more thoughts of my husb*and.

"Brian ... I just want to thank you and Alexis ...."

He shook his head and pulled me into his arms once again. "No thanks necessary. You just go to New York and bring Jefferson home."

And then in the quiet that followed, I said the prayer again ...

Please God ....

Now I sighed, so grateful for what I called my middle-of-the-night friends. That was how I'd always referred to Alexis in the past and she'd proven last night that was who she was, arriving at my door still practically dressed in her pajamas.

I gasped a bit as the plane's wheels bumped off the runway and the jet glided into the air, defying gravity as it headed over the Pacific Ocean before making its U-turn, taking me East to where I needed to be.

It had surely taken long enough. At around two this morning, I began to wonder if walking was an option. Anything to get to my husband.

My husband, my wonderful husband. The man who'd already been wonderful when we'd met all of those years ago ...

I felt like I was going to die from the suffocating heat. Even now, outside on the porch, I felt waves of all of that warmth threatening to smother me here, too.

"Some party, huh?"

Turning around, I had to squint through the darkness to focus on the mocha-skinned brother dressed in red and white fraternity paraphernalia. He swaggered toward me and then sloped against the outside wall.

"Yeah." I nodded. "A little hot, though."

"I like things hot," he said with a half-smile ....

I'd had a half-smile then, but I was full-out grinning now re-membering that time at the Back-to-Campus party at the Kappa Alpha Psi House on Queen Street, right off of Hampton's campus. He'd told me his name, then asked mine before he serenaded me as if he were the lead singer of the Ohio Players ....

"Fire! Fire! The way you walk and talk really sets me off to a full alarm ... "

I sighed, remembering the way he'd sang, then told me that I was gonna be his wife. We had never seen each other on cam-pus before, but he'd spoken that line with more than the usual male upperclassman bravado. He'd spoken with almost a divine certainty...

"Oh yeah – you're gonna be my wife."

"You don't even know my name." I chuckled.

"Okay, wife, tell me your name."

I stepped closer to him, just so he knew that I wasn't intimidated by all of his testosterone. "My name is Kyla. Kyla Carrington."

He brought the beer can that he held to his lips, took a swig, then said, "That's all I need to know. The rest I'll learn over the lifetime of our long and happy marriage."

It was only because I wanted to show him that I had toe-to-toe capabilities, that I said, "So, Jefferson, if we're going to be married, don't you think I should know your last name?"

"Is that a yes? Does that mean you will marry me?"

I laughed ....

That had been only our first laugh together and we'd had a billion more of those moments. And we'd shared so many other amazing times, too:

Like the way he'd been the one standing at the altar with tears coursing down his face on the day when we really did marry and we held hands in front of Pastor Ford.

"I now pronounce you man and wife. Jefferson, you may ...."

Our pastor didn't even have a chance to finish before his lips were on mine, lingering in the gentlest, longest kiss we'd ever shared.

I would always remember that moment, especially since our journey to the altar hadn't been the easiest road ever taken. From the moment our first date had come to an end, that's our struggle began...

"This was really nice, I had a good time," I told him.

His smile was huge as he leaned against the doorpost to my room, then moved in for the kiss. I kissed him, so pleased that it was a gentle meeting of our lips. But then, he tried to probe his tongue further and I knew I had to stop.

"I think we should end this now."

"Really?" His voice was husky, but he sounded a bit amused. "I was thinking that I could come in."

I shook my head. "I don't think so."

He leaned back and frowned. "I thought you said your roommate was away for the weekend."

"She is."

"Well," he returned his hands to my waist. "I figured we'd have some private time."

I kept my smile even though I knew we were coming to the hard part. I'd been here before … and I'd sent more than my share of guys running.

I said, "There's something you should know."

"You talk too much." He kissed my neck and I trembled. "Because whatever you have to say isn't what I want to know."

It was so hard concentrating when his lips felt so good against my …. "I don't do this."

His frown was so deep, I hoped he wouldn't give himself a headache. Then, he grinned, like he was sure my words were a joke. But I swiped that smile away with the words, "I'm a virgin."

His hands dropped from me so fast, I really couldn't say that I saw him move. "Uh … well …."

I laughed. "That's exactly what everyone says."

"Uh … well … I should say …."

He stopped like he didn't have any other words. So, I filled in the blanks for him. "Good night?"

"Yeah … uh … well … good night."

I stood there, watching him walk away. Those were not new words for me, but this was the first time those words hurt because I liked Jefferson and I knew what would happen next. Like the others, Jefferson would see me in the cafeteria and look the other way. He'd see me on the street and cross to the other side. Being a virgin was like having the world's worst contagious disease — no one wanted to catch virginity.

But Jefferson hadn't left me alone. No one even needed that feather to knock me over when he called a few days later and asked me out again. He'd interrogated me on our next date, boldly ques-tioning my motives as if what I'd told him was some kind of game. I explained it to him simply, explained that I was a Christian who'd kept the celibacy vow I'd made at thirteen.

Of course, Jefferson gave me all the lines that I'd heard before: it had been a long time since I was thirteen — things and times had changed — in the Bible, God wasn't talking about the twentieth century — the Lord certainly wasn't talking about us.

Of course, he hadn't been able to convince me, but what was shocking was that I had changed him. He still called me, even though after our second date, it wasn't very often. Until it became more often, until it became exclusive, until we fell in love.

But not even love could change my mind. Nothing could do that, not love, not pressure, not temptation.

"Jefferson, as much as I love you, I love God more."

It had been a battle, though I wasn't just clashing with Jefferson. I'd been fighting my own flesh, too, because Jefferson Blake was hot. Period. It was hard not to give in to the walking temptation that he was.

But then, our wedding night …

"Mrs. Blake, what would you like to drink?"

The first-class flight attendant startled me away from the memory of the consummation of our marriage. I'd been so into it, I had to shift in my seat.

I really needed some coffee since I hadn't been asleep. That was what I told her, but then I added, "And a glass of water, please. With ice."

Less than two minutes later as I took alternating sips of cof-fee and water, I stayed on this stroll down this single lane of my memory. Because I only wanted to think about this man who had been my dream.

We'd had so many amazing moments in these years. From the best of times to the worst. There was the way he leaned over and kissed me just moments after Nicole's birth. There was so much love in his watery eyes when he said:

"Kyla, you have given me the greatest gift, the most beautiful gift. And I will always love you. Both of you."

Then, there was the way he held my mom right after my dad passed away and she was trembling with grief and fear:

"We will take care of you, Mom. You don't have to worry; we will always be here. Because you're my mom, too."

I pressed back the tear that had pooled in the corner of my eye. There was no way that I could lose this man who made my heart beat. He was a giant among men, my partner in our perfect marriage.

Perfect.

Except.

For that one time.

For that one thing.

Except.

For Jasmine Cox Larson.

I shook my head. Why had I allowed that devil to pop into my mind? There was no reason for me to even think about that single betrayal by Jefferson. No reason to think about that scar on our otherwise decades of ecstasy.

Decades.

God, that was not enough.

I needed more. I needed a century, a millennium. I needed a million lifetimes.

That was why I closed my eyes. And began to pray.

Please God, please God, please God!

chapter 3

Jasmine

All kinds of thoughts were swirling through my mind. Kyla had been kidnapped, Kyla was still lying in the store away from the eyes of the police, Kyla had been dazed and was walking around New York scared and lost.

As if my husband heard my brain at work, he reached across the backseat of the car and squeezed my hand.

I was sure Hosea was wondering about the burden I was carrying. How could I be so concerned about a woman I hadn't spoken to in twenty years?

But Kyla wasn't an ordinary woman. And neither was our friendship from the moment we met ....

It was the first day of school and I wasn't sure yet, but I think I hated it. I didn't want to play with these kids. The girls were silly and the boys wouldn't let me play kickball with them.

My baby sister, Serena, was much more fun and she had just been born. She was like a real live babydoll, better than any I'd ever had because she cried for real. And she wet her diaper for real, too. That was fun, so all I wanted to do was go home and play with her.

But then, I saw this little girl leaning against the fence. She had been sitting at the table next to me in the classroom, but now, she was crying for real ... like Serena. When she looked at me, she started crying harder.

"What's wrong with you?" I asked her.

At first she looked like she didn't want to tell me, but then, she pointed to three girls on the other side of the school playground.

"Those girls over there," she hiccupped, "are picking on me." I wondered what was the big deal with that. I shrugged and told her, "So? Just punch them out."

Just remembering the way Kyla's eyes had widened made my lips curl into a smile for the first time since I saw the news an hour ago. Horror was all over her face when she explained that her mother had told her she couldn't do that because Christians would make God mad if they fought.

With all the wisdom of a five-year-old, I told her that her mother didn't know squat and then with all the bravado within me, I marched across the park and threatened those girls, telling them if they wanted to keep their two front teeth they needed to leave that other little girl (I didn't even know her name) alone.

When the teacher called us to go back to the classroom, I grabbed Kyla's hand and dragged her back into the school.

That was how it all started. On that day, a lifelong sisterhood had been born. At least through the years as we got closer, I'd thought it was going to be lifelong.

From that moment, Kyla and I had been through so much, but we'd always been through it together. Through middle school, high school, then college and beyond, next to Kenny (who eventually became my first husband) Kyla had always cheered my celebrations and shared my tears. She held my hand and helped my heart to heal when my mother died, and she'd done the same after my divorce.

But somewhere and somehow right after that, something happened to me. I hurt Kyla — though no one would ever believe me if I told them that had never been my intent. I'd loved her. Truly.

I sighed and Hosea squeezed my hand, making me open my eyes; I didn't even realize I'd closed them. When the car rolled to a stop at the corner of Malcolm X and 135th Street, we thanked the driver and slid from the car. Hosea held my hand as we walked so fast that we were almost trotting into Harlem Hospital. But then, once we stepped inside, Hosea's steps slowed and I knew why.

My husband had to come through these doors so often as a pastor, but there was one time when it was personal, a moment that Hosea always remembered. That time back in 2009 when we'd received the call in the middle of the night — about his father. My father-in-law had been shot, too.

I made sure my steps matched Hosea's until his memories faded. I was able to tell when that happened by the way his pace picked up and the dread drained from his face.

As we made our way toward the Information Desk, I watched the woman behind it glance up and in an instant, her eyes shined with recognition. My husband, Pastor Hosea Bush, received many privileges that stemmed from him leading City of Lights at Riverside, the largest church in Harlem. With that and with both of the Sunday services televised, Hosea was recognized by most Harlem residents, whether they were church members, attended other churches, or were Bedside Baptists.

I wasn't sure which category the woman at the Information Desk belonged to when she exclaimed, "Pastor," but she was a member of one.

After they exchanged greetings, Hosea asked about Jefferson in less than a dozen words.

"Oh," her voice lowered a couple of decibels. "Is he a friend of yours?"

"Yes," Hosea said.

"I was here last night when they brought him in." She spoke to Hosea like she had no problem sharing information. I guess that was another one of those privileges of being a well-known pastor.

She whispered, "He was admitted under a different name. You know, standard procedure with these kinds of shootings in case it's gang-related."

That made me frown. It was all over the news that Jefferson was here at Harlem Hospital, though anyone could have guessed that this was where he'd been brought. Was Jefferson still in danger from the shooter?

That question made my heart sink and my stomach do a triple

backflip. Maybe my thoughts weren't so out of line. Maybe Kyla was being held by the man who'd shot Jefferson because he knew she could identify him.

I was able to keep my moan mostly inside as Hosea took my hand. After she'd made her announcement about Jefferson under a different name, I'd checked out and hadn't even realized it. Thank God for my husband because obviously, Hosea had heard everything.

He led me to the elevator and then, inside, I trembled more with my thoughts.

When we stepped off on the fourth floor and walked up to the nurses station, if any of the three women (one standing, two sitting) behind the counter recognized Hosea, they didn't show it. Because when Hosea said, "We're here to see Doctor Jefferson Blake," all three gave us stares as if my husband had never spoken.

Hosea continued, "I know he was admitted under John Robinson," Hosea said. "And, I was told the reason why."

Now, the standing nurse spoke. "And you are?"

"I'm Pastor Hosea Bush."

She raised an eyebrow as if to say: that don't mean nothing to me. "Unless," the nurse rotated her glance to me, "she's his wife …."

"This is my wife."

The nurse nodded, then shook her head. "John Robinson hasn't been cleared for any visitors, except for his wife."

"Is his wife here?" I asked.

Right away, the nurse gave me one of those there-really-are-dumb-questions glances. "No, that's why I asked if you were his wife."

Dang! If I would have known that, I would've lied. "Do you know where she is?"

Before the last word was out of my mouth, I knew it was another dumb question, but I still needed to know the answer.

"I don't have any idea," the nurse replied with a little bit of an I'm-getting-sick-of-these-questions attitude.

"So, you don't know if she's been contacted?"

"Debra …." The nurse who'd been sitting right behind the one who'd been speaking, stood up.

Even though she didn't say anything else, some kind of unspoken demand had passed between them because Nurse Debra had nothing more to say except, "I'm sorry. That's all I can tell you."

"But you didn't tell us anything," I said. "And we need to know."

Hosea cupped my elbow and led me away right after he thanked the nurses and right before the volume of my voice started to match my rising blood pressure. I stopped moving when we were just a few feet away and let my eyes roam one hundred and eighty degrees, taking in each of the rooms on this side of the corridor.

"Darlin'."

My husband spoke in a tone that told me he knew what was on my mind and he wasn't going to let me just take off running from room to room until I found Jefferson.

"I just …."

"I know."

"I'm really worried … about Jefferson and Kyla."

He nodded and kissed my forehead. "Okay, we'll go to the police."

I exhaled.

Hosea paused, and looked around at the doctors huddled in the hallway. "I'm surprised no one is up here. But let's go downstairs, I'll make a couple of calls and then, we'll check in with Dan," he said referring to a member of our church, though Detective Dan Foxx was more than that. He was my earthly savior, the hero who'd found my daughter when she'd been kidnapped six years ago.

Hearing his name was like oxygen for me. Now I could breathe because if anyone could help us, Detective Dan Foxx would do it. He would find Kyla. "Thank you," I said and hugged my husband.

Like he always did, Hosea had made me feel better, although fear still gripped my heart. I didn't want to be afraid, but I was. I was very, very afraid that something terrible was about to happen.

chapter 4

Kyla

There's power in a praying woman.
The sound of Pastor Ford's voice in my mind made me lift my head and open my eyes.

"Oh my God," I whispered.

I hadn't thought about calling my pastor last night, though I knew for sure that she would have been there with me, just like she was when my dad passed away. She'd been at Cedar Sinai when the doctor told us that there was nothing more that they could do. She'd held me while I'd held my mother as we cried and cursed the aneurysm that had attacked my father's brain and taken away his life.

But maybe that was why I hadn't thought about calling the woman who was like my second mother. Because didn't pastors usually show up at the end of life? No, I wasn't ready to see her. I would call her, of course. Just not now, not yet.

I tried to turn my thoughts to a happy place as my Uber crawled across the bridge. I wasn't sure what bridge because I didn't know a lot about New York. But I knew enough to know that this bridge was taking me into Manhattan because of the skyline in front of me that was framed through the car's windshield. My eyes zoomed in on the Empire State Building and fresh tears sprang into my eyes. The island of Manhattan held one of the best memories of my life. That time when I'd come to New York for the first time. With my boyfriend, though, I'd left with a different man ....

I felt like such an adult, away on a trip without my parents. Of course, through my years at Hampton, I'd traveled home with friends, mostly Alexis. I'd gone with her to Savannah several times.

But this was different. This was New York. This was just me and Jefferson.

He wrapped my hand inside his and led me into the packed lobby of the Empire State Building, keeping me close as people hustled by us, rushing, eager to go home, I supposed. We maneu-vered through until we found the Observation Deck elevators.

Inside the elevator, Jefferson wrapped his arms around me from behind and I leaned into him — this was my favorite place to be.

Even though the elevator operator stood just feet away, Jefferson kissed my neck, then whispered, "Are you having a good time?"

"Yes," was all I could get out. It was so hard to breathe when Jefferson was this close. It was always this way and that was why it had been a monumental feat to keep the promise that I'd made to God almost ten years ago. I was a child then, but whenever I was with Jefferson, I felt like a woman. So, keeping this vow ... whew! There was a reason why the women on campus called my man Hot Chocolate and so many times, I'd wanted just a sip of that drink.

But I'd stayed strong and Jefferson had stayed with me. Graduation was this coming weekend and he had surprised me with this two-day trip to New York, complete with separate hotel rooms, so that we could spend time together before it got crazy with my parents and other relatives arriving to see me walk across that stage to receive my degree.

But then the elevator doors opened, and all of my thoughts of our past and this coming weekend were swiped away as Jefferson and I stepped out and onto the top of the world.

Of course, we weren't even on top of the Empire State Building, but being 86 floors above the streets of Manhattan made it feel like we were standing at the apex of the earth.

"Oh, my," I whispered.

"Isn't this amazing?" Jefferson asked.

I nodded, doing a slow turn, taking in the urban jungle that was spread out before us. It was a mass of concrete, some tall buildings, others short, none coming close to the giant tower where we stood.

Turning to my boyfriend, I began, "Jefferson, this ...." I paused in the middle of my words and pressed my hand over my mouth.

Normally, I had to look up to gaze into the eyes of my six-foot-two man. But not at this moment. Now, I had to look down. Because he had lowered himself onto one knee. And as the sun still hung high behind him, casting a halo-like glow over him, he reached into his jacket and pulled out a small velvet box.

Maybe if my knees hadn't started knocking, I would have been able to wrap my mind around this moment. But I couldn't capture a single thought because all of my mental effort was focused on breathing. In, out. In ....

I stopped, not even able to do that much when Jefferson flipped up the box's cover. And before he could utter a word, I shouted, "Yes. Yes."

Jefferson laughed, but he was not alone. I heard the other chuckles and giggles, but I didn't look around. All I did was hunch down so that Jefferson and I were eye-to-eye.

"Uh ... Kyla," he whispered. "This isn't the way it's supposed to be. You're supposed to be standing and I'm supposed to be down here."

"But I wanna be where you are ... always."

He blinked a couple of times and then, slipped the ring from the box. I knew this was the moment when women were supposed to examine the diamond for the four c's: cut, carat, clarity and color. My mother had taught me that. But none of that mattered. Jefferson could have purchased this ring from Woolworth's. Truly. That was how much I loved this man.

As Jefferson slipped the ring onto my finger, he whispered, "Kyla Carrington, I want you to be Kyla Jefferson. I want you to be my wife. Because I so want to be your husband."

I told him yes again, this time with a kiss. Around us the air filled with applause and moans of approval. Then, he took my hand and helped me to stand. So many people had surrounded us that they had to part like the Red Sea to let us through. Jefferson led me to the edge of the observation deck, wrapped his arms around me, and I leaned back into the man who would be my husband ....

Using the tips of my fingers, I wiped away the tears that always came with that memory. At that time, I thought Jefferson was the most romantic man on this planet. Who else would think to propose on top of the world?

Of course now, I knew of all the movies that played out a similar scene. But that only made me love it when I watched "An Affair to Remember" and "Sleepless in Seattle." It gave me a chance to live our moment on repeat, as many times as I wanted to. I wanted, I needed to somehow live that moment again — with Jefferson.

When the driver said, "Here we are," I glanced up at the massive building. "Harlem Hospital."

I didn't move, not quite sure what to do. The driver glanced at me through the rear-view mirror, frowned, then turned around in his seat to face me. "Are you all right?"

"I'm fine." The tears that moistened my cheeks belied my words.

He nodded because what else was he supposed to do with a crying woman in the back of his car? He popped open his trunk, jumped out and before I could make it to the curb, he was standing there with my small roller-bag. As he pulled up the handle and turned the bag toward me, he said, "I hope everything will be all right."

"I hope so, too," I said before I thanked him for the ride.

As the music of New York sounded all around me, I stood there, watching the driver get back into his Toyota Corolla and then roll into traffic. For a moment, I wished that I could call him back. Because how was I supposed to walk into this hospital by myself? I'd thought I could make it on my own, but now, I knew for sure that I couldn't. I needed someone: Nicole, Alexis, my mom, Pastor Ford ... the Uber driver.

With that thought, I pulled out my cell. But just as quickly, I tucked my phone into the pocket of my suitcase. It was ridiculous that I needed to speak to Alexis or my mom or Pastor or anyone before seeing Jefferson.

Turning around, I faced the hospital, set my shoulders back, then pushed through the maze of people rushing down the sidewalk. A new wave of fear washed over me. God, I was scared. But I loved Jefferson — and that memory gave me all the strength that I needed.

There were so many people inside the lobby, making it feel more like an office building than a hospital. In the center was a circular desk with a gold Information sign sitting above. As I moved forward, the security guard nodded at me and I greeted him the same way.

I rested my suitcase beside me, and then waited as the two women behind the desk finished talking. It looked like they were changing shifts and I just wished that they moved faster.

When the shorter woman finally sat down, I said, "I'm here to see Doctor Jefferson Blake." I paused. "I'm his wife."

The woman spread her lips into one of those I'm-doing-this-because-it's-part-of-my-job smiles and tapped on the computer keys.

It took her way too long before she said, "I'm sorry," and looked up at me with a frown. "We don't have a Doctor Jefferson Blake on staff here."

At first, I didn't understand her, and then, with a breath, I said, "I'm sorry, I wasn't clear. My husband, Doctor Blake, he's not a doctor. I mean, he is, but he's a patient ... now. He's a patient here."

"Oh, I'm sorry." This time, her smile was more genuine and her fingers moved quickly across the computer keys. She kept typing and typing. "You said the last name is Blake?"

I tapped my foot. "Yes, Jefferson Blake."

She typed some more, I tapped some more.

Then, she apologized again. "We don't have anyone here by that name." She looked up at me. "Are you sure you're at the right hospital?"

"Of course I am." My voice rose. "This is Harlem Hospital, right?"

"Yes." The woman nodded.

"My husband is here," I said, though there was no confidence inside my voice nor inside me. Travis had said Harlem, right? There was no way I would have gotten that information wrong, right? "Can you look again?"

It must have been the tears in my eyes that made her turn to the computer once more. This time, when she looked up, she didn't even say a word. The expression on her face apologized.

My husband was not here.

Where was he?

How was I going to find him?

My shoulders that had been squared were now rounded and I felt the tremors rising within me, but I pressed them down. I couldn't lose it. I had to think, I had to find Jefferson. Then, I remembered: Travis.

I prayed that his plane hadn't yet taken off. Fumbling inside my purse, I searched for my cell. I pushed aside my wallet and my makeup case and my tablet.

No cell phone.

I pushed aside my pen holder and my tissues and my brush.

No cell phone.

Oh, my God! Where was my phone? Where was my husband?

I was in New York, by myself, and I couldn't find my husband, or my phone.

It was all of it. Everything. All piled up on me at once. It was my fear and my frustration that boiled into tremors that this time, I could not stop. The tremors rose and rose within me and I stood in the middle of that lobby in this New York hospital and I cried. Not the kind of tears that had watered my eyes on the plane or that had streamed down my cheeks in the Uber.

No, now, I cried for real. I cried like a child. The kinds of tears that came with heaving and hiccups. The kind of tears that wouldn't let me speak.

"Miss," the woman said to me. "I'm so sorry. Is there anything I can do?"

"You can find my husband," I said as if she had personally misplaced him. "And my cell phone, too."

Behind her, the security guard stepped closer. "What's going on?" he asked.

I sobbed, not able to speak, at first. But finally, I was able to get out, "I ... I ... " And then, I felt a hand on my shoulder.

Oh, my God. Travis had decided to stay in New York.

Whipping around, I was ready to hug my friend.

Except when I turned, I faced my enemy.

"Jasmine," I whispered her name as if I couldn't believe the sight before me. I didn't believe it and just figured that somehow now, I'd stepped into the middle of a nightmare. That was what happened when you dreamed sometimes. You're in Los Angeles, then, you blink, and you're in Pittsburgh. That was how I felt. Like I was dreaming and had just gotten off at the wrong stop.

Then, she said, "Kyla."

When she spoke, I knew for sure it wasn't a dream. But what was this? What was Jasmine doing here? Then, she wrapped her arms around me as if she were still my friend.

The only reason I didn't stop her was because I needed a place to cry. So, I leaned into her shoulder and wept.

Through my tears, I told her my story, "Jefferson, he was shot here in New York."

"I know."

"But now, I can't find him. He's not here at the hospital."

"He's here," she whispered. I leaned back and looked at her. "He's here," she repeated and nodded.

"He is?" My voice sounded so small to me. I pointed to the woman behind the desk. "She said he wasn't," I hiccupped.

The woman sat stiff and still with a look that said — don't blame me.

Jasmine said, "That's okay, I know where he is. Let's go. I'm going to take you to your husband."

The way she took my hand and led me toward the elevators reminded me of a long, long time ago. When we were in kindergarten. Jasmine had handled everything that day. Just like she was handling everything now.

I followed her, but after only a few steps, I stopped. "My bag," I said before I turned around.

Right behind us was a man. With kind eyes and an even kinder smile and right away, I knew this was Jasmine's husband. Alexis had told me that a good and gracious spirit surrounded this man and she was right. It was like he carried peace with him and I felt calmer and steadier just because he was here.

Jasmine said, "Don't worry about your bag. My husband has it. My husband, Hosea."

He nodded. And then, he held up … my phone! "It was sticking out of the side pocket of your suitcase."

They'd found my husband and my phone, so I let Jasmine lead me away. The woman I'd once loved like a sister. The woman who had violated our bond in the most egregious of ways.

I still hated her, I still didn't forgive her. But she was doing what I needed most right now. She was taking me to my husband and that was all that mattered.

chapter 5

Jasmine

My heart ached, but inside, I had hope. At least now, the only one I had to be concerned about was Jefferson.

Almost an hour had passed since I saw Kyla in the hospital's lobby after returning from the police station. We had gotten a bit of information from Detective Foxx. He wasn't working the case, but he shared all that he knew.

Jefferson had been shot … trying to stop some teens in one of those flash robs … one boy pulled out a gun and fired three shots … there had been a woman with him who they needed to find … and the store had a surveillance camera.

"It's because of that woman that we're here," Hosea had told Detective Foxx.

In as few words as I could, I explained that I knew Kyla and Jefferson and I knew that she was the woman who'd been with him last night so now, I was afraid for her life because if there was one thing I knew for sure, Kyla would have never left her husband's side.

"Is there any way that I can see the video? So that I can let you know if the woman with Jefferson is Kyla?"

Detective Foxx shook his head. "We don't have it here yet, but maybe I'll be able to arrange that. She's a witness, so we need to talk to her."

I raised an eyebrow. Clearly, he wasn't taking this seriously enough. "She's his wife and you have to find her."

"I promise you, we're doing all that we can to find whoever was with Doctor Blake. Now, we've already made some progress, we know there was no gang affiliation with the flash rob, so that's good news. The hospital will be alerted. But everything else, we're still working hard. You can trust that."

It was only because of what he'd done for me with Jacqueline that I didn't press the detective anymore. He'd already proven to me that he always handled his business, and this time, would be no different.

When he sent me and Hosea back to the hospital and told us that he would do his best to arrange for me to see the video, I left, not satisfied, but hopeful. And then, that hope turned into ultra-relief when we walked into the hospital and saw Kyla just standing there.

Right away I was taken back to the first day we'd met. And just like that first day, all I'd wanted to do was rescue her.

The only thing about doing that, though, was that I hadn't thought this whole thing through. It wasn't until Kyla had turned around and stared at me that I wondered if I'd made a mistake. I had been so concerned about her safety that I had all but forgotten that she probably still hated me. She had to — because if anyone I knew tried to sleep with Hosea, I would (gladly) catch a case for sure.

That was the way Kyla had looked at me. Like if she only had a knife and if I only had a heart.

But then, she cried and I held her like the sisterfriend that I wanted to be, especially under these circumstances. As I led her up in the elevator, we didn't exchange a single word. Even at the nurses station, it was Hosea who did all the talking, the liaison between Kyla and the nurses.

I stood back and took in my friend. The years had done nothing to her, except matured her from pretty to beautiful. Kyla wasn't attractive in that model girl sort of way. Although she was older, she had the aura of Monica Calhoun, a quiet sophistication that was so sweet — until it wasn't. Maybe that was why I watched "The Best Man" so much. Maybe it was because Monica reminded me of my best friend.

Even now as she stood there in jeans that were more like leggings and a white tailored shirt, Kyla could rival anyone who walked in wearing a ball gown.

Her voice had broken through my thoughts. Kyla said, "Would you mind holding my purse, Jas?"

It was more than her voice that surprised me. It was her tone and what she called me.

"Of course."

I'd taken her bag, shifted it onto my other shoulder, and then watched Hosea and a nurse escort her to a room that was just feet away from where we'd been standing.

Really? If I'd known this morning that we'd been that close to Jefferson's room ....

"Darlin'?"

Hosea's voice and then his hand on mine, brought me back from those memories of earlier in the day. I gave him a smile and then, rested my head on his shoulder as we sat just waiting.

I said, "I'm so scared for her."

"I know."

"I hate to see her hurting this way."

"I know." Then, he lifted my chin until our eyes met. "I not only see, but I can feel your concern." He entwined my fingers with his and brought the back of my hand to his lips. I stiffened a bit. Because that was such a Hosea move. Not that my husband wasn't affectionate. He always was, everywhere. And he especially loved embarrassing our eleven-year-old daughter, inside our home and out.

But this kind of move, specifically, was the prologue to what would be an interrogation. And before he even began, I knew where his questions would lead.

"You care so much about Kyla and I could tell that she cares about you, too. So ... why haven't you two been in touch? Why did you disconnect?"

I tried to hold his gaze, but it didn't work. I turned away, afraid that he would see the betrayal from all those years ago still in my eyes.

I'd shifted, but that didn't stop my husband. "What happened? Why did you two stop being friends? Because after what we went through this morning, it's obvious that at one time you were very close."

I sighed, my way of stalling. And in those moments, I scanned the ICU waiting room. First, my glance settled on a couple, a man and a woman, both wearing crowns of silver hair. The two clung to each other in what looked like desperate fear. Quickly, I turned away from them only to focus on a Hispanic woman, who clutched her rosary, and mumbled words (probably prayers) in Spanish. I would have been able to keep my eyes on her, except for the woman who sat directly across from me and rocked back and forth.

All of these people — their pain was as apparent as their clothing and I felt such an urge to go into my Lady Jasmine role; I wanted to kneel before each of them and pray.

Until, my eyes rested on the woman who sat closest to the waiting room door. There weren't any tears in her eyes, there wasn't any fear in her countenance, there wasn't any pain in her demeanor. She just flipped through a magazine, though every couple of seconds, she did glance up at me. I was sure though that I wasn't the target of her gaze. She was probably studying Hosea, probably recognized him, though it was hard to tell. It was a challenge to see her eyes through the fascinator that she wore; the veil half-covered her eyes. I was fascinated with her fascinator. Really? Who would wear that kind of a hat to a hospital ... on a Tuesday?

"Darlin'?"

I guessed I'd let too many seconds pass without answering my husband, but now I couldn't concentrate on anything except for this woman. She seemed so out of place, not only because she wore a hat instead of any kind of concern, but the rest of her outfit was just as curious — a form-fitting red dress that seemed more appropriate for an after-five affair rather than the ICU waiting room.

"I guess you don't want to talk about it, huh?"

It took a bit for me to break my stare and I turned to my husband. It wasn't that I didn't want to tell Hosea about what happened with Kyla, it was just that — I didn't want him to remember the woman I'd been when we'd met. I didn't want to take him back to the time when I'd been so scandalous that I married him while carrying another man's baby. I only wanted him to think about who I was now, not who I'd been then. And if I told him that I'd slept with my best friend's husband ....

But I wasn't going to lie. Lying was part of my old ways and I was now a woman who still fell short, but always wanted to do better, always wanted to be better. So, I'd have to tell him the truth, no matter the consequences of what I would see in his eyes.

"Pastor Bush?"

Hosea and I looked up and we both smiled, though Hosea was smiling because he was looking into the face of a friend. My smile came from the fact that his friend had saved me in that moment.

"Doctor Knight," Hosea said, though outside of the hospital, he called his friend, Roger.

Not only was Roger Knight a long-time member of City of Lights, but he was one of the doctors who had worked to save Hosea's father's life when he'd been brought here to Harlem Hospital in a situation that was quite similar to what happened to Jefferson.

"I got your text about Jefferson Blake." The doctor looked around at the other occupants and then cocked his head. "Let's step into the hallway."

We stood to follow him and as we passed the lady in red, I expected her to glance up. It seemed, though, that she was engrossed in some magazine article and by the time I stepped into the hallway, I'd forgotten about her.

When we were a few feet away from the waiting room entrance, Dr. Knight stopped. "So, Jefferson Blake is a friend of yours?"

I spoke up, "He's married to my best ... he's married to a friend of mine. But I know him ... well."

Dr. Knight nodded. "Well, it's been all over the news."

"We saw the reports," Hosea said.

I said, "I was just wondering if you could tell us anything." Then, out of the corner of my eye, I saw a flash of red. Turning just a degree or so, I saw the woman who'd been sitting in the waiting room. Now, she stood outside the door, too close to us, as if she were eavesdropping.

I turned my head, just a little more, to make eye contact with her. But she looked down at the cell in her hand. Maybe the signal in the room was bad and she'd stepped into the hallway to check her messages. I shook off thoughts of her and turned back to Dr. Knight.

"I'm sorry, I wish I could help, but you understand the HIPAA laws."

Hosea nodded, but I didn't. What I understood were the rules of friendship. Dr. Knight knew that whatever he shared with us, stayed with us. But he was one of those stand-up kind of guys. Following all rules that he'd been given and oaths that he had taken. I guess that was why he and Hosea were friends.

"But his wife is here now, right?" he asked me.

"Yes, we just brought her up and she's in with Jefferson now."

"Great. Well, the neurosurgeons will talk to her. I think Doctor Reid did the surgery. If you have any general questions after she fills you in, let me know."

"So that's it?" I asked, hoping that Dr. Knight would be moved by my anxiety.

He shook his head. "I'm sorry. All I can tell you is what's already been on the news. Doctor Blake is in critical condition."

Once again, my peripheral vision distracted me and I watched the woman dab at her left eye as if she were trying to keep a tear from falling. Then, she glanced up and it was the way her glance locked with mine that I knew she wasn't standing there to check her messages. She was listening.

Why?

"Excuse me," I said, as I took a step toward her.

Behind me, I heard Dr. Knight say, "I have to get back to the fifth floor," but my ears couldn't focus because all of my energy was on my sense of sight — and this woman in front of me.

She held my glance for only a moment more before she turned and power-walked toward the elevators. I was amazed at how she moved in stilettos that looked like they'd been dyed to match her dress. She turned to the left, disappearing from my view for a couple of seconds.

As I rounded the corner to the elevator banks, I expected her to be standing there. But she wasn't amongst the three who were waiting.

Glancing around quickly, I saw the exit and rushed to that door. The moment I opened it, I heard heels clicking on the concrete steps. Looking over the railing, I saw her three flights down already, sprinting like she was wearing track shoes.

"Hey," I shouted, but she did not look up.

Who was that woman?

The question was still swirling in my mind when I stepped back into the hospital and almost bumped into my husband.

"Where did you go?" he asked, though he didn't give me a chance to respond. "It's Kyla. She's looking for you. She just spoke to the doctor and it's not good."

"Oh, my God."

"She needs you, Jasmine."

I nodded and then, took off like now I was the one running a race. Of course, that woman was still on my mind, but I had to push her aside. Because all that mattered right now was my friend. I had to take care of Kyla.

chapter 6

Kyla

I glanced down at the card that Dr. Reid had given to me and I leaned against the counter at the nurses' station because I needed that surface to steady myself from all that I'd just seen and all that I'd just been told.

For a moment, I closed my eyes, wanting a little reprieve. But behind my eyelids, the image remained: Jefferson, looking like he was just sleeping, the rise and fall of his chest under the cotton sheet seeming so natural. Except that there wasn't anything natural about any of it. Because his brain was held in place by the heavy gauze cap that he wore. And his face, so swollen it made him look like he'd gained at least fifteen pounds, right after Evander Holyfield had punched him in both eyes. There was a thick tube that was lodged deep inside his mouth, down into his throat. And then, there were the two machines, one with blue lines, the other with green that were attached to my husband and, for now, were giving him dear life.

At first, the look of Jefferson and all of that equipment that was an extension of him had shocked me, but once I'd steadied my legs, I had rushed to his side and taken his hand before I leaned over and pressed my lips, as best as I could, against his. There was a part of me that had hoped that just my kiss would bring him back to life. But this was no fairy tale. So, I'd shifted just a bit, brought

my lips so close to his ear and told Jefferson that I loved him and
Nicole loved him and my mother loved him and Alexis loved him
and Brian loved him ....

I had continued down the line, giving him lots of names and
reasons to come back to us. I had told him that he was loved until
my back ached from leaning over for too long.

My plan had been just to stand for a moment, to get the crook
out of my muscles and then go back to talking to my husband. But
the moment I stood up, the doctor walked in ....

*"Mrs. Blake." The doctor spoke my name as if he already knew me,
with familiarity yet concern. Coming across to the side of the bed
where I stood, he reached his hand toward mine. "The nurses told me
that you were in here. I'm Doctor Reid, the lead neurosur-geon on your
husband's case."*

*I was about to tell the doctor that it was nice to meet him, but
then, I yanked those words back. That wasn't the truth. I wish I'd
never had to meet this man. But I didn't want to be rude, so I said,
"Thank you."*

*Dr. Reid glanced at Jefferson, then when he faced me again, he
said, "There's an office right down the hall where we can talk."*

*My eyes were on my husband when I nodded at the doctor and then
followed him into the hallway. It wasn't until he turned to the left that
I wondered if I should go the other way to find Hosea. I didn't know
him, but I could tell that Hosea Bush would stand by me and with me
and help me to navigate through since I had no one else.*

*But if I found Hosea, I'd probably find Jasmine, too. That
thought of Jasmine made my decision. I followed Dr. Reid alone.*

*He led me into a small office, with just a desk and a couple of
chairs, clearly not Dr. Reid's personal space, probably shared among
the doctors in the ICU. He held out a chair, then sat be-hind the
desk. Opening his tablet, he tapped on a couple of screens before he
began, "I usually find that it's best for me to describe the patient's
condition and the care the patient's being given. Then, if you have
any questions, I can answer them all for you."*

I had to take a breath to get enough oxygen, to have enough energy to nod.

"I'm going to be completely honest," Dr. Reid continued, and I wondered why didn't he just get to the parts that I needed to know.

"If at any time you want to stop me to ask questions ...."

I couldn't take it anymore. "Doctor Reid, I'm a doctor's wife. I can take whatever you have to tell me. The hard part is not know-ing and the waiting."

He nodded as if he understood. "The first thing is your husband is a blessed man."

It was only then that I realized I'd been holding my breath ... and now, I breathed. Dr. Reid was not only a man of medicine, but it seemed like first, he was a man of God. To me, that just increased my husband's chances exponentially.

Continuing, he said, "People rarely survive gunshot wounds. About ninety-percent don't make it. Yet, your husband was con-scious when he came in."

"I didn't know that," I said. But then, I hadn't asked Travis any-thing — except was Jefferson alive.

Dr. Reid nodded. "Doctor Blake had what we call a through-and-through wound, meaning that the bullet entered right above his eye and exited at the back of his head."

Oh, my God. That image was so vivid and I closed my eyes at that thought. A bullet had traveled through my husband. Traveled through his brain.

I wasn't sure if Dr. Reid was aware that I was about to faint, but he kept on, "This is a very good thing."

I opened my eyes.

"This means that the bullet didn't break into fragments nor did it lodge in his brain. And he was more than conscious. He was able to follow a few simple commands."

He survived ... he was conscious.

"We performed the surgery — another good thing. Less than an hour after the shooting and we were able to extract skull frag-ments from his brain and determine the path of the bullet." He paused to breathe. "The bullet passed through Doctor Blake's head without crossing the midline of the brain." It must have been my

blank stare that made him add, "That's the third very good thing because if not, we'd be talking about a critical injury here."

"He's not critical?"

"Oh, he is. Make no mistake, he's had trauma to his brain. Like I said, we removed skull fragments, stopped the bleeding, but then, we did have to perform a decompressive hemicraniotom."

A decom what?

The doctor heard my thought, that was the only way to explain why he repeated the name of the procedure. "A decompressive hemicraniotomy. We removed a portion of your husband's skull, giving his brain room to swell, because it will swell in this case."

I shuddered, then, I spoke, "His skull. Removed?"

"A portion of it," the doctor said. "That sounds scary, but it's become a common procedure to protect the brain after such a severe traumatic injury. And that's why we felt it was best to put Doctor Blake into coma. He's been given pentobarbital that will allow his brain ... and his body to rest. Depending on his progress, we'll gradually begin to wake up your husband in the next few days. And at that time, I'll be able to give you a better assessment and prognosis."

"A prognosis. So, you don't know if ...."

"We don't know anything, Mrs. Blake." He closed his tablet. "The truth is while I've given you the facts and some good news, your husband was shot at close range in the head. A bullet traveled through his brain. And so, we have to wait to see if he wakes up, what kind of damage has been done."

I'd only heard four words. "If he wakes up ...."

He nodded as he stood. "I hope to have more information for you tomorrow. In the meantime, do you have any questions for me?"

I opened my eyes and remembered the only question I'd had was how could I roll back time's hands? How could we all go back twenty-four hours or even seventy-two hours? Then, I would have kept Jefferson safe at home in Los Angeles.

If he wakes up ....

God, what was I going to do?

If he wakes up ....

"Kyla."

When I heard Jasmine call my name, I turned. Her arms were already outstretched before she was even close to me. And when she was just inches away, I collapsed into her embrace.

"What's wrong?" she asked.

If he wakes up ....

I just shook my head.

She said, "Jefferson. He's not ...."

"No!" I leaned back, then snapped, "Don't say that. Don't you even think that."

"Okay." She nodded. "I didn't mean anything." Her voice was gentle, caring. Like the Jasmine I knew before.

So I reeled it back a little. "I'm sorry," I said. "It's just that, I just spoke to the doctor."

"Do you want to talk about it?"

This time, I was the one who nodded.

A voice over my shoulder said, "Is there a place where my wife and her friend can talk?"

I hadn't even seen Hosea come back with Jasmine. The nurse who'd been attending to Jefferson earlier, nodded. "Right over there," she whispered as she pointed across the hall.

I hadn't noticed the room before — Quiet Room.

Hosea said to me, "It might be good if you talk to Jasmine in there."

An image flashed in my mind:

I was shaking when the doctor walked out of my father's room and when I grabbed my mom's hand, I felt her trembling, too.

He said, "Let's go talk in here."

I glanced up to where the doctor pointed. A room down the hall. With a sign on the door. Quiet Room.

That was when I knew, I just knew that my father hadn't made it ....

Snapping back to the present, I heard Hosea say, "It would be good if you talked in there rather than in front of Jefferson."

He was right. I didn't want to have any kind of negative or even doubtful conversations in Jefferson's room. Because I was sure that my husband could hear me, or at least feel me and so when I was in there — when anyone was in there, I wanted nothing but good thoughts, God thoughts.

I glanced at the door to the Quiet Room and then, I returned my gaze to Jefferson's room.

Hosea said, "While you're talking to Jasmine, I can sit with Jefferson if you don't want him to be alone — if it's all right with you." Then, he added, "I can pray with him."

That made me smile and gave me a little bit of peace. "I'd like that. He'd like that." I paused. "Thank you."

Turning to the nurse, I asked, "What do I have to do to add my friend," I paused and glanced at Jasmine, then corrected myself, "add them to the list of people who can see my husband?"

The nurse said, "All you have to do is tell me and we'll put their names into the computer."

I nodded and Hosea said, "I'll take care of that, too."

"Yes, please. And thank you again," I said. "I feel that's all I'm saying is thank you and I haven't even had a chance to say nice to meet you."

He gave me a smile that could warm up the world. "Maybe that's because we met before."

I tilted my head. "You remember? I didn't think that you did since we only spoke on the phone that one time."

He glanced at Jasmine and from the corner of my eye, I saw the deep frown on her face.

"Of course I remember," he said. The wattage of his smile dipped just a little. "It was an important time, back in 2008, I think it was." But once he got those words out, all of his warmth was back.

"Well, thank you again. For being here, for taking care of me, and for praying with my husband." I paused and this time I faced Jasmine when I said, "Thank you to both of you."

He led me and Jasmine to the Quiet Room, and gave us both a nod before he left us alone. I stood for a moment and pushed back the memory of the last time, the only time that I'd been in a room like this — the day my father died. I sank into one of the four leather chairs and Jasmine lowered herself into the one next to me.

For a few moments, we respected the name on the door, but finally, Jasmine broke the silence with, "I wonder why this room is here."

Her statement made me sigh and I leaned forward, holding my face in my hands. I expected memories of my father to return to my mind's eye, but all I could see was Jefferson. And fear began to rise like bile up in me.

The soft hand on my back made me turn my head so that I was looking straight at her. It was so weird sitting here ... with Jasmine. I said the first thing that came to my mind. "I never thought I would see your face again."

My words pushed her back a bit, but she was Jasmine, so she recovered right away. "I know. I moved as far away from you as I could so that you would never have to see me."

I smirked. "Really? You moved away *for* me?"

She nodded. "I moved away for both of us." Another moment of quiet, and then, "But here we are now."

Slumping deep into the chair, I said, "I know."

More quiet seconds before she said, "So what did the doctor say?" She paused. "I mean, if you want to tell me." Another pause. "You don't have to." More hesitation. "We can talk ... about anything ... it's up to you ... whatever ...."

"Jasmine!"

Her lips snapped together.

"Why are you rambling?"

"I guess," she lowered her eyes, "I don't really know what to say to you. I mean, I'm really sad about what happened to Jefferson and I was so afraid that you'd been kidnapped."

I fast-blinked a couple of times. "What?"

She waved her hand. "I'll tell you about that later." She leaned back. "It's just weird, I guess. I mean, I want to be here for you, I want to help in any way that I can. But ...."

I said, "But ... the last time I saw you, I wanted to punch you right in the throat."

She laughed, though I guess it was more like a hearty chuckle.

Whatever it was, I didn't crack a smile.

"What's so funny?" I asked her.

"You. Punching anyone anywhere." That was what she said, but I noticed that she shifted a bit in her seat, moving a couple of inches away from me. As if she didn't want to test her theory about who she thought I was.

I said, "Well, I've changed."

She shook her head. "There is no one in my life, except for Serena, that I've known longer than you. And even though we haven't seen each other in a while, I know that you have not changed that much."

She was amused. I was not.

I sat up straight in the chair. "Yes, I have. Especially with women who sleep with my husband."

"Ouch." She looked down and away from me.

But, I sat boldly. "I told you I've changed. Twenty years ago, I wouldn't have said anything like that to anybody."

When she looked back up at me, I saw something in her eyes that I had never seen before. A softness that revealed ... what? Sorrow? Regret?

She said, "Well, I've changed, too." Her words were soft and without any bit of the attitude that I was giving to her.

I wasn't finished, so I said, "I guess you have, being married to a pastor."

But while my words agreed with her, it must have been my tone, my stiffness, my entire countenance that told her that I knew a snake could shed its skin, but not its heart.

She said, "I hate the circumstances, but I hope we get the chance to talk. Because there is so much that I want to say to you."

Before we walked into this room, before we sat down together, before we had this little chat, I had almost, almost forgotten about what Jasmine had done to me. It was my grief and fear that pushed that memory aside.

But now, talking to her like this, for the first time in twenty years reminded me. Reminded me that the Bible talked about forgiving, but there wasn't a word in there about forgetting.

I didn't have the chance to stew in those thoughts, though because there was a quick knock on the door and Hosea stepped inside.

The sight of him made me jump up and speak fast. "Did something happen to Jefferson?"

Hosea held up his hands. "No. He's fine. I mean, he's the same. I prayed with him a bit, but these gentlemen, these detectives want to talk to you."

I hadn't even noticed the men, one Black, one Latino who followed Hosea into the room. "Detectives?"

"Yes," the Black one said, reaching for my hand. "My name is Detective Green and this is Detective Hernandez." I gave him a quick handshake as well.

"You're here about my husband, right?"

They both nodded. "Yes, ma'am," Detective Green said and I figured he was the designated driver of this conversation.

I asked, "Do you know exactly what happened?"

The detective kinda nodded his head from side to side in a 'sort-of' move. "Well, it was a flash rob."

"What is that?" I asked.

He shook his head. "When a group of … usually it's teens … run into a store and steal whatever they can. There are so many of them, there's nothing anyone can do. But it seems your husband tried to stop at least one of them. The wrong one."

I closed my eyes and shook my head. I could imagine that. Jefferson wanting to do the right thing.

The detective said, "We really want to get this shooter, so we want to talk to his companion. The woman who was with him last night."

Of all the words that the detective had just spoken, a spotlight shined on two. I frowned. "His companion?"

Behind me, Jasmine cleared her throat, but I didn't turn around. I kept my eyes on the detective.

"Yes." But then, he changed the subject. Detective Green asked, "Do you have any idea why your husband would have been out that late … and up in Washington Heights?"

I shrugged. "I don't know. I guess he was hungry or something. Is being there a problem?"

"No," Detective Green said, then glanced at his partner before he finished with, "but he was a bit away from his hotel. He was staying in midtown, near the convention center. So we're trying to figure out why he was all the way uptown."

I'd been to New York a few times, but I didn't know midtown from Harlem from Washington Heights. I didn't know if this was a big deal or not, though these detectives were making it almost sound like Jefferson being away from his hotel was a crime. "Well, all I can think is that Jefferson wanted to get something to eat. Maybe someone told him about this place to grab a quick bite ...."

There was that exchange of glances again before Detective Hernandez uttered his first words. "Where he was wasn't the kind of place to grab anything to eat. It wasn't a restaurant or a fast food joint. It was a store or what people in the neighborhood call a bodega."

He said that as if that was supposed to make some kind of difference. "Well maybe he had a headache or wasn't feeling well. Maybe he needed to buy some aspirin or cold medicine, I don't know."

"Did he have a cold the last time you talked to him?"

"No, but you're asking me for reasons and I'm trying to tell you everything that I can think of."

The detectives nodded before Detective Green asked, "When was the last time you spoke with your husband?"

"Yesterday before their last session. It was about two in LA, so five here in New York. He said he would call me once he got back to the room last night, but he never did."

"Did you try to call him?"

"I did, but when I didn't reach him, I didn't think anything of it. I figured he was out with some of his friends. Some of the doctors that he only gets to see once a year at this convention." When they did that glance thing between each other again, I said, "Look, I want to know what's going on? Why are you asking me questions when you should be out finding who tried to kill my husband?"

"We're still trying to get descriptions of the shooter."

I knew my tone was full of impatience and sarcasm when I said, "I certainly can't tell you what he looks like."

Jasmine said, "What about the video? Didn't the store have a surveillance system?"

Detective Green nodded and said, "Yes, they did."

Detective Hernandez shook his head and said, "But it wasn't working."

Jasmine groaned, but I just stood there, trying to get all of this to make sense.

Detective Green said, "That's why we want to get in touch with the woman who was with him last night." He finally returned to what I wanted to talk about. "Do you have any idea who was with your husband?"

I shook my head. "No. But if I had to guess I'd say that she was one of the doctors from the convention."

This time when the detectives glanced at each other, I folded my arms. They didn't have to say another word; I knew what they were implying.

"Okay, well, we're going to keep working this case, but we're definitely hoping to find this woman. We need to speak with her."

I tightened my arms across my chest. "Okay."

"We'll be working the conference today, but here's my card." Detective Green added, "Call me if you can think of anything else."

"I will," I said, even though I knew I would never call him for anything. Not after this.

Then, Hosea turned to the men and led them out of the room. The moment they stepped over the threshold, I plopped back into the chair and stared at the card. Of course, I was grateful that the police were working this case, but their questions infuriated me. Questions about some woman. Their inferences were all in their tones. She probably hadn't even been with Jefferson. They'd probably just happened to walk into the store at the same time.

The woman who was with him last night.

I shook my head to push the detective's words aside. Because if I thought about his words, I'd have questions. And if I started asking questions, that meant that I didn't trust Jefferson. And I did trust my husband. He had worked hard to earn my trust again and he had it. Completely.

When I felt a hand on my shoulder, I looked up. And into the eyes of Jasmine Cox Larson ... at the moment, I couldn't remember her new last name. But while I couldn't remember her name, I remembered back twenty years — to what she'd done.

And because of what she'd done, questions rushed into my mind, overwhelming me.

The woman who was with him last night.
"Kyla?"
The woman who was with him last night.
"Are you all right?"

I tried to blink, but I couldn't. It was like my eyes were steady on Jasmine and my mind was steady on that woman. Like Jasmine and the woman were the same.

But Jefferson ... my husband wouldn't hurt me like that again ... would he?

No!

Never!

At least ... that was what I thought.

chapter 7

Jasmine

With sluggish steps, Kyla trudged from one end of the waiting room to the other and when she almost bumped into the wall, she started the route all over again. I watched her with her head a bit down, her glance squinted as she stared at the floor, her hand pressed to her mouth as if she were trying to force words that were about to be spoken back inside.

I wondered what she was thinking. Was she wondering about the detective's words? Did she wonder like I wondered — who was that woman?

As Kyla paced, my thoughts wandered to another woman. The woman who'd been listening to our conversation with Dr. Knight just a few hours ago. I didn't know why, but I had such a strong feeling that the woman who'd been eavesdropping on us and the woman the detectives were searching for was the same.

But who was she? Why had she been with Jefferson? Why had she been with Jefferson at midnight?

I closed my eyes and asked the question that summed up all of my suspicions — was Jefferson cheating on Kyla?

"Sweetheart."

My eyes popped open at the sound of Kyla's voice. No, it wasn't the sound. It was that word: Sweetheart? Was Kyla cheating, too? What was going on with the Blakes?

Kyla said, "I'm sorry I didn't call. I've been with your dad from the moment I walked into the hospital. And, I didn't want to call you in the middle of the night."

I breathed — sweetheart. Nicole.

The thought of Kyla and Jefferson's only child made me smile and made me feel a new ache. I'd been so in awe when Nicole had been born. That brown-haired, brown-eyed, brownish-pinkish little baby was a brown ball of niece joy. Of course, we weren't related by blood, but no one could have told me nor Nicole that we didn't share some kind of DNA. That little girl had my heart from the moment I peeped her in the nursery.

I so loved her, but when I'd unplugged from her parents, she was part of the disconnection. She'd crept into my thoughts over the years, but I'd always blinked her away.

Now though, I let the image of the nine-year-old girl rest in my mind. Or had she been ten the last time I saw her with her bouncing pigtails and a personality that outshone the sun? So many years had passed and that meant that Nicole Blake was now grown.

I wanted to know all about the woman she'd become.

"No, the doctors are in with your dad now."

Looking down at my phone, I pressed the Home button, wanting to take my attention away from Kyla's conversation.

"Okay, well, I'll call as soon as they come out. I promise, this time."

My email account opened, but I didn't read one word; my focus was still on Kyla. I wasn't trying to eavesdrop, but it was fascinating that Kyla and I were physically in the same room and mentally on the same side. I could have never imagined circumstances that would have brought us together this way.

"I haven't even had a chance to think about that, Nicole." Kyla paused her pacing. "I'll get on-line or something, but I don't want to check into a hotel. I really don't want to leave your father." She paused and sighed. "I know, but I can just as easily sleep in his room. Right now, he's my priority."

There were just a few seconds of silence before she said, "Of course." A beat. "I will." Another beat. "I love you, too." Then, she hung up, looked up and caught me staring.

"I'm sorry," I said. "I wasn't trying to listen."

She shook her head and waved her hand. "It's all right. It's not like this is a private room." She sat down in the chair next to me.

"That was Nicole?"

Her eyebrow raised in a none-of-your-business kind of way. My question had been natural, but only if it had been asked by a friend.

Then almost as quickly, she gave me a quick nod, but nothing else. That was the sign that she was grateful that Hosea and I were here, but that I didn't need to twist anything up — we were not friends.

"Where's Hosea?" she asked.

I guessed since she hadn't slept with my husband, she could ask me all kinds of questions.

"He went downstairs to make some calls."

"I guess that's what I really should do. I need to call Alexis and my mom and Pastor Ford, but …."

"You don't want to be far from Jefferson," I finished for her.

She nodded and gave me more than a moment's stare. As if she'd had a sudden flashback the way I just did, remembering how everyone used to ask if we were related because as different as we were, there were so many things that were the same — especially how we used to finish each other's sentences.

I said, "If you want to make any more calls, maybe you can use the Quiet Room." Not giving her a chance to respond, I pushed myself from the chair. "I'll go ask the nurse."

"No," Kyla stopped me. She glanced around at the waiting room. We shared the space with only one person. The woman, who still clutched a Bible to her chest and rocked back and forth. Kyla said, "I don't really … like that room."

I frowned and wondered what that was about, but I wasn't going to ask any more questions.

She glanced at her watch. "Gosh, is it really after six already?"

I nodded. "As soon as Hosea comes back up, we'll take you to get something to eat."

Before I even finished, she was shaking her head. "I'm not hungry." Then, she leaned back, her head hitting the wall behind us. "Whew! This!" She closed her eyes and took deep breaths — in her exhales, I felt her fear.

I looked down at her hands resting on the arm of the chair and before I could change my mind, I did what I would have done if we hadn't had this history between us — I covered her right hand with my left.

She flinched just a little, but she didn't open her eyes. And she didn't make a move to punch me in my throat. So, I kept my hand in place as she took yoga-style cleansing breaths.

When her lashes became moist with tears pressing from behind her closed eyes, I whispered, "Jefferson is going to be all right."

Slowly, her eyes opened and the way she looked at me, I was sure that she was about to burst into full-fledge tears. "You think so?" Her voice was so tiny.

I nodded. "I know so. We went through something like this a few years ago with Hosea's father."

"You did?" Now, she sounded like a little girl waiting for the next line in a fairytale.

"Yes. Hosea's dad was shot, but he's fine now. And he was right here in Harlem Hospital, too. This is a really good place."

"I know." Kyla nodded. "Two of Jefferson's partners at the clinic started here." She nodded again as if that move gave her strength. "Okay, Jefferson is going to be good." Then, she looked at me and a second later, she burst into tears.

I scooted from my chair, crouched in front of her and pulled her into my arms. When she didn't resist, I tightened my hug. She sobbed and I blinked back my own tears, some that had nothing to do with what we were facing now. Some that were all about my regret.

"Kyla."

Both of us turned to the sound of Hosea's voice. Kyla leaned back and with the back of her hand, wiped away her tears while I blinked back my own.

My husband came to us, offered me his hand and helped me to

stand. Then, turning to Kyla, he said, "Mrs. Taylor is here to speak with you."

I hadn't noticed the woman who'd walked into the waiting room with Hosea. With her hair pulled back in a tight bun, her cat-eyed glasses and her navy sheath, Hosea didn't have to say anything more than her name. Her look screamed 'administrator.'

"Hello, Mrs. Blake," the woman spoke in a robotic tone.

Kyla nodded her hello.

Mrs. Taylor said, "I'm from the billing department. We have some paperwork we need to go over with you."

"Does she really need to do this now?" I interjected. "It's not a good time."

The woman's tone was sympathetic, though still a bit robotic. "Unfortunately, we do need to take care of this. It won't take long."

Kyla's voice cracked with emotion. "I can't."

"I am so sorry," the woman replied. "But I'd hate for Doctor Blake to be placed in our indigent status. And the only way to prevent that is to get his paperwork completed."

"You know what?" Hosea sat in the chair where I'd been sitting. "I can do this with you. I can go with you to Mrs. Taylor's office."

Kyla didn't even hesitate. "All right, but I was waiting for the doctors to come out of Jefferson's room. I really want to speak to them first."

"They're not in there." Hosea looked at Kyla, then at me. "I came up and checked his room first, thinking that you two were in there."

"They were supposed to come talk to me when they finished!" Kyla said, her voice escalating with each word. "Something must be wrong …."

"No." Hosea's tone was soft, as if he were speaking to a child, though without any condescension. "Because if anything was wrong or if things had taken a turn, believe me, they would have found you." He paused. "Look, why don't we do this. First, we'll go with Mrs. Taylor and then, we'll find Jefferson's doctor, okay?" The stiffness eased from her shoulders and then, Kyla took a couple of easy breaths.

Even though I'd seen it a thousand times, even though he'd done it to me a million times, I was always amazed watching my husband's gift. Hosea's voice, his tone, his words, his countenance and confidence was a balm in Gilead.

Now Kyla stood, practically springing to her feet as if she'd been given ten shots of espresso intravenously. And, she almost smiled when she said to Mrs. Taylor, "Okay, let's do this."

Kyla followed the woman, now with strength in her steps, and Hosea glanced back at me. "You coming?"

I shook my head. "No, I'll wait for you." I dropped down in the chair, feigning a bit of exhaustion.

He nodded and leaned over to kiss my cheek. "I'll meet you back here. We won't be too long." Then, he trotted to catch up with the women.

I counted to ten, then popped up from my seat. My words to my husband weren't a lie — I told him that I'd wait for him; he was the one who'd assumed that I'd wait for him here.

I'd be waiting, but while he was taking care of Kyla, I had something I had to take care of as well.

When I stepped outside of the waiting room, I glanced at one end of the hall and then the other. It was clear, and time for me to see if I could figure a few things out.

***

I paused once again, right outside of Jefferson's room and formed the lie in my head — in case Kyla had convinced Mrs. Taylor and Hosea that she just had to see Jefferson first and the three of them were inside. When my lie was ready and my breathing was steady, I pushed open the door, paused, peeked in, then stepped inside.

The room may have been clear, but it wasn't silent. The drone of the machine filled the air. I took slow steps until I stood just a few feet from Jefferson's bed. He may have been in a medically-induced coma, but all I could think was that the years had been more than a little kind to him. Kyla once told me that the woman at Hampton called Jefferson Hot Chocolate, and I guessed like wine, chocolate did that same finer with time thing because even with his head covered in that cap, and even with his face swollen, he just looked like a chubby, but still so, so, so fine version of the man that I'd known.

It was the way he looked that made me remember ... that night ... when he'd believed my lie and had been kind enough to me to let me stay at his house ... when Kyla was away in Santa Barbara with her parents.

I had tricked him, seduced him; really, it had been too easy. Now, I wanted to know — had he been tricked, had he been seduced again?

Taking two more steps, I stared down. The sheet that covered Jefferson rose and fell with the rhythmic inhales and exhales of his chest. If I ignored the mounds of gauze and all the swelling, it really did just look like he was sleeping, like he was at peace ... and like ... he was in love.

I would never be able to explain it to anyone, but even as he slept, even with his injuries, in all of his unconsciousness, it was hard for me to see anything but the love he had for his wife on his face. He was fighting to come back to her, only her. Like I said, I couldn't explain it, but I could feel it.

I sighed, my thoughts going back to that night again. All of those years ago, he'd loved Kyla and still, I'd won in that moment.

Shaking my head, I tried to toss that doubt aside. I knew most women believed once a cheater, always a cheater, but that was not what I felt in my heart. Jefferson Blake was the exception. He and Kyla were the exception. Just like I was with Hosea.

"So, who is she?" I whispered. "Why was she here?"

Then, I waited, as if I expected Jefferson to open his eyes, sit up, and give me some kind of answer. Maybe he would squeeze his eyes together twice as a signal that he had no idea who I was talking about.

"This is ridiculous," I muttered. What did I expect to find when I came in here? Did I really think that I could look at Jefferson and know the truth? Did I think that he would, through some kind of osmosis, explain it all to me?

No, I wouldn't have any help in this. I was on my own, but that was okay. I would find that woman and force her to tell me what was going on.

This time when I moved, I stepped so close to the bed that the rail pressed against my waist. I closed my eyes, said a prayer, then stared at him for a couple of moments. I remembered when my father-in-law was in a coma; he later told us that there'd been times when he'd been aware of our words, of our movement.

That was why I leaned over and began to speak to Jefferson. "I know I owe you and Kyla all kinds of apologies. And even though I haven't been in touch over the years, I've been filled with regret." Moving closer to his ear, I added, "I'm so sorry, Jefferson. I'm so sorry for what I did to you and Kyla. But I promise you, I'll make up for it. I'll take care of Kyla until you come back to her. I don't think we'll be the friends we once were, but she'll know that she can count on me. And I want you to know that, too."

An urge rose in me to reach out and touch Jefferson. It wasn't from the place that had driven me twenty years ago. That feeling was so long gone. My heart had been filled by Hosea and there would never be enough room for another man in my life, in my heart, in me … again.

What I felt for Jefferson was that brotherly love, the flip side of the sisterly love that I still had for Kyla.

It was with that, that I reached out and squeezed his hand. It was with that, that I leaned over and kissed his forehead.

And it was with that, when the door to his room swung open and Kyla stepped inside.

I jerked upward, standing straight, my eyes wide because I felt like a cheater who'd been caught cheating.

And Kyla glared at me as if she felt the same thing. As if she knew I was a cheater, and she had, once again, caught me, too.

chapter 8

Kyla

I moaned a bit as I pushed myself up from the chair. My bones ached — half from exhaustion and half from trying to twist myself like a pretzel into that chair during the night. I steadied myself on my feet before I dragged to the side of Jefferson's bed.

"Good morning, sweetheart," I said, as I leaned down and kissed his forehead.

Just as I did that, the door swung open. I looked up.

Jasmine paused at the entry and I straightened up — exactly the way she'd done yesterday.

"Good morning," she said with a bit of a smirk that I wanted to slap off of her face.

"He's my husband. I'm supposed to be kissing him."

She raised an eyebrow. "All I said was good morning." She let the door close behind her.

"I don't want your lips anywhere near my husband." I spoke with a little bit of a smile and as much levity in my tone as I could muster. I wanted to sound like I was kidding, that this was just a joke. But I was not, and it was not.

I didn't trust Jasmine Cox Larson Bush.

She said, "You know I had just come in here to pray for Jefferson, yesterday right?"

Those were almost the exact words she'd uttered when I walked in and found her lips pressed against my husband. It had taken every bit of everything in me not to march over to her, snatch her from Jefferson's side, and give her that drop-kick beat-down that I owed her from 1997.

But before I'd had a chance to do that, she had backed away with her hands up and had given me that I-was-just-praying-for-Jefferson spiel. She didn't explain what prayer had to do with a kiss and I hadn't asked since she'd had the good sense to follow up that transgression by asking where was Hosea and then saying she was going down to the cafeteria to find him.

Only Hosea had come back to the room with a tuna sandwich and a bottle of juice for me. Only Hosea had asked where was I staying and then, told me that he wanted me to stay at their place.

When I'd said, "I really don't want to leave Jefferson tonight," that had been ninety-nine percent truth. The other part of that equation — I didn't want to be near his wife.

But now in the light of day, and given the fact that I'd thought about it a lot last night, I came to the conclusion that Jasmine wasn't trying to seduce my husband. Not even she would try to do that to a man in a coma.

She handed me a cup of coffee. "Three creams, four sugars." She spoke in a tone that sounded like she was trying to call a truce. I guess she knew that we were still in some kind of war.

I said, "You remembered."

She nodded. "Yup, I used to tell you that one more sugar and you'd be drinking coffee-flavored Kool-Aid."

I kinda chuckled at that. It was funny then, and still funny now.

She said, "I remember how you like your coffee. But can you do me a favor and try not to remember who I used to be?" She shook her head. "I'm telling you; I'm not that woman anymore."

My answer: I removed the green splash stick from the cup, then took a sip.

That seemed to be good enough for Jasmine because she said, "So how did you sleep?" And then, she glanced at the chair where the blanket was sprawled on the floor.

Was that another smirk in her tone?

I wanted to smack her — except I was grateful that she was here. I hated to admit that, but it was true. There was no way I would've been able to handle the eighteen hours that I'd been here without her and Hosea.

"It wasn't the best sleep I'd ever had. But at least I was here with Jefferson and I got to wake up next to him … in a way." I yawned, and then did a semi-stretch since I was still holding my coffee.

"Hosea called first thing this morning," Jasmine said as she took a step closer to Jefferson's bed. "They told him there'd been no change, that Jefferson was still resting."

I sighed. "Yeah, the doctor said that he'd be here around ten. I can't wait to speak to him. I'm hoping that he can tell me *something* different than yesterday." This time my yawn was longer and wider.

Jasmine said, "I'm taking you home with me." Before I could say anything, she added, "You don't have to stay. Just take a nap." Then, she sniffed. "And you could use a shower, too."

I narrowed my eyes and tried my best not to smile. "It hasn't been that long; I know I don't stink."

"I'm just sayin' …."

This time, all I could do was smile.

She said, "Ky, we're only twenty minutes away and Hosea will have a car service on standby for you, to take you back and forth or wherever you want to go."

I tilted my head. Jasmine had asked me to forget who she used to me. So, I blinked and tried to see who she was now: Jasmine Cox Larson Bush. First Lady of a mega church, the wife of a preacher. I had to stop and think about that again — Jasmine, the wife of a preacher. That sounded like the punchline of a joke.

She said, "I know you've got to be famished, too."

Her words made my stomach rumble as if my body were on her side, even if the conscious part of me was not. Because no matter how tired, or how hungry or how funky I was, I needed to be with Jefferson every moment.

I shook my head, but she nodded hers.

"This is not open for discussion, Kyla. Just a couple of hours so that you can refresh. So that you can be strong for Jefferson because he needs you."

Her tone was firm, the way it used to be when we were kids and she was always trying to be the boss of me.

But now, I thought about her words. *Strong for Jefferson because he needs you.* It was only because she reminded me of that fact that I said, "All right."

"Good."

"But, I don't have to go to your place. I need to get a hotel anyway. I need to have someplace to put my luggage and to get settled."

"You can do that with us."

"I don't want to put you out."

"And I don't think we have time to go back and forth over this." Jasmine sounded as if she had no plans to relent. "Plus, with the convention in town …." She stopped as if she were sorry that she'd mentioned that. As if that were a reminder of what happened to Jefferson.

I sighed. "I guess …." Turning, I glanced at my husband. Why was I so unsure? Why didn't I want to go anywhere with Jasmine, not even to her home?

"Okay, let's go," Jasmine said as if the decision was already made. I hadn't even heard her move across the room, yet now, she stood by my side, gripping the handle of my carry-on bag. "This is the only one you have, right?"

I hesitated before I nodded.

"It's barely seven, Ky. You said the doctor won't be here till ten so you can be back by then … if you want."

Taking another glance at my husband, I acquiesced. "Okay," I told her and then stepped over to Jefferson's bed. Holding onto the rail, I leaned forward and kissed his forehead. "I'll be right back sweetheart." My fingers trailed his jawline. "I'll be away for just a couple of hours." Leaning over once again, this time, I kissed his lips.

With a final goodbye, I turned away, and faced Jasmine. We both stood, staring at each other like we were the stars in one of those old Western showdowns. Then when Jasmine turned toward the door, I followed her and wondered: was I going home with the woman who once was my dearest friend or with the trick who'd tried to steal my husband twenty years ago.

***

I was weary, but I felt like I had a shot of energy when I walked into Jasmine's apartment. "Wow," I said when we stepped inside the black and white marble-floored foyer. The morning sun shone through the sky light above and highlighted the rounded staircase. But I didn't have a moment to appreciate the space as I followed Jasmine through the mammoth mahogany double doors that led to the massive living room.

There was so much for my senses to appreciate, but I was drawn to the enormous windows that framed a ten million-dollar view of Central Park.

"Wow," was all I could say as I stepped across the room and walked right to the windows.

From this penthouse level, the people below looked like ants and the cars looked like toys. But the park with its sprawling acres of greenery — it was like the best of New York was laid out at my feet.

"This is fabulous, Jas …." I faced her and pulled back my enthusiasm. "I mean, Jasmine."

She tilted her head. "You used to call me Jas all the time."

"Yes." I nodded. "Back … when we were friends."

She opened her mouth, as if she were about to protest, but then, sighed as if she realized her words would do no good. Reaching for my suitcase, she said, "Come on," her voice tight now. "I'll show you where you can freshen up."

From the grand room, we walked down a long mahogany paneled hall, and then, I followed her into a bedroom that was just as elegant as everything else in the apartment.

Jasmine rolled my suitcase into the room and set it next to the canopied-bed. "Your bathroom is here." She pointed toward a door. "There are fresh towels and everything that you'll need. It's a Jack and Jill bathroom, another guest room is on the other side. The kids' rooms, along with our nanny's and our office are upstairs and the master suite is on the other side of the apartment. So you have complete privacy."

I listened to Jasmine give me the facts, so impassively as if she were not impressed by what was clearly impressive. There was not a bit of braggadocio in her tone, which was so different from the Jasmine that I knew. That Jasmine would have still been in awe of her accomplishments. This Jasmine was not.

At the window, she drew open the velvet drapes before she faced me. "Mrs. Sloss will be getting the kids up for school soon. What would you like for breakfast?"

"Your kids."

The smile that lit her face was nothing that I'd ever seen on Jasmine before. "I have two, can you believe it?" She scooted onto the edge of the high bed and kicked up her feet. "Me, married with two kids."

She laughed and I couldn't help but chuckle with her.

"Ky, I never knew that I could be so happy."

"Wow." I sat down next to her. "The Jasmine I knew had a hard time being happy."

The ends of her lips dipped. "I keep trying to tell you that Jasmine is gone. She was looking in all the wrong places for happiness. But once I settled down, I found my happiness in Christ."

I thought back to all the times when I'd tried to talk to Jasmine about God and all the times that she'd laughed at me. "So, you really did that? You gave your life to Christ?"

"Uh-huh." She nodded. "It hasn't been the easiest journey for me, learning how to bow not just my knees, but my heart to God, too. But it's a journey that I'm still traveling and I'm enjoying the trip."

I let her words settle. "Who would have ever thought that I'd be sitting in this magnificent apartment with you, talking about God and your kids."

"I know, right?"

She laughed, but I brought her down a notch when I said, "So this is real, it's not just an act?"

If she'd been a candle, my words had just blown out her flame. She lowered her eyes as if my words had really hurt her. Inside, I shrugged. I wasn't trying to be a mean girl in any kind of way. I just ... didn't trust her.

"I know why you would ask me that." She looked down at her folded hands. "There have been so many things in my life that I wish I could take back." Then, looking up at me, she shook her head. "No, I don't. I wouldn't change anything about my life because all of that dirt that I did and stuff that I caused ... I know I hurt a lot of people, and I'm really so sorry about that part. But I also know that God used all of that to bring me right here. Without any one of those things, I wouldn't be here today, Ky. I'm a better person today because I wasn't so good before."

I knew she was talking about a lot of things in general; I knew she was talking about Jefferson in particular.

She confirmed my thought when she said, "I don't think I will ever be able to apologize enough to you for what happened with me and Jefferson."

This was where I was probably supposed to tell her that I forgave her. What I said was, "So, you must have pictures of your kids."

Now, it was like I lit that wick again. She grabbed her cell phone from inside her purse, flipped through a couple of screens, then held out her phone for me. "This is Zaya."

"Oh, my goodness," I said, chuckling at the photo of a young man in a wide-legged stance, wearing a dark pinned-striped suit with his hands pushed into his pockets. His open-collar made him look so cool, and what was even better was that he held the exact pose as his father, who stood behind him. "He is so handsome. My goodness, Jasmine, he looks just like his father. A mini-Hosea."

There was nothing but love in her laughter. "He does, doesn't he?"

I said, "And his name, so unusual. Zaya?" I looked up at Jasmine.

"He's actually Hosea the second, but when he was born, Jacquie was only two and when she said Hosea, it came out Zaya, so that's how he's known to the world."

"Ah! I get it." I laughed.

Jasmine reached for her phone and flipped to the next picture. "And this is my eleven-year-old diva, Jacqueline."

I took the phone back from Jasmine and froze, though unfortunately, my mouth didn't. "Oh, my God. She looks just like Brian." I paused so that I could breathe and my mind pressed repeat. "She looks like Brian."

I was shocked, though I didn't know why. I guess I'd forgotten just how scandalous Jasmine had been. She'd slept with my husband first, but then a few years later, had gone after Brian. She had slept with two best friends, almost destroying two marriages, getting pregnant by one of the men.

I shuddered thinking how this could have been me, how by the grace of God (because I did ask Jefferson if he'd used a condom) I wasn't looking at a photo double of a mini Jefferson. I wasn't sure if Jefferson and I would have survived that.

She took the phone from my hand, though she had to tug a little bit since I was still kinda in a frozen state. She said nothing and I'd said too much.

She tucked the phone back into her purse, then stood. "Mrs. Sloss, my housekeeper, makes a mean breakfast," she said as if her plan was to just roll over what I'd said. Looking down, she added, "She doesn't believe in the kids eating just cereal, so after you freshen up, you can have breakfast if you want," she looked up, "or not." She paused waiting for me to say something. I didn't. "You can take a nap, too. Anything that you want."

I nodded.

She did the same, then moved toward the door. Right when she stepped to the threshold, I called out to her.

When she turned back, I said, "Thank you."

She gave me just a single dip of her chin, then closed the door behind her. I didn't wait even a half a moment before I grabbed my cell phone.

Pressing the name, I then held the phone to my ear, not even wanting to take the time to plug in my earbuds.

After just two rings, I heard, "Hello."

Alexis's voice was filled with sleep, and that was the first time I glanced at the clock. The clock hadn't clicked to eight, which meant the sun wasn't even thinking about rising in Los Angeles yet.

"Oh, my God, Alexis. I'm sorry."

"No, no, that's okay," she said, her voice coming to life. "You know you can call me at any time and your mom and I thought you were going to call last night."

"I know." I paced at the foot of the bed, though it was hard to pick up any kind of speed since my feet kept sinking into the thick carpet. "I was; I was just so exhausted."

"That's what we figured."

I said, "But I'm not too tired to talk to you now. I had to talk to you."

"Why? What's up?" She was at full attention now. "Did something happen with Jefferson?"

"No, I'm going to speak to the doctor as soon as I get back to the hospital."

"Back? Where are you? Did you check into a hotel?"

"No." I settled onto the bed and lowered my voice even more, just in case Jasmine had her ear pressed to the door. "I'm at Jasmine's house."

There was a pause. "Jasmine who?"

I was sure Alexis knew who I was talking about. Still, I clarified, "Jasmine Cox Larson."

Another pause. "Jasmine Cox Larson who?"

"Come on, Alexis. You know who."

"Yeah, I do. But I was thinking it was five o'clock in the morning, so something had to be wrong with my ears or your mouth. So ... what are you doing there?"

"They met me at the hospital yesterday. As soon as I got there. I was having a breakdown, long story. But Jasmine and Hosea were there and they've been there ever since."

"So, Hosea was with her?" Alexis didn't give me a chance to respond. "Then, her showing up there was legit. He's a good guy."

"He is. He's exactly like you said."

I could almost feel Alexis nodding. "I'll never forget meeting him when he was in L.A. with his show and when I found out …." She paused. "When I found out that Jasmine had screwed my husband and had a baby."

"That's why I called. All this time since I've been here, I couldn't stop thinking about what she had done with Jefferson. I'd forgotten about her … and Brian. Alexis, she just showed me a picture of the little girl."

"Jacqueline."

"Yeah. And she looks just like Brian."

"I know. I told you that, you just forgot. That was how I found out, remember? I took one look at that little girl and wondered how had Brian's face gotten onto that little body." Alexis paused. "So, I guess she hasn't grown out of that."

"She hasn't. Anybody could be her mother because she took everything from Brian." There was silence, and I said, "Alex, I'm sorry. If this is too much. It's just that I was so shocked. I wasn't prepared."

"No, don't be sorry. Actually I'm glad to know that she's okay. That everything is okay back there."

"Really?" I scooted back on the bed, kicked off my shoes, then, sank onto the silk duvet. "I don't know how you did it. How did you forgive Jasmine?"

"Well," she paused as if she needed to really think about her answer, "first of all, Jacqueline is still Brian's daughter, so how could I wish anything bad for her … or her mother? I really want the best for that little girl."

"I get that part, but what about Jasmine?"

Alexis took another pause. "I'm not sure if I can really explain it, but once I decided to get back with Brian, I had to forgive Jasmine first. I needed to kick her out of our bed because at one point, she was right there with us. But once I forgave her, I let her go — I let all of those images in my mind go. And then, I could really forgive Brian and get us back together. It wasn't easy, though."

As close as Alexis and I were, I was trying to remember had we ever had this conversation. When she'd divorced Brian, she didn't want to talk about him at all. But when they worked to get back together, it never seemed appropriate when we were working so hard to focus on the positive.

I said, "I thought I'd forgiven Jasmine — until I saw her."

"Yeah, it's easy to be a good Christian from a distance. The true test is when it's right there in your face … whew. I don't know if I could stay in her house."

"I'm not staying." I shook my head as if she could see me. "I have to get out of here."

"Now, wait," Alexis said before I got the words completely out of my mouth. "Just because I said I don't know if I could stay there, I think you should. I mean, it's hard enough worrying about you being three thousand miles away and handling Jefferson by yourself. But knowing that you're there with Hosea, at least that makes me feel better."

"I don't know."

"Come on, you said so yourself — Hosea is a good guy."

"Then, what's he doing with Jasmine?"

Alexis laughed. "Good point. But seriously, though, you need to stay there so that you have some kind of support. You don't have to be her best friend; that position is filled. But you do need somewhere to rest and someone to lean on. And in New York, there's no one better than Hosea Bush."

"Well, Nicole is trying to get here."

"Good, but in the meantime, just until Nicole makes it there, hang out with Hosea."

It sounded like it could be a good idea, but the only challenge was Hosea came as a package. I didn't say that to Alexis, though. I changed to, "How's Mom?"

"Sleep."

I chuckled. "I know that."

"Well, that's her current state. You want me to have her call you when she wakes up?"

"Yeah. That would be good. I hope I have some better news to give her, to give you, too."

"You will. That's my prayer. So get back to your husband and

I'm going to get back to sleep. And call me if anything changes."

"I will. I love you, girl."

"I love you more."

When I ended the call, I did it with a sigh. Besides Pastor Ford and my mom, Alexis was always such a guiding spiritual light. She had more of a reason to hate Jasmine, than I did. Yet, she really sounded like she had forgiven her — at least from afar.

I crossed my ankles, pulled my knees to my chest, and wrapped my arms around my legs. After talking to Alexis, I wondered how much of this situation had to do with me and Jasmine. Could all of this be some kind of divine set-up to bring me and Jasmine together? I just never knew with God — He would use the craziest situations to teach. Maybe hidden somewhere in all of this pain, was a lesson on forgiveness, the real kind that came with forgetting, the way Alexis seemed to have done. I'd given complete forgiveness to Jefferson; did I owe that to Jasmine, too?

I placed my cell phone onto the nightstand, then rolled off the bed. From the canopied bed to the cherry-stained nightstands, matching ceiling fan, along with the antique leaning mirror in the corner, this room looked like it was straight out of an upscale designer magazine.

If her surroundings were any indication, if the clothes she now wore told the story, Jasmine was different. Maybe I needed to do what she asked:

Can you do me a favor and try not to remember who I used to be?

As I made my way to the bathroom, I vowed that I would try my best. I'd try to see her for who she said she was now. The only thing: in order to do that, I'd have to trust her.

And trusting Jasmine Cox Larson Bush — that was going to be the hard part.

chapter 9

Jasmine

I walked into our bedroom, just as Hosea was coming out of the bathroom. Usually, my husband being wrapped in a towel was enough to take my thoughts all the way to the right. But at this moment, I just nodded at him, tossed my purse onto the chaise and then, flopped down on the bed.

He frowned, then walked over and sat next to me. "Is everything all right?"

I shook my head, but knew that I needed to fill him in quickly. So, I said, "Nothing's changed with Jefferson," before I sighed.

Hosea didn't seem to notice, though. He released his own long breath. "But I guess you wanted Kyla to come back with you and she didn't, huh?"

"No. She did. She's downstairs in the guest room."

Confusion clouded his face and filled his tone. "Okay, that's good, right?" He didn't give me a chance to respond. "She can get some rest, get something to eat, and maybe you can even talk her into relaxing a bit. I can go to the hospital so that Jefferson won't be alone while you stay here with her."

"I don't think she's going to be here that long."

"Oh." He nodded. "She wants to get right back."

"That … and she wants to get away from me."

He twisted his waist so that he faced me full-on.

After a moment, I said, "Hosea, there's something I have to tell you. There's something I want to tell you because I really need your help."

Now, I pivoted so that I faced him and my glance hit right in the center of his bare chest. His skin glistened from the moisture that remained from his shower. "You're gonna have to get dressed." I shook my head and waved my finger. "I can't focus when you're dressed ... or undressed like that."

He grinned. "It's that serious?"

"It is."

The way I said it, the way I looked at him made him nod, made him stand, made him go into his closet and then come back wrapped in his bathrobe.

He'd done that much too quickly, not giving me enough time to come up with a story that would portray what I had to tell my husband in a brighter light. Now, I'd be forced to just go with the straight truth.

When Hosea sat back down, I took a breath. When he reached for my hands, I was so grateful.

He said, "This is a safe place, Jasmine. You know that."

I did. That was one thing that I knew for sure with Hosea Bush. Through the years, he'd shown me nothing but unconditional love, even through our trials. And so I had no fear sharing this, it wasn't something that would drive him away — especially since it was twenty years ago.

Still, I hated revealing who I used to be to Hosea. He knew that I'd been a liar, he knew that I'd been an adulterer (though he only knew about Brian. I hadn't given him the slew of married men I'd been with). And then, there was the ultimate sin — I'd tried to pass off Jacqueline as his daughter. But all of that had been not only forgiven, but forgotten. Now, I tried my best to live up to what Hosea saw in me.

But what I had to tell him was a reminder ... of my old self.

I wasn't going to prolong this pain, though. I needed to get this out as quickly as I could. "Before you met me, Hosea, I wasn't the best person."

"Well, to be honest, Darlin', you had some challenges when we met, and after we got married, too."

He spoke with a smile and his words were meant to add a bit of humor to make this easier. But I couldn't even smile because the truth, even in jest, really hurt. Looking into my husband's eyes, I said, "I need to tell you what happened with me and Kyla. I have to tell you why it's a miracle that she's even here in our apartment." He took my hands as if he were trying to give me courage and like always, I was filled with so much love for this man who sat next to me and who stood by me always. "I was in a really bad place after my divorce from Kenny. It just seemed like there had never been anything good about my life. I know now, that wasn't true, but I didn't know it then."

He nodded, another gesture to encourage me.

But it wasn't enough; I needed more air, too, so I inhaled. "I coveted everything, Hosea, especially everything that my best friend had."

"Kyla."

I nodded. "I'd known her practically my whole life, she was like my other sister, really. In a way, I was closer to her than Serena because we were the same age. But the thing was, Kyla had every-thing. I'm telling you, she never even had a bad hair day in her life."

"I'm sure that's not true."

"It's not, but you couldn't have told me that then. And once I divorced Kenny, her days seemed to get brighter. Her husband opened that clinic, her daughter was a star even when she was seven and eight, and Kyla didn't have to work." It bothered me a little that I remembered all the facts of that time so well. "A jealousy rose inside of me that I couldn't have controlled, even if I understood it. It was weird, I loved Kyla, I really did. But I wanted what she had — even if I had to take it from her."

He began nodding his head slowly like he knew where this story was going and the old me would have stopped right here. I would have found some reason not to go on. But because of who I really wanted to be, I continued, "That was when I did one of those things that now, looking back, makes me so ashamed." I inhaled, then exhaled the truth, "I seduced her husband. I slept with Jefferson."

Hosea was still bobbing his head and for a moment, I froze. Had I made a mistake? Till now, I'd been able to tell him anything, everything. But over the years, I'd revealed my past to him in a drip-drip-drip fashion. And maybe it had all become too much. Maybe he was finally drowning in my truth and it was now too much to bear.

The way he sat there, saying nothing, just nodding, I wanted to take those words back. Dang! Why had I told him anyway?

But then, he responded: he lifted his arms and wrapped me inside a hug that I didn't know I needed until I rested my head on his shoulder.

My voice trembled when I said, "She's never forgiven me and I don't think that she ever will."

He leaned back. "Did you ask for her forgiveness?"

"I did, but … there's still this chasm between us, this break that no matter how hard I try, I can't seem to fix."

"Well, Darlin', she's been here for what? It hasn't even been twenty-four hours. Give her some time. Yes, forgiveness is supposed to be instant, but you know, we ain't the Lord, and some of us need time to work it out."

I waited a beat. "So … you don't think twenty years is enough?"

He chuckled. "And how much time would you need if someone had done that to you?"

That was a good question and I was glad that Hosea didn't expect an answer because I would have had to tell him the truth. I would have had to tell him that forgiveness would never be an option if any woman stepped to him that way and that he and our kids would have to come to prison to minister to me.

He wrapped my hands inside of his once again. "You've done your part. You've asked for forgiveness and you've repented." He paused and gave me kinda a side glance. "You have repented, right? You're not going to sleep with your new best friend's husband, are you?"

I rolled my eyes, not even going along with this little attempt at a joke. "My best friend is Mae Frances. She's not married."

"Well, I don't know what she's doing down there in Smackover, talkin' about that's her summer place. Who has a summer place in Arkansas?"

When he said it like that, I couldn't help but crack up.

He kept on, "In the last year, she's spent more time down there, than she does here in New York."

"That's true," I said through my laughter. "But how in the world did we start talking about Mae Frances?"

"I wanted to see you smile, Darlin'." Then, his tone returned to his serious ministerial baritone. "I'm just sayin', you've done all that you can do. The rest is on Kyla."

"I just want to prove to her that I've changed."

He shook his head. "The Bible doesn't say anything about you having to prove yourself for forgiveness. Just be honest with her and be yourself. Beyond that, there's nothing that you can do. God has to change her heart."

I hesitated for a moment, wondering if I should tell Hosea about the plan that was at the formulating stages in my mind. About the woman who'd been with Jefferson the other night.

But I held back because I knew my husband. I didn't know if there was anything there, I didn't know if there was really a story behind this woman and Jefferson, but I didn't want Hosea talking me out of it before I got started. So, I kept it to myself — for now.

He said, "Listen, all you can do is be there for Kyla in the way she allows you to be. You're not gonna be able to do anything to force it."

I lowered my eyes so that I wouldn't be telling a bold-faced lie to his face. "I know."

"You know what I want to do now?" he asked, but didn't pause. "I want us to pray so that this won't be so heavy on your heart. God has already forgiven you, Jasmine. Now, you have to forgive yourself."

"I just wish Kyla would."

"Well the truth is, God is the only one you gotta worry about, 'cause as nice as Kyla seems to me, she doesn't have a heaven nor a hell to give to you."

If I hadn't still been filled with shame, I would've given my husband three snaps and two twirls on that one.

He said, "But … I understand how you're feeling, and I want to pray that you will release the guilt because you know that's not of God."

My husband lowered his head and then, I did the same. "Father God, we come to you this morning with hearts filled with praise and thanksgiving …."

My thoughts wandered. It wasn't that I didn't want to pray; I needed this because I wanted to release the heaviness that I'd carried for twenty years. It'd been such a burden to bear and I knew that prayer would help. But I had a chance to assist my prayers, to move things along a little faster because prayers without works were dead.

Now, I knew the scripture wasn't exactly that way, but the premise was the truth. I could wait for something to happen or I could go out and just do what I do.

So as Hosea prayed, one half of my brain prayed with him and on the other side, I tried to figure out my next steps. And what I would do if I found out that woman was having an affair with Jefferson. How would I handle that? How would I protect Kyla?Then once I solved this whole thing, maybe in addition to God, Kyla would be able to forgive me, too.

***

"And, I told Holly, that I was going to be the one to play Jesus's mother, Mary in the Christmas play because Jesus was really black and since there're only five black girls at Caldwell and I'm the only one in drama, she could just give up that idea of getting that part."

I drummed my fingers atop the kitchen table as I sat with Jacqueline and Zaya. They chatted as they ate their breakfast but my mind felt like a galaxy of shooting stars, thoughts bouncing from one end of my brain to the other.

"Mama!"

"Huh?"

"You're not listening to me."

That made me focus my attention, or at least my eyes on my daughter. "Yes, I am."

"Then, what did I say?" my pre-teen challenged me like she was a grown woman.

"Uh …."

"I can tell you everything she said, Mama," my nine-year-old heart came to my rescue. "She said, she told Holly …."

Then, my son went on to tell me the exact words Jacqueline had spoken. But not even that was good enough for my diva. "Yup, that's what I said, but you should have been listening, too, Mama."

"I'm sorry." I covered her hand with mine, looked up, then jumped up.

"Kyla!"

I didn't know how long she'd been standing there, but the way she was staring at my children, it seemed she'd been there for a while.

We stood there in the midst of a few passing moments and I wished that I could read her thoughts. After I left Hosea, I'd knocked on her door, but when there was no answer, I joined my children for breakfast the way I always did.

I said, "I'm sorry. I didn't see you."

Moving toward her, I beckoned her to come into the kitchen. "Come on, sit with us. What do you want to eat? Mrs. Sloss can make you whatever you want."

Kyla took slow steps toward me, but her eyes were fixed on Jacqueline and inside I moaned. How was I supposed to help Kyla forget about my past when Brian's face was connected to my daughter's body?

But I didn't sound as if I'd had any kind of apprehension when I said, "Kyla, I'm so glad you're getting a chance to meet my children."

Before I could say more, Jacqueline stood and marched over until only a few feet separated her from Kyla. I studied my daughter, hoping that she didn't see the wonder in Kyla's eyes.

I told my daughter, "Jacquie, this is one of my best friends. I grew up with her in Los Angeles. This is Auntie ... "

Kyla interrupted with, "Kyla. Just call me Ms. Kyla." Then, she pulled my daughter into a hug. "It's so nice to meet you, Jacqueline."

The way Kyla stopped me told me that she didn't want that kind of connection to my children and that made my heart ache. But I played it off, standing straight, standing strong.

"Hi, Ms. Kyla," Jacqueline said as she returned Kyla's hug.

Then, Zaya stood and did the same. Kyla stood back and holding both of their hands, she stared at my children some more, although this time, she was careful to give equal time to my son.

"It is so nice to meet both of you," she said.

"Do you have any children?" Jacqueline asked.

Kyla nodded. "I do. I have a daughter."

Jacqueline's eyes brightened as visions of a new friend danced in her head.

I said, "But her daughter is a little bit older."

She tilted her head. "How old?"

Kyla responded, "Nicole is thirty."

"Thirty," Jacqueline and Zaya exclaimed as if they couldn't imagine such an age.

Then with eyes wide, Jacqueline asked, "You have a daughter who's thirty?"

Kyla laughed. "I do."

"Wow!" Zaya said. "So how old are you?"

"Son!" I jumped in. "It's not polite to ask a woman her age," I said, as Kyla laughed.

"That's right," Jacqueline said, her tone filled with the exasperation of the embarrassed big sister. "Everyone knows that."

"Sorry," he whispered.

"Oh, that's all right." Kyla put her arm around him. "I wouldn't mind telling you my age, but I'm not sure you can count that high."

He looked up at her with wonder, as if he were trying to imagine what number could that be? She squeezed his shoulders, assuring him, then turned to me.

"I took a shower and changed my clothes." She swept her hands down the length of the maxi dress that she wore under a denim jacket. "So, I was thinking that I should get back to the hospital."

"What about having something to eat?"

She shook her head. "I'm fine. I can't eat anyway."

"Okay," I said. "Let me get the kids out the door and I'll go with you."

"No, Jasmine. You don't have to do that."

"Of course she does." Hosea's voice came into the kitchen before he did and when he entered, I noticed the way Kyla smiled at him, a genuine one that rose from her lips to her eyes rather than the polite, but plastic grimace that she gave to me. "Good morning." My husband squeezed Kyla in a hug. "So, you're ready to get back up to the hospital?"

"I am. I'm so grateful." She glanced at me. "I needed the break."

"Well then, maybe you should stay a little longer," I said, hoping that she didn't hear my hope. "You should try to eat something."

Hosea said to me, "Kyla can get something at the hospital, right?"

When Kyla nodded, I did, too. I guess I was trying a bit too hard and my husband was pulling me back.

Then, he said, "So why don't you two do this, go on to the hospital, I'll get the kids off to school …."

"Daddy, I don't need anyone to get me off …."

He ignored our daughter. "And then, I have to check in at the church, but I'll be up there in a couple of hours to support you in any way that you need."

I watched Kyla exhale and do that genuine smile thing again. "Thank you."

"All right, then," I said. "Well, we can get going," I told Kyla. "I called the car service," Hosea said to both of us. "They're downstairs, but you don't have to rush."

"No, I'm ready to go now."

Hosea said, "I'll carry your suitcase down for you."

That was the first time I noticed it. Kyla's suitcase at the edge of the archway that led to the kitchen.

"Oh," I said. "Why are you taking your suitcase? Aren't you

staying here?"

"I don't want to impose."

"I told you," I took a step closer to her, "it's not an imposition. We want you to stay."

It was the way she took a step back that told me that what she wanted was to leave.

Hosea said, "Okay, another suggestion. You can leave your suitcase here and then tonight, depending on how you're feeling and what you decide, I'll bring it wherever you need it."

Kyla didn't even hesitate. "Okay."

As I hugged my children goodbye, Kyla hugged my husband. She said, "Thank you, Hosea. Thank you for everything."

I left her in the kitchen saying goodbye to my children as I dashed into the bedroom to grab my purse. Kyla wasn't turning to me, but at least, she had Hosea. She was depending on him and I understood that. It was the same way that I'd depended on Jefferson all those years ago.

As I grabbed my purse, I said a little prayer, giving God thanks that Kyla Blake wasn't anything like Jasmine Cox Larson.

chapter 10

Kyla

This didn't make a lot of sense to me, but I couldn't stop the tremors. Not my hands, not my legs. I wasn't trembling because of fear. Before we'd left, Hosea had taken my hand and standing in a circle with their children and Jasmine, he had prayed for me and Jefferson.

When he'd finished, Jacqueline and Zaya had hugged me and told me that they hoped Mr. Jefferson got well soon. They didn't know me nor my husband, didn't really know what had happened to him, yet, their words were sincere. They had the heart of their father and I'd walked out of their apartment and into the waiting black Sedan with such peace.

But now, it felt like a bit of peace inched out of me with each block we drove. Because though I had left three of the Bushes behind, the fourth one was sitting next to me.

My eyes were on the window, watching the cars that rolled along beside us. It wasn't nine yet, so I guessed rush hour was the reason for this crawling traffic. But even as I kept my gaze away from Jasmine, I felt hers on me.

I knew Jasmine only wanted to help. That was why she insisted on accompanying me and I hadn't objected because Hosea had agreed. But her presence wasn't aiding me in any kind of way.

Truly, I wanted to find some way to wash away my thoughts of the past. I wanted a tsunami of memories featuring all of Jasmine's good deeds to overcome me, forcing me to forget so that I could truly forgive. But that felt like such an oxymoron to me — Jasmine and good deeds.

"Are you all right?" Jasmine touched my arm.

For the first time, I faced her and did my best to give her a smile. "I'm good. Thank you again for …."

"You don't have to keep saying that, Kyla," she interrupted me. "I just did what I was supposed to do."

I nodded even though I wanted to ask was that how she justified what she'd done with Jefferson? Was that what she was supposed to do?

Inside I sighed. I needed that tsunami of good deeds.

As the car slowed in front of the hospital, I glanced at my watch. "I'll still be able to talk to the doctor."

"With time to spare," she said as the car stopped and the driver jumped out to open the door curbside. Together, we thanked him, and I moved to the door of the hospital refreshed and with a renewed purpose. Jasmine stayed silent as we walked through the lobby into the elevator. Even though we were alone in the chamber, she still said nothing.

When we stepped from the elevator, I almost bumped right into Dr. Reid.

"Oh," Jasmine and I said at the same time.

The doctor stepped back, as if he were surprised to see me. "Mrs. Blake. I had to check on another patient and was going to come back, but if you have some time now …."

"Yes," I told him. "I'm glad I caught you."

"Definitely perfect timing." He led us from the elevator to the side of the nurses station. He looked around as if to assess if there would be listening ears. Then, he said, "I had a few questions about your husband's medical history." He tapped his tablet and when he looked up, his glance fell to Jasmine.

She said, "I'll be over there."

I nodded, and turned back to the doctor, but just as I did, I watched a woman ease out of one of the rooms. Was that Jefferson's room?

As the doctor droned on, I counted — one, two, three, four, five.

Yes! That woman had come out of my husband's room. I probably wouldn't have noticed her — it was the hat that caught my attention. The big floppy hat and shades — on the fourth floor of a hospital. As if she were trying to be incognito and was too dumb to know that she drew more attention to herself.

She took two steps our way, looked up, then, swiveled and went the other way.

"Mrs. Blake?"

My eyes and ears focused on the doctor. "I'm sorry, Doctor Reid."

But then, over his shoulder, I saw Jasmine rush behind the floppy-hatted woman, as if she were trying to catch her.

My antenna shot straight up to ninety degrees, but I was torn — did I want to know what was going on with Jasmine and this woman — whoever she was? Or did I want to do everything I could to help my husband?

I chose Jefferson, the way I would all day, every day.

But as I tried to concentrate on the doctor's words, my eyes kept wandering to that woman. And Jasmine. She'd caught up to her and now they stood at the end of the hallway, by the staircase.

They knew each other, I was sure of that. It was the way they spoke. The two were too far away for me to hear anything, but I could see their gestures — familiar.

All kinds of thoughts bombarded the walls of my mind:

The police had asked me about a woman.

Jasmine was a liar.

A woman had been with Jefferson.

Jasmine was a cheater.

I wanted to do everything that I could to save my husband, but I was drawn to the drama playing out in front of me. It almost felt like this had something to do with saving Jefferson's life.

"Doctor Reid, I have to take care of something."

I hated that I walked away from the man who was trying to save my husband, but I felt as if this woman had something to do with all of this. I quickened my steps.

The woman turned; her hat hung low across her face, so her eyes were hidden. But she stiffened when she saw me coming. Like before, she swiveled, pushed the door to the stairwell and disappeared.

Jasmine stood there, but by the time I was within feet of her, she faced me.

The look on her face made me want to do what the woman had just done. Made me want to turn and run away. But I stood my ground.

"Who was that?" I asked.

If Jasmine wasn't black, right now, she would have looked white. I was sure of it. Because it was like every bit of blood drained from her face. But even though she looked as if she'd just had an encounter with a ghost, her only answer to my question was, "Who?"

That single word was like a punch to my gut. It was a one syllable lie and this was why our friendship could only be spoken about in past tense. "The woman who you were just speaking to."

"Oh ... her." A beat. "I ... I don't know."

"I saw her coming out of Jefferson's room, Jasmine." My voice had raised; my voice was tight. "Who is she?"

Now, more than a beat passed. Jasmine's eyes fluttered. "I don't know."

My insides became a brewery for my anger. "You were talking to her. Don't play with me."

"No, really, I don't know." She shook her head with every word that she spoke.

For just a flicker of a second, it sounded like, it looked like she was telling the truth. Because of the way she looked right into my eyes, not flinching, just pleading.

But since I knew her, I knew it was a performance because there was no truth within Jasmine. "You were talking to her."

Another beat. Another. Then, another. Then, Jasmine's face went blank, now void of any expression. Except she had that look, that look where I could almost see the lies percolating inside of her.

She said, "I don't ...."

Already I knew — that was the prologue to another lie and I held up my hand. If I wasn't a woman of a certain age (and a certain class), I would have palmed her, smashed her face so hard that she would have been sniffing her brain.

But really, all I wanted to do was to get away from her. I never wanted to hear another lie, never wanted to see another fake smile, never wanted to be around her again.

I had tried to repair the irreparable and that was impossible.

Turning, I stomped back down the hall. Dr. Reid was gone and that was fine. I'd catch up with him later. Right now, I had to protect my husband in another kind of way.

I pushed the door to his room open and stomped inside. By the time I reached his bed side, I'd calmed down. By the time I held his hand, my heart had returned to its normal pace.

"Hey, baby," I said and kissed his forehead.

But while my heart was now steady, my mind was not. I needed to get Jefferson away from here, back to Los Angeles where he would be away from all of this. Comatose patients could be transferred, I knew that. That was what I wanted to do with my husband because I had a feeling that he wouldn't be safe until he was far away from Jasmine Cox Larson.

After a few minutes, I walked to the door, peeked into the hallway and was relieved when there was no sign of Jasmine. Good! I'd half-expected her to follow me, but I guess even bad liars had good sense.

I spotted the nurse who'd been taking care of Jefferson during the first shift. She smiled when I approached.

"Good morning. I heard you got a chance to get away from here for a couple of hours."

"Yes," I told her, though I didn't return her smile. "Would you mind paging Doctor Reid? I need to speak to him." Without waiting for a response, I half-turned to Jefferson's room. But then, I faced her again and added, "Stat." I paused. "Please."

chapter 11

Jasmine

Around me, Harlem sang and I cried. Tears may not have been rolling down my cheeks, but I was crying. And wondering — what had just happened?

It was after nine now, yet New Yorkers rushed passed me, around me, dashing down the subway stairs as if somehow they could still make it to work on time. But even though I was bumped and nudged a couple of times, I kept my pace slow and steady because that was the only way I could keep my legs moving.

Passing the Schomburg Center, I paused. Where was I going? All I knew was that I had to get away from the hospital — even for a little while. I had to get away from Kyla and that look. That look on her face that was a fusion of disbelief and disdain. That look that summarized all that Kyla thought of me. The only thing that was missing was the hate and I knew that if I'd stayed in that hospital, hate was not far away.

I shook my head and once again, propelled forward, walking toward nowhere. I couldn't believe this happened. Kyla and I had made progress, but the few steps that we'd taken forward had just been washed away like footprints in the sand.

Kyla had looked at me as if I were a liar. But how was I supposed to answer her questions? It wasn't like I had any answers; I had far more questions now than I did before.

The memory of my conversation with that woman made me take an extra breath, made me do more than just slow my steps. I had to stop in front of one of the stoops on 135th Street. I just stood there and remembered ....

As I stepped away from Kyla and Dr. Reid, the door to Jefferson's room opened and a woman eased out. She took a couple of steps toward us, then pivoted and tiptoed the other way. If she were try-ing not to be noticed, she had the wrong approach because it was hard to miss her. She'd stood out yesterday in the waiting room in her red hip-hugging dress and matching fascinator, and today, she did the same. Clearly, she had a penchant for those polyester-spandex blends that had been fashioned into dresses that caressed every bend and curve of a woman's body. Because the dress she wore today was the same — same style, same fit, only blue. And today, it was accessorized with that ridiculous wide-brimmed hat that hid every part of her face, except for her lips that were painted the same shade as the dress she wore.

It looked like she was actually trying to walk on her toes, truly tiptoe away, which had to be challenging in her stilettos. That was why once I started moving, I knew that I would catch her. Her stilettos were no match for my sneakers.

Right before she reached the stairwell, I darted in front of her, covered the knob and blocked the door.

Her head leaned back, so that now, in addition to her blue lips, I saw her nose and one eye. "Excuse me."

"I'm sorry," I said. Then, I asked, "May I talk to you for a second?" The floppy hat quivered as she shook her head. "I'm really in a hurry and I don't have anything to talk about since I have no idea who you are."

She tried to step around me, but I was that tree — now that she stood in front of me, I was not about to be moved.

"Really?" She threw up her hands in exasperation. And with that gesture, her face was exposed. She was a beautiful woman ... I'd noticed that yesterday, though she had caked on too much make-up, even for me.

She was like the color yellow — not in terms of her skin-tone;

clearly she was an African American woman. But it was like sun rays bounced from her. Her features looked almost sculpted, though the sculptor could have used a bit more collagen in her lips. Besides that, though, she was probably the perfect art model.

Down the hall, I saw Kyla straining to look over the doctor's shoulder, though he blocked most of her view. I wanted to drag the woman into the staircase so that Kyla wouldn't see any of this, but I couldn't take the chance of her getting into that space and then, getting away. Here, she couldn't turn away from me. She couldn't go in the other direction because if she did, she'd have to pass Kyla and I had a feeling that she didn't want to do that.

I angled my body just in case Kyla had taken a lip-reading class in the last twenty years and turned my attention back to the woman. "Look, I'm taking a big guess here, but I'm thinking you don't want to make a scene. So, I'll keep my voice down, if you tell me what I want to know."

She folded the brim of the hat back so that now, I could clearly see her. "What do you want?"

A moment ago, I'd pegged her as an art model, but with her voice, I gave her a new profession. She could make major cash on one of those sex-after-dark phone lines.

With her face in full view, I did my assessment in seconds. She was a woman who used every bit of what she had to get what she wanted. I didn't have a single doubt — she could lure the most faithful of men.

Is that what happened with Jefferson? Had she drawn Jefferson into her web and her bed?

Another glance down the hall at Kyla — her eyes were still on me. My time was dwindling because I knew my friend. "How do you know Jefferson?" With my tone, I let her know that my ques-tion was a demand for answers.

The woman folded her arms and in one second flat, she went from vamp to sistah. Her blue lips became duck lips before she said, "I have no idea who you're talking about," and her neck rolled with every syllable.

"Don't play dumb; I don't have time to go through twenty

questions with you," I said. "This is what I know: you were here yesterday, you listened to my conversation with the doctor, and you were just coming out of Jefferson's room. So ... who are you?"

She did those lips and rolled her neck again. "I wasn't here yesterday and as far as coming out of the room, I was lost. I was in the right room, wrong floor."

My being nice, asking simple questions, expecting direct answers wasn't working, so I stepped closer, though I made sure that my body still blocked the door. She would have to pull an all-star linebacker move to make it past me. "How do you know Jefferson?"

She   sighed,   then   smirked.   "He's   a ...   friend."

She'd said friend, but with the way she purred, she might as well have just come on and said lover.

"A friend?" I repeated, hoping that maybe she would correct what I was thinking.

She shifted her small handbag from one hand to the other. "Yes." She gave me a one-shoulder shrug. "A friend."

"How do you know him?" I asked again. "What kind ... of friend?"

She leaned forward. "The best kind." She did that purring thing again. "The kind that comes ... with benefits."

I almost collapsed with shock and disappointment. But I was the hunter, and surely, couldn't let the hunted see my weakness.

"I don't believe you," I said.

"And I would care what you believe ....why? You're not even his wife." She glanced over her shoulder, letting me know that she knew some facts.

My plan had been to confront her, to intimidate her, to get her to confess and spill everything that I needed to know. But she had taken that script and flipped it upside down and then turned it inside out and now I was the one who wanted to run away. Since yesterday, I'd wanted to figure out the mystery of this woman so that I could help Kyla. But in this instant, I was so sorry that I'd asked any questions or knew anything. Because now, what was I supposed to do with this information?

This was between Kyla and Jefferson and I had just put myself in the middle.

"So, now that you know, you can get the hell out of my way."

There was a part of me that wanted to step aside, let her go, pretend that I hadn't heard a thing, and then just go home and pray that Kyla and Jefferson would work it out. But now that I knew, I wanted to know more, needed to know more, was about to ask more. Except I saw Kyla coming our way.

"Are you going to move, or do I have to move you?"

There were so many reasons why I wanted to take her up on that challenge. I wanted to kick her ass just because she was sleeping with my best friend's husband. And then, I paused. Had I really just had that thought? I had been this woman — twenty years ago. I stepped aside and she rushed past me into the stairwell right before Kyla reached us ....

Then, Kyla began asking me all of those questions and I had no idea how to answer. In one ear I heard Kyla, and in the other, I heard that woman. Kyla demanded the truth from me, but what was that? What did I know?

Well first, I knew that the woman in the floppy hat knew Jefferson. That was a fact. She knew him and she knew Jefferson had a wife — and she knew Kyla was his wife. At least, that was what I assumed with the way she'd told me that I wasn't married to Jefferson.

And I knew the big news — that she was involved with Jefferson. Or so she said; maybe she was lying. But why would she lie? Why would she say that she was his friend ... with benefits ... if it weren't true? Why would she be hanging around the hospital if she wasn't the side chick?

I rolled the conversation back through my mind, and the more I thought about what she'd said, the more I doubted her. If she were Jefferson's jump-off, then why was she so forthright about it? Why would she tell me because if she knew so much about Jefferson and Kyla, then she should know that I was a friend — at least she could assume that with the way I'd been at the hospital. So, wouldn't she be afraid that I'd tell Kyla? She wouldn't want Kyla to know, would she?

Shaking my head, I thought back to my time with Jefferson — I did want Kyla to know. Because with the way my mind was set up back then, I figured that once she knew, she'd leave Jefferson and he'd be mine.

Maybe this trick had the same plan. Maybe she wanted Kyla's life and was going to confront Kyla at some point because that was what I would've done.

I moaned. The thought of that with what Kyla was already going through made me sick. It would be horrible for her to have to deal with Jefferson's throw away while Jefferson was in a coma.

There was no way that I could let that happen. First, I had to get back to the hospital and somehow keep the truth from her while at the same time, getting her to trust me. Once I did that, I'd be able to move forward with the business of taking care of business.

Swiveling around, I turned back toward Malcolm X Boulevard and with each step, my plan became clearer in my mind.

chapter 12

Kyla

"I understand you wanting to get him home," Dr. Reid said to me, "but we only move a patient when there's a reason and when it's in his best interest. Truly, what's best for your husband is to just rest now. He's getting the best of care here and that's what matters most."

For the last twenty minutes, I'd been pleading my case to take Jefferson across the country where he could be cared for by the top doctors and loved by his family and friends. But if this had been a trial, I'd just lost the case. Dr. Reid had me at 'what's best for your husband ...' I couldn't make this about me — and Jasmine.

Thanking Dr. Reid, I assured him that I understood and that from this point, I'd be the supportive wife.

"I know you slept here last night, Mrs. Blake. Maybe what you need is to really get some rest. Is there someone you can stay with or are you going to check into a hotel?"

"I went home with a," I had to pause for a second, "friend ... for a few hours this morning. But, I'm fine now."

He gave me a look that told me I was far from fine and that my idea to move my husband three thousand miles was proof that I needed to close my eyes and go to sleep for a while.

"Let's make a deal," Dr. Reid began. "I'll do my job and take care of Doctor Blake. And you do your job and get some rest."

I shook my head. "No, I'm fine. I want to be here for my husband."

"I understand, everyone says that. But here's the thing — your husband, he's resting, you're not. So when he wakes up, he's going to be ready to get out of here, maybe hit a couple of clubs, stay out all night. But you ... you'll be too tired." He shrugged before he gave me a smile and I couldn't help but give him a little laugh.

Gently, he rested a hand on my shoulder. "Promise me, you'll at least consider my advice."

I nodded, then he tapped something onto his tablet before he stepped away. Turning back to Jefferson's room, I paused before I pushed the door open — I needed a moment to gather all of this in my head.

Slowly, I strolled back down to the waiting room, and was a bit relieved when I saw just one woman in there, holding a rosary. Sitting near the door, I let everything that happened this morning settle in my mind. All I wanted to do was focus on my husband, but my thoughts kept returning to Jasmine.

What was up with her? Why was she lying? Who was that woman?

As soon as I asked myself those questions, I pushed them aside. Yes, Jasmine had cleaned up over the years, but no amount of designer outfits or red bottom shoes or cash in the bank could change her soul. Clearly, not even her husband nor the Lord had been able to do that, so why was I trying to figure it out?

I sighed. I just needed to get my tablet, get online and check into a hotel. Hosea said that he'd bring my suitcase wherever I needed, and I would tell him as soon as he got here. Pushing myself up from my chair, I turned to the entry, and there was Jasmine.

She took a step toward me which made me want to take two dozen steps back.

She said, "I ... is everything okay with Jefferson?"

My eyes narrowed. "He's the same. Nothing's happened in the last hour."

She nodded, looked around, then ran her hands up and down her arms like she was suddenly chilly.

I felt the question rising inside of me and I was angry at myself for one: wanting to ask this question and two: for thinking that if I'd ask, I'd get an honest answer from the woman whose face showed up under 'Notorious Liars' and 'Famous Skanks' in Wikipedia. But even though I knew I wouldn't get the truth, I couldn't help myself. "Jasmine, who was that woman you were talking to?"

First, she gave me a blank stare, then in seconds, I watched that blankness melt and in its place was what? Honesty?

She nodded, then motioned for me to return to where I'd been sitting and she followed. She inhaled a big gulp of air before she said, "I don't know."

"Really, Jasmine?" She had done exactly what I knew she would do. I sprang up from that chair, but before I could take a step, she reached for my arm.

"Wait! No really, Kyla. I don't know her, but I can tell you what we talked about."

I squinted as if somehow that would help me discern the truth better.

She said, "I asked her about … Jefferson."

That made me open my eyes, wide, this time. Made me back step and sit down. Made me take a couple of yoga-style inhales because now, my heart was jumping.

She did the same breathing exercise that I'd just done, then said, "Remember when you spoke with the police yesterday? Remember when they asked you about a woman?"

I gulped, nodded, then wondered if I should tell her that I'd changed my mind. I didn't want to know anymore.

But I stayed silent, so she continued, "Well to be honest, Ky, I was really curious or maybe it was just that I was suspicious, I don't know which one. But I wanted to know who'd been with Jefferson."

When she paused, I wanted to grab her shoulders and shake the rest of the story from her because now that she'd started I wanted to know what she knew. But she'd paused … why? My heart didn't have this kind of patience. If she didn't keep on talking, surely, I would stop breathing.

Probably no more than five seconds passed, though it was longer than a couple of eternities for me, when she finally continued, "When I saw that woman coming out of Jefferson's room earlier, I immediately thought she was the one the police were asking about."

I swallowed and tried to keep my lips from trembling. "Was she?"

It wasn't until Jasmine shook her head that I breathed.

"No," she said. Then, with as much gaiety as she had when we used to gossip back in high school, she added, "That chick is just trying to get with Doctor Reid."

I blinked. "What?" I blinked again.

She nodded and leaned forward as if she were about to share something so scandalous, she didn't want to take the chance of being overheard. "She says that the doctor is her boo and they'd had some kind of argument so she came up here to the hospital to talk to him." Jasmine didn't even pause, she kept talking — just like when we were in high school. "She found him in Jefferson's room, but he wouldn't talk to her because he said it was so unprofessional. And girl," Jasmine lowered her voice so much that now, I had to lean forward, "she said Doctor Reid told her it was over between them." Now, she leaned back. "That's why she was still in Jefferson's room when Doctor Reid left. Because he told her to get herself together and then get out."

She paused, and I sat there, waiting for more.

"You can close your mouth now, Ky," Jasmine said and I clamped my mouth shut.

But I had to work hard to stop it from opening wide again because this story was just so unbelievable ... that it was believable.

I waited a few more moments before I said, "Really?"

Jasmine nodded and gave me a little conspiratorial side-eye — just like in high school.

"Well, why didn't you just tell me this before?"

Her grown demeanor was back when she sighed. "I know. It was just that she asked me not to say anything and you have to admit, it is pretty embarrassing. Plus, I didn't want you to be upset with Doctor Reid."

I frowned. "Why would I be upset with him?"

"I don't know." She shrugged. "Maybe you would have thought that he should have called security. Maybe you would have thought that he shouldn't have left her alone in Jefferson's room."

"Well ... that part is true."

"See," she exclaimed like she had just made a major point. "And I didn't think there was the need to bring anymore drama into your life."

I stared at Jasmine and wondered if she understood that by her not telling the truth before ... that was the drama.

She said, "I was just trying to protect you and I didn't do it the right way. I lied and for that, I'm really sorry because while I know that we'll never be what we were, what I want you to know now is that you really can trust me." Jasmine covered my hand with hers. "Hosea and I really want to be here for you, Ky. Know that."

I looked down to where her hand touched mine and that made me remember how Jasmine had always played the role of protector. Maybe that was all there was to this. Maybe Jasmine was trying to take care of me and I'd read more into the situation because — well, because she was Jasmine Cox Larson.

When I looked up, I nodded and she nodded back.

"So," she said. "Now that that's out the way, can we go back to being friends?"

The words she spoke were just as genuine as the distrust that was still in my heart. Why couldn't I take a measure of this woman — add up all the years of friendship we'd had, all the good times we'd had, all the wonderful things she'd done and let all of that override her one transgression. Why was the worst thing that Jasmine had ever done worth more than all the goodness?

"Ky?" she interrupted my thoughts. "Friends?"

I opened my mouth to tell her my truth, but before I could get, "No," out, I heard the most beautiful sound.

"Mom!"

I looked up and my heart jumped up, but I stayed still because shock kept me right in my seat. My daughter rushed to me and by the time she was in front of me, I found the strength to stand.

"Nicole!" Pulling her into my arms, I burst into tears. "I've been calling you. How did you get here? How did you get here so fast? Why didn't you tell me you were on your way?"

She laughed. "Which question do you want me to answer first?"

"All of them," I said.

"I will, but I have a question for you." She pulled me down into a seat. "How's dad?"

"He's the same." I squeezed her hand. "But the doctor said that he's hopeful."

"I want to see him."

"Of course." We were still holding hands when we stood and it wasn't until then, that I remembered.

"Oh." I faced Jasmine.

When I looked at her, Nicole did, too. "Hello," my daughter said, her tone filled with the politeness reserved for strangers.

"Nicole, I don't know if you remember Jasmine," I said.

Nicole's eyes spread into the size of half-dollars. "Oh, my God. Auntie Jasmine?" She threw her arms around Jasmine's neck for a couple of seconds before she stepped back and took Jasmine's hands inside of hers. "It's been years. What are you doing here?"

A mist covered Jasmine's eyes as she stared and took in all of Nicole. "Look at the beautiful woman you've become." Her voice shook a little, and that filled me with emotion, too.

"Thank you, but look at you. I'm so glad to see you," Nicole said, embracing Jasmine once again. She was still talking when she leaned away to look into Jasmine's face some more. "Mom told me that you moved away and the two of you just lost touch. I have always wondered what happened to you."

"I live here in New York and when I heard about what happened to your dad, I came running."

"Oh, my God. You live here? So you've been here with Mom the whole time?" Nicole looked from Jasmine to me and then back to Jasmine.

I answered for Jasmine. "Yes, she has, sweetheart. She and her husband have been very supportive."

"Oh, thank you. Thank you so much, Auntie Jasmine. I didn't want my mom to be alone."

"You're welcome. But why don't you go see your dad and we'll catch up later. I'll be right here."

"Okay." She gave Jasmine that smile that I loved so much, and then holding onto me with one hand, and rolling her suitcase behind her with the other, we made our way to Jefferson's room.

I was so grateful in this moment that I almost forgot about what had happened between me and Jasmine this morning.

Almost.

chapter 13

Jasmine

It was hard for me to sit and wait. What I wanted to do was rush into Jefferson's room and just stare at Nicole. Even now, I wiped away a tear. Who would have thought a year, a month, or even a week ago that I'd be sitting here with Kyla and her daughter?

It didn't feel like old times, but I didn't feel that awkward separation either, especially now that Nicole was here. Kyla and I were far from being friends, but once again, I had hope — because of Nicole and because I had told a lie.

My lie was brilliant, it was gargantuan, and it was kinda, sorta, close to the truth. But it was a lie that had worked. I had pulled off an Oscar, Tony, and (if I'd sung a few words) Grammy award winning performance, reaching back to our high school days when I used to love spilling some major tea.

When I'd sat next to Kyla, I'd had everything that I needed to convince her: the persona, the demeanor, everything to get her to believe me when I told her that woman was involved with Dr. Reid.

Now that she did believe, I could focus on earning her trust. And that would come with me solving this mystery of the mysterious woman. But before I did that, I planned to spend the rest of the afternoon bonding with my friend and her daughter.

I was in the waiting room alone, which was the only reason why

I pulled out my cell. Pressing the number under 'Hubby' I grinned as soon as I heard my husband's voice.

"Talk to me." That was always his greeting.

"I'm still at the hospital, but Nicole's here." When he stayed silent, I realized just how little of this part of my past my husband knew. "Nicole, Kyla's daughter."

"Oh. Good."

"I know. She's made a major difference for Kyla. You should see her; she feels so much better, looks stronger."

"I'm happy about that. So, I'll have Mrs. Sloss get the other guest room ready."

"Yes." I knew that I was wearing one of those tips-of-lips to tips-of-ears grins. "I'll give you a call when we're on our way. It may be later. I'm sure Nicole will want to spend as much time as she can with her dad."

"Of course. Just let me know and I'll have a car sent for you. Don't even worry about Uber."

"You know you're the best, baby."

"It's easy to be the best when I've got the best."

Then, together, we said, "I love you," before we clicked off our phones.

While I waited, I checked my Twitter timeline, then switched over to Facebook, but I couldn't focus on any of the postings. There was nothing going on in the world right now that was more important than what was going on right here.

My hope was still floating when Kyla and Nicole returned, about an hour later.

"How is he?" I stood as they approached.

With the tip of her finger, Nicole dabbed a tear at the corner of her eye.

"He's good," she said. "Well, not good, but the doctor came in for a little while and I was glad for that." She nodded. "I was able to talk to him and it was good to hear from the doctor that dad's just resting. He said that's what comas are all about."

"That's right, sweetie." Kyla rubbed her daughter's back. "Since I've been here, I'm convinced that your dad will be fine."

Like I'd told Hosea, Kyla's voice was stronger now, filled with steadiness and sturdiness. She even stood taller. As if having Nicole by her side renewed her fortitude — made her wear the armor of a mother's might.

"I agree with your mom," I told Nicole. "I believe with all of my heart that your dad will be fine."

She glanced up, nodded, then reached for me in another embrace. I glanced at Kyla as I held her daughter. She stood, without a smile — at first. And then, the ends of her lips curved up, though some might have said that it was closer to a grimace than a smile. But whatever, it wasn't a frown.

I was still holding Nicole when Kyla said, "Nic, sweetheart. Let's go get something to eat."

She stepped back, sniffed and looked at her mom. "Should we leave Dad?"

"Well, the doctor told me that I should rest, and I'm sure the same applies to sustenance. You should eat and I know you didn't eat much on the plane for all of those hours."

She nodded, then said, "Okay."

I stood there, not quite sure what to do. But after taking a few steps, Nicole turned back. "Auntie Jasmine? Aren't you coming?"

My glance shifted to Kyla and that slight upward curvature of her lips was gone. Now, her face was as stern as stone. But when Nicole asked me again, Kyla nodded, almost imperceptibly, but enough for me to see, to know that she approved. Kind of.

I hated these circumstances, but I was filled with joy as I walked behind Kyla and Nicole. I followed them ... until we got to the lobby. Then, I took over.

"I'm going to take you to one of my favorite restaurants," I told them as I opened my Uber app.

"I don't want to take a lot of time, Jasmine," Kyla said.

I didn't even look up when I said, "No worries. We're going to Melba's and not only do I know her, but I know everyone there. Once we get in the car, I'll call ahead and they'll get us in and out."

"Wow, Auntie Jasmine. You got it like that?"

"Yup." I grinned and led the two out of the hospital. By the time we got to the corner of 135th Street, the black Hyundai was waiting. Inside the car, Nicole sat in the middle and she held her mother's hand. That warmed me. I wasn't looking forward to Jacqueline and Zaya growing up, but seeing this relationship with Nicole and Kyla made me believe that there were wonderful life's chapters ahead.

As we drove up 135th Street, then made a left onto Frederick Douglas Boulevard, I texted Melba and was thrilled when three minutes later, I received a text back:

I'm not there, but they're waiting for you. They'll get you in and out. Tell your friend I'm praying for her.

Like Melba promised, when we drove up to the restaurant and stepped inside, Louis, the manager, was waiting by the door, then sat us right away and we had menus in our hands before we even blinked.

"It won't matter what you order," I told them, "you will love it."

Kyla sighed. "It does look good." She placed her menu down. "I'm just not very hungry."

"Me neither." Nicole did the same, then looked at me. "Sorry, Auntie Jasmine."

I couldn't say the same. From the moment Melba's came to mind, I'd been thinking about the grilled jerk shrimp, the pecan-crusted tilapia and the cheddar grits. But even though my mouth watered, this wasn't about me. So, I came up with a plan.

"Why don't we do this," I began. "We'll order our food to go. And when you get hungry, I'll heat it up for you in the cafeteria or we can take it home with us tonight and ...."

Kyla shook her head. "We're not staying with you." Then, looking at Nicole, she added, "We'll stay in a hotel. We'll get one tonight."

"Mom," Nicole said looking between her mother and me with my wide opened mouth, "I think if Auntie Jasmine is offering and it's not an imposition ...."

I jumped in. "It's not. I told your mother that this morning. We have adjoining guest rooms, so that you'll each have your own, but share the bathroom and ...."

"No."

"The kids would love to have you there," I continued, as if I couldn't stop. As if I could change everything by keeping my lips moving. "And Hosea and I would love to have you there, too."

"No."

A single word. So emphatic.

"But, Mom," Nicole began again, "I'm thinking that it might be good for us to have the support."

"No."

A single word. So final.

I was sure that Nicole and I looked like twins with shock in our eyes and our lips pressed together. The only difference between us was I understood and Nicole didn't. I thought I'd made inroads, but Kyla had just shut me up and shut me down. Yes, she might have believed my lie about that woman, but she didn't trust me. She may have forgiven me for sleeping with her husband, but she hadn't forgotten about it.

Talk about having a cracked heart.

"Well," my voice sounded so small, "I still think you need to eat. We can order and have them pack it to go."

"That'll be fine." Kyla picked up her menu and held it high, hiding her face.

Nicole looked at her mother, then turned to me. "That would be great, Auntie Jasmine. Thank you for bringing us here."

She lifted her menu, too, but spoke as if the silence was just too awkward to bear. "I'm not hungry, but everything does look good."

I became her ally in this battle to normalize what was far from normal. "Well, like I said, you can't go wrong. I'm going to have the tilapia."

The cheer in our voices sounded like we were talking about Christmas dinner. So inappropriate, but better than addressing what felt like oxygen seeping from the room. Once we put in our orders, Kyla pushed her chair back.

"Excuse me for a minute. I'm going outside," she said. And then, turning more to Nicole than me, she added, "I'm going to call your grandmother and Alexis. And I need to check in with

Pastor Ford, too."

"Okay, tell them all I'll speak to them later."

When Kyla left us alone, I expected Nicole to ask me what was going on and I prayed for a good lie within me because there was no way I could explain the truth to this woman who was still a little girl in my mind.

But instead, Nicole looked at me with the saddest of eyes. "Mom never acts like this, you know that, right? It's just everything that's going on with Dad."

"I know that, sweetheart. It's all right. Your mom just ... doesn't want to impose."

"I get that — I guess. But to me, at times like these, you need your friends. And since Aunt Alex can't be here, I wish we were staying with you."

My glance turned to the windows in the front of the restaurant and I wondered what Kyla would tell her child if she'd heard Nicole compare me and Alexis. I watched Kyla with her cell pressed to her ear, pacing to the corner, then turning around and marching the other way. Her hands moved as she spoke, something she always did when she was emotional. Was she talking to Alexis about me?

I shook that thought away. *This isn't about you, Jasmine.* But shaking away that thought, didn't shake away the sorrow.

"Do you like living in New York?" Nicole asked me.

Turning back, I nodded. "I do. I like the city, but I love my life with my husband and children." I went on to tell her about Hosea and his church.

She said, "Wait. You're *that* Jasmine? Lady Jasmine? You're married to that Hosea Bush? Oh, my goodness."

Her glee made me smile, at least on the outside. I went on to tell her about Jacqueline and Zaya and she told me about her life in Beijing.

"I work for the State department, the U.S. embassy."

I asked, "How in the world did you get there?"

She laughed. "I know, right? I'm just an LA girl. But you know what? This was my dream, actually. Mom and Dad took me to China when I was thirteen, and I fell in love with the country, but more than that, I loved the language. Then, Dad told me that I could study that in college because anyone who spoke any of the Asian Pacific languages would always be employed. Globalization, you know. So, I was hooked."

"Wow. At thirteen you knew that?"

"Yup. You know my parents. To live in their house, I had to be focused. Remember when Dad taught me how to read the stock reports?"

"I do remember that. You were like six and could do it. I'm ...." I paused because I never said my age aloud. That was between me and God and I'd lied about it so much, I wasn't sure that God knew anymore. So, I amended my words. "Even at my age, I still can't read them."

She laughed and this time, my smile almost reached the inside. Almost. I was happy, though, because at least, I was able to help her forget why she'd flown to New York ... even if it was for a few minutes.

"Yeah, I had the best parents." Then, quickly, she corrected herself. "I mean, I have, I have, I have the best parents."

I reached over and squeezed her hand, just as the waiter returned with the wrapped-up food. Kyla was right behind him. As soon as he handed me the package, I could smell the pecan-crusted tilapia, but not even the aroma could douse the dejection that I felt with the way Kyla looked at me.

"Okay," I said, right as I handed the waiter my credit card.

"No, I got this," Kyla reached for her purse.

"Mom!" This time, it was Nicole who spoke in a tone that made her mother pause. Made her mother look up. Made her mother turn to me and just say, "Thank you."

After that, though, I couldn't get out and away fast enough. I accompanied them back to the hospital, though once we arrived, I sent Kyla, Nicole and all of the food (including my order) inside.

"I'm going home," I said. "To check on the kids," I lied.

"Oh, okay. It was so good to see you again, Auntie Jasmine." She hugged me. "We'll see you tomorrow?"

I nodded and then turned to Kyla. I wasn't sure if I should reach for an embrace, but once she stayed steady, I stayed back. "I'll send Hosea back with your suitcase."

"Thank you." She nodded. And then, she added another, "Thank you for everything," because she'd been raised right. Then, with another nod, she took her daughter's hand and dragged her away from me.

I stood on the corner of 135th and Malcolm X feeling like a fool to ever think that after I'd slept with her husband, she'd accept me back in her life as her friend.

With a sigh, I opened my Uber app. It was time for me to go home to be around people who not only loved me, but who liked me, too.

chapter 14

Kyla

"*Bless the Lord, O my soul: and all that is within me, bless his holy name. Bless the Lord, O my soul, and forget not all his benefits: who forgives all thine iniquities; who healeth all thy diseases ....*"

I stood next Nicole as she sat at Jefferson's bedside, whispering healing scripture after healing scripture over her father. Even when I leaned over and kissed her forehead, she didn't stop. She kept reading Psalm 103, and then moved to another verse.

Watching her, there was a scripture that so filled my heart: *Train up a child in the way he should go: and when he is old, he will not depart from it.*

This was Proverbs 22:6 in action and that was why I knew I could leave the room and give Nicole this time with her dad.

Stepping into the hospital's hallway, I waited for the door to close behind me, then I leaned against the wall, not having the energy to take another step.

It was hard for me to believe that not even forty-eight hours had passed since I'd received that call. It felt more like forty-eight days with all that had happened: me getting to New York, Nicole arriving ... and Jasmine.

Jasmine Cox Larson was a layer in my life that I really didn't need right now. A layer that brought questions that I couldn't answer. Like, why was she even here?

Thoughts o f h er m ade my h ead throb. Had s he t old me t he truth about that woman? Had Jasmine ever told me the truth about anything?

I closed my eyes, just to escape thoughts of Jasmine for a moment, but that was not what happened. I closed my eyes for rest, but instead, I had a flash. Back twenty years, back to 1997:

I ran up the stairs, so eager to see my husband. About midway up, I heard the faint sound of water; Jefferson was in the shower. Not knowing that I was coming home early, he was probably on his way to church.

Pressing my hand against my mouth, I muffled my giggles. I'd already told Alexis that I'd meet her at the second service because for the next three hours, I planned on having some serious, hot, married, I-missed-you-so-much sex with the man who made the word foine be just a regular ole adjective.

At the top of the stairs, I was shocked to see the double doors to our bedroom closed. Even when Nicole was home, we rarely closed our door. So why had he closed the door when he'd been home alone?

There were already questions in my mind when I pushed the door open — and I thought that was why I was immediately confused. Because the first thing that hit me was the smell, slightly musky, the aroma that lingers after exercise ... or sex.

And then, my sense of sight took over ... and I saw Jasmine ... naked ... in my bed ... naked.

"Oh, Kyla," she said in a tone that sounded — regular. As if my walking into my bedroom and finding her naked in my bed was something that was — regular.

All these years later, I still felt the same way I did on that Sunday morning. All these years later, tears filled with pain still pushed forward, but I squeezed my eyelids, hoping to press back every one because I did not want to cry. Hadn't I cried enough that day and for the rest of 1997? Hadn't I cried enough in 1998, even as Jefferson and I worked so hard to build and bond again? Hadn't I cried enough in 1999, and 2004, and 2009 on those few occasions when my heart didn't allow me to forget that my best friend (and my husband) had stolen something so sacred from me?

Yes, I'd cried enough, but I guess I wasn't finished.

I opened my eyes and at first, the vision in front of me was blurry. But I blinked through my tears and looked straight into the eyes of Hosea.

He stood there for a moment, watching me cry. Then, he rolled the suitcase that he held in his hand closer to me, stood it up, and pulled me into his arms.

It was like his embrace was filled with permission. So, I sobbed. And sobbed. Then sobbed some more. I cried until there was nothing left within me.

Even after that, Hosea gave me a few moments before he stepped back.

"I'm so sorry," I said.

Again, he didn't use any words. Just took my hand, leaving my suitcase by the door, and he led me away. I didn't even ask him where we were going when he guided me past the nurses station, then around the corner and down a long hall. I was so exhausted that it felt like we'd been walking a mile when Hosea finally pushed through double doors and we entered a small sanctuary.

"Oh, wow," I whispered. "I didn't know they had the chapel up here. In ICU."

"This isn't the main chapel," he said, his voice as low as mine. "But a couple of years ago, they put this in for visitors of patients in critical care. My dad and I have used this room often."

He led me to the second pew, which was just a long wooden bench. I slipped in, then, he sat beside me.

We were alone in the small space that wasn't filled with much: just wooden benches, a make-shift altar, one stained-glass window ... and the overwhelming presence of God. His peace permeated every inch of this space.

I bowed my head, not because I was going to pray; I figured Hosea would have that part covered. I did it because I was just so tired.

Lots of quiet seconds passed before Hosea said, "Kyla ... did anything ... Jefferson ...."

Lifting my head, I sniffed. "No, I wasn't crying because of Jefferson." I wiped away a straggling tear.

He faced me and frowned and I wondered if he knew about his wife and what she'd done. I wondered what he would think if he knew I cried because of what my husband and I had suffered through because of his wife.

In a way, I wanted to tell him. Because if he didn't know, this would be a way for me to get back, to hurt Jasmine. But that was just my pain speaking, because aloud, I said, "It's nothing, it's everything. My daughter is here."

He gave me that smile that went all the way from his lips to my heart. "Well, that should make you happy."

I tried to match his smile. "It does. I needed her here."

"I get that," he said. "You need that support."

I nodded, then turned away from him. And stared at the golden cross that hung high on the wall above the altar.

He said, "We'd love to support you, too."

I let a few moments pass. "Jasmine told you that I'd prefer to stay in a hotel."

"She did."

I waited for him to say more, to protest in some kind of way, but when he didn't, I said, "It's just that ...." I left it there. Because if I said anymore, he'd leave this chapel knowing that his wife was a skank.

He shifted a bit so that more of him was facing me. "You don't have to explain. This is all about what's best for you, Jefferson, and your daughter. The best way that I can help you," he pressed his hand against his chest, "is to pray for you and to help you do whatever you want to do."

This man. His voice. His words. "Thank you."

"So, if you want to stay in a hotel, that's where you'll be. You and your daughter will stay at the Plaza."

The Plaza? Anyone who knew anything about New York City, knew about the Plaza, one of the most famous hotels in the world. And if you didn't know that history, then certainly you knew about all the movie cameos, especially one of my favorites, The Way We Were.

But what I knew most about the Plaza was the reason why people with last names like Vanderbilt and Rockefeller stayed there. This five-star hotel only had rooms that approached one-thousand dollars a night.

I shook my head. "Thanks, Hosea, but Nicole and I will need something a little more aligned with my budget."

"Did I ask you about all that?" His question came with another grin. "It's taken care of. For however long you need." He held up his hand. "And before you protest, hear me out. First of all, with the convention in town, hotel rooms are not only scarce, but the ones that are available are exorbitant. You know, that supply and demand thing."

The ends of my lips curled up just a little. "Look at you. I thought you were a pastor, not an economist."

"I ain't always been saved."

Then, right there in the chapel, we laughed before he continued, "And, I have an account at the Plaza because that's the hotel we use when the church has guests in town. We've given the Plaza a lot of business over the years, so in times like these, they want to help out. That's called, you take care of me and I'll take care of you. Another economic principle." He paused, and then looked up from the corner of his eye as if he were trying to figure something out. "Or is that a political principle?"

More laughter before he wrapped up his case. "Plus, I'm a pastor. People like helping a pastor out, especially one who's on television. So there you have it. You have to stay at the Plaza."

All I could do was shake my head, though I didn't do that because I was saying no. I did it because how could I not say yes?

"So, you'll stay there because it's close to me and Jasmine, but ... far enough away ... from Jasmine for you to feel comfortable."

Those words took my smile away and I had to press my lips together to hold what I wanted to say inside. I wondered again and this time, I wanted to ask — had Jasmine told her husband that she had slept with mine?

No, she hadn't. Liars were cowards, that was why they lied. Of course, Hosea knew that she'd slept with Alexis's husband — Alex had told me all about that encounter and the dinner that she'd had with Hosea about ten years ago. But once Hosea had found out that Jasmine was a liar and a cheater, he still stayed with her. I shook my head again. How could such a good man end up with such a bad woman?

"What?" Hosea said, I guess responding to my silence. "What're you thinking? Talk to me."

I glanced up at the cross again and even though I was in this sacred place, I didn't tell the truth. I said, "I'm thinking that you could have been an attorney, before you were saved, of course."

When we laughed again, I realized that just minutes before, my heart had been aching, the tears had been pouring. Yet, here I was now, inside this chapel, just sitting, just chatting, just having a few good moments.

He glanced at his watch. "It's almost ten, you know."

"Wow." I paused. Twisting my wrist, I checked my own watch. Not that I didn't believe Hosea. But even though my watch showed that it was a little before seven LA time, my body felt like it was well after ten. "I didn't know it was that late."

"The only thing that I'm going to ask you to do, besides stay at the Plaza, is to leave now so that you can get some rest. Because without rest, you have no strength — physical nor spiritual. And that's what you must have for your husband. You and Nicole, too."

I said, "You're right," because there was no fight left in me. I guessed I was going to the Plaza.

"So let's go back to Jefferson's room, we'll pray, and then, I'll get you and Nicole over to the hotel." He paused. "Oh, and we have to figure a way for me to go over to Jefferson's hotel and pack up his things."

I pressed my hand against my mouth. "Oh, my goodness, I hadn't even thought of that." Then, after a moment of contemplation, I added, "Maybe I can just stay in his room."

"No," he said as if he'd always made decisions for me. "You don't need to be around all that. I'll take care of it." He stood, took my hand and lifted me from the pew.

And then, I didn't know why, but this time I was the one who pulled Hosea into a hug. This time I was the one who held him. It took him a few seconds, but he put his arms around me. And held me.

Right there, in front of God.

When I stepped back, I said, "Thank you," to Hosea and to the One who had sent him.

Again, Hosea used no words, but the way he said, "You're welcome," was by taking my hand and leading me from the chapel, back down the hall and to my husband's hospital room.

chapter 15

Jasmine

It had taken me two days to get into the back of this Uber. That was the amount of time I needed not only to put together a plan, but I needed the time to lay kind of low. My feelings were still hurt by what Kyla had said and what she'd done on Wednesday. She had shut me down, shut me out, shut me up.

So even though I'd wanted to spend some time with Nicole, I'd only gone back yesterday with Hosea. We'd stayed for about an hour and I'd spent most of my time talking to Nicole. But while I had stayed in my place, I was only biding my time. My desire to heal our friendship would be forever futile — unless I figured out this thing with that woman and Jefferson. I wasn't quite sure why I felt that way; but I just knew somehow that was a key.

"Miss, is this where you wanted to go?"

I didn't even realize the driver had stopped and I peeked out the window of the Corolla. We were high up in Manhattan on 178th Street, a neighborhood called Washington Heights that I had visited a few times with Hosea — once when he spoke at a church, and another time when we visited the mother of one of our church members.

Eyeing the bodega where Jefferson had been shot, I nodded to the driver. "Yes," I said before I thanked him, then opened the door, slipped out of the car and stepped into the Dominican flavor of this neighborhood.

It was Manhattan, but almost like another land. The Dominican Republic gyrated through the streets in this part of the city. From the bachata that filled my ears and caressed my soul, almost making me want to raise my hands high above my head and shift my feet in the little bit of the merengue that I'd learned from watching Dancing with the Stars to the aromas that tickled my nostrils, then made my stomach growl in hopes that I would satisfy my appetite with just a taste of the spicy stew whose scent sailed from an open apartment window.

I had come in the middle of the day, thinking this would be a quiet time. But I should have known that there was nothing muted about the pulse of Washington Heights. It was always lit, as my eleven-year-old would say. Even now, at just a bit before three on a Friday, the block was packed with people: parents walking their young children home from school, teens in clusters, boys checking out girls who pretended like they didn't even care to notice.

The driver had let me off between two older Chevys parked at the curb where a bunch of guys stood, leaning against the cars that blasted music through their rolled-down windows.

"Excuse me," I said, as I passed them.

"Que lo que es," one of them sang.

I paused, settled my eyes on the one who'd called out to me, looked him up and down, before I gave him a little nod of my head. "What's up with you?"

His eyes got big as if he couldn't believe that one: I'd stopped to speak, and two: I understood what he'd said, and three: that I'd responded appropriately. His boys cracked up and I smiled as I pivoted and marched toward the store that I'd seen on the news.

My attention was already back to my objective. I had my questions ready — kind of. No, the truth was, I didn't really know what I was looking for. Yes, the woman, but I was working on so many assumptions, not even knowing what I would do once I found her.

Shaking my head, I brushed those thoughts aside. No need to second-third-fourth guess myself now. I'd figure it out as I went along. This was the first step — find the woman who'd been with

Jefferson in this store that night.

Before I could step to the glass door of the bodega, a hand came around and pushed the door open for me. "Thanks," I said glancing over my shoulder at the teen who'd just spoken to me.

He nodded his 'You're welcome,' with a lopsided grin that would have been sexy if he didn't have his mother's breast milk still on his breath. Then, once we stepped inside, he shouted, "Hey Luka," before he headed to the other side of the small store.

"What's up, Jamal?" the man who stood behind the counter replied.

It seemed an unlikely exchange between the middle-aged East Indian man who wore a gorgeous purple turban and the teen, whose pants were barely above the crack in his butt. But Mr. Luka spoke to Jamal like they were buddies.

While Jamal went one way, I moved straight to the counter. There were two young girls standing in front of me, and I waited as they paid for their candy. Then, I stepped forward to the man who was protected by the thick plexiglass. "Hi, Mr. Luka?" Although I knew that was his name, it still came out as a question.

"May I help you?" he replied in a thick accent.

My first thought was that he'd forgotten to say hello to me. Then, I said, "I have a couple of questions about the shooting that happened here Monday night."

He shook his head and waved his hands. "I don't know nothing," Mr. Luka said. "I already spoke to the police."

"I know you did," I said, seeing already that this was not going to be easy. Not with the way he reacted. Like he wanted me out of his store right now. "And I thank you for that. I'm here because I'm trying to get some information."

He had never stopped shaking his head. "I have no information. Just a bunch of kids."

We'd only exchanged a few words, but I could tell that he was determined not to give me anything. Well, what he needed to know was that I wasn't going to be deterred either. He was going to answer a question, give me a clue, tell me something. "The police said your surveillance camera wasn't working that night?"

He grunted, then glanced over my shoulder and I couldn't believe it. That quickly, four people had lined up behind me. I stepped to the side; I wasn't trying to mess with the man's business.

As he took care of the customers (who all looked me up and down as if I didn't belong in their store) I studied the small space which seemed to have been put back together from the chaos of Monday. It was jammed with four rows of the kinds of products you found in all convenience stores: candy, cakes, and cookies. Lots of potato chips and plantain chips, and stacks of other nondescript edible products and household goods. Of course, there was one wall lined with refrigerated shelves for the sodas, juices and beer — lots of beer. It hardly looked like there'd been a mob robbery or a shooting in this store at all.

As I took it all in, I tried to imagine Jefferson before the shooting in this store … with that woman. Why was he even here? This was the place a man like him would stop for a pack of cigarettes or a six-pack, but Jefferson didn't indulge in either — at least he didn't back when I knew him. Yet, he was here, and he was with her. What was he doing so far up in Manhattan, especially that late at night? Why had they stopped at this store?

Not that it wasn't safe. Back in the day, Washington Heights had its share of crime, just like the rest of the city. But when many of the gangs had been broken up and driven out, this area was now one of the safest in New York.

Except for what happened on Monday.

"Miss, are you going to buy something?" Mr. Luka asked. "Because that's all I can do for you."

I hadn't noticed that Mr. Luka had cleared the line and now his impatience was back to me.

"If you don't want to buy anything …."

I knew his next words would be to tell me to go away, so I grabbed a pack of gum from the packages below the counter, dropped it in front of him, then fished in my wallet for my credit card.

When I handed him my American Express, he gave me a look that in any language shouted 'what-the-hell' and I said, "I'm sorry,

I don't have any cash."

It was only the partition that separated us that stopped his glare from setting me on fire. He tossed my credit card back to me, then grabbed the gum and dumped it behind the counter.

"Look, I really don't want any trouble," I said. "The doctor who was shot here, he's a good friend." I sighed. "I was just hoping that you could help."

"I don't know what I can tell you. I didn't know those people. The man, the woman, all of those kids. There were so many."

"Well, what about the woman who was with him? Was she shot?"

He shook his head. "No. She helped him. She covered his head with paper towels and then she left, right before the police came." He waved his hands. "Please, I have to get back to my store." With a nod, he motioned for whoever was standing behind me to step up.

I blew out a long breath of frustration. Either Mr. Luka was right and he didn't know anything or I didn't have much of a future in police investigation nor interrogation. He did confirm, though, that Jefferson had been with a woman — the woman of many hats, if I were into betting. I wondered if I should have asked if the woman had worn a hat that night. Then, I would have known for sure that it was her.

"Yo, Luka," Jamal called out, "I was about to walk out of here with this soda."

"And I would've called the police." Mr. Luka didn't even crack a smile.

"Yo, you know I'm only kidding. But dang, you were only paying attention to her."

When Jamal jabbed a finger my way, Mr. Luka gave me a you're-still-here? glare.

I nodded, letting him know that I got his message, and moved toward the exit.

But before I could pull the door open, like before, a hand reached around and did it for me.

Turning to Jamal once again, I said, "Thank you."

"Yo, it's what I do."

Stepping back outside into the Caribbean sounds and smells, I glanced down at my phone to open the Uber app once more.

"Yo." Jamal's voice made me look up. "You Five-O?"

My question was in my frown before I said, "Excuse me?"

"The police." He raised his voice to speak above the music. "Are you the police?"

I squinted and shook my head. "No. Why in the world would you ask me that?"

"'Cause I don't talk to Five-O, but I'll talk to you."

"About what?"

"About what you were asking Mr. Luka."

My stomach fluttered just a bit. "Do you know something about the shooting?"

"You weren't asking about the shooting. I heard you asking about the woman."

I nodded. "Do you know her?"

"Maybe." He shrugged, then with a gentle cupping of my elbow, he led me a couple of feet to the side of the store's entrance. A little bit away from the music that streamed from the car, he lowered his voice. "Depends on how much it's worth to you."

My eyes narrowed as I studied him in his white T-shirt and jeans that looked like they were about to drop to his ankles. This dude thought I, dressed in my tailored navy pants suit, was an easy mark. "You know what? I don't have time for some scam."

He leaned back, like he was offended. "Look, lady, I don't have a need to scam you. I was trying to help a sistah out." He grinned. "Provided you help me out."

My answer to that came in the way I rolled my eyes, turned, and began my march down the block to the corner. Forget about waiting for an Uber. It would be quicker to hail a cab.

I hadn't even taken a dozen steps when Jamal called out, "I got video."

I stopped, I hesitated, I turned back to him, but I didn't move. I waited for Jamal to come to me.

He was still wearing that grin when he held up his cell phone and tapped the screen. "I don't know what you can get from it, but it's better than nothing."

"What is it?" I reached for the phone.

He immediately pulled it away. "Ahhhh, you know this is the concrete jungle. Up here, you don't get nothin' 'less you ready to give somethin'".

I hooked my hobo on my shoulder, then crossed my arms. "I don't have any money, I never travel with money, so unless you take credit cards ...."

He laughed. "That's a good one, maybe I should start carrying around one of those things that you can hook up to your phone."

"Whatever. 'Cause if you don't have one of those now ...."

I did another one of those stiletto pivots, but before I could take a step, he said, "Okay, okay. I'mma help you out just 'cause you're cute."

I was smiling when I turned back to him.

But right before my smile could turn into a grin, he added, "Yeah, you remind me of my great granny."

My first thought was to slap him, but my second thought was then, I might not get the chance to check out the video. And what was more important than him insulting me by comparing me to his ... not grandmother, but great grandmother — was me seeing this video.

He lifted the phone so that the screen was eye level.

"Me and my boys were shooting a rap video outside the bodega. Luka gives us a hard time, but he's cool people and I hate what those dudes did to him. But anyway, we saw the guy who got shot and a lady go in before the others got here. I remember 'cause her whip was tight and she wore this big hat."

Big hat? Bingo!

Jamal continued, "She parked right here." He pointed to the spot where his boys were still blasting music from the car.

I squinted, trying to see the video through the glare of the sun. On the screen, three boys were preforming some God-awful rap, spouting words I couldn't understand. Then all of a sudden, they stopped. A man walked into their shot — Jefferson.

He seemed distracted, as if he wasn't even aware of what was going on around him.

"Hey!" one of the boys shouted.

Jefferson looked up and right into the camera. "Sorry guys." He waved his hands and quickened his steps away from them.

The moment Jefferson was out of the shot, the three went back to their singing-rapping-noise-making.

Looking up at Jamal, I said, "This doesn't help. I was looking for the woman."

"Hold up," he said. "You just like my great granny. Cute, but impatient."

He grinned and I scowled.

I rolled my eyes right back to the screen.

As the video played, Jamal said, "Now, I'm not all that sure that ol' girl was with him. I mean, I think she was because I saw them inside talking to another dude through the window. But the dude who got shot came in another car, I think one of those Ubers. And she drove up right behind him. But she peeped what we were doing and stayed back for a couple of seconds until we stopped rolling. Even then, she told me that she would sue me if I put her on camera." He gave me that lopsided grin again before he added, "But she ain't said nothing about me making her car a star."

The screen went dark for a moment, then picked up with, "Yo, Jamal, get me spitting these bars on this whip," one of the boys said.

"Dawg, you crazy." That was Jamal's voice. "Sitting on that lady's ride? She come back out here and see you ...."

"Just get the shot."

The camera turned as the guy sat on the hood of what looked like a Mercedes, and the three continued their show. Jamal zoomed in on the guy on the car, then dropped his cell lower to show the hood ornament. And right below the Mercedes symbol was ... a license plate. A license plate number!

"Oh, my God," I squealed, as I tapped the number into my Notes app.

Jamal had just given me exactly what I needed. I wanted to see more, but then, the video ended.

"Everything got crazy after that," Jamal said, his grin gone. "We knew something was going down when all those dudes rushed the store. And then, at the sound of that first shot, we were ghost."

That was okay. I had enough.

I flipped back the flap of my purse, dug deep into the side zipper and pulled out the one hundred dollar bill that I always carried.

When I handed it to Jamal, he grinned. "Hey. I thought you said you didn't have any money."

"I guess that makes me a little different from your great granny, huh? I'm like you; I got game, too."

He laughed as I walked away. Maybe I did have a future as an investigator.

Now, I had to get to work.

chapter 16

Jasmine

That was the best insult that I had ever let go by. Because I had a license plate number. The problem was, a license plate was just a license plate when the number was in my hands. But there was someone I knew who could turn license plate information into a full ancestry.com analysis.

"Mama, where are you?" Jacqueline called out. I could tell she was at the bottom of the staircase.

I stepped into the hallway from the office. "What's up?"

"Can you help me put together a gospel playlist for our Christmas play?" She didn't give me a chance to say that I would. "'Cause Susie Gottlieb is in charge of the music, and I just have a feeling that the songs she knows will be boring. I want the music to be poppin' like at church. So, I'm gonna be proactive and give them a playlist before Susie comes up with hers."

My take-charge daughter. "Okay," I told her. "We'll do that in a little while. First, I have to make a call. You finish your homework and then, I'll be down."

"Mom, it's Friday. We don't have homework."

"Well, just let me make this call and then I'll help you."

"Yes!" She pumped her fist into the air. "The play is gonna be lit."

I blew out a breath as I watched my daughter dance away. I wasn't sure that her Christian academy was looking for a lit Christmas play, but I would handle that, right after I made this call.

I rushed into the office, closed the door, then clicked on my cell and swiped the number. The phone on the other end rang once, and then went right to voicemail.

For a moment, I just stared at the cell that I held. "Really?" I spoke to the phone as if it were the cell phone's fault that my best friend had sent my call to voicemail.

What I wanted to do was grab my purse, get in the elevator, call an Uber, and pay him extra to speed over to Mae Frances's east side apartment. The problem was, my friend wasn't there. In the last year, I could count the days, probably not even using fingers on both hands, that she'd spent in the uptown, upscale apartment that allegedly she still called home.

Mae Frances wasn't in New York and the challenge was, she could be anywhere. She could be in Sicily or Santa Monica, but most likely, that woman was probably back in Smackover.

Yup ... Mae Frances knew everybody, had connections all over the world, and had visited places I'd never heard of. Yet for the last year, she'd spent most of her time in that country town, Smackover, Arkansas.

Just a thought about that place put a pinch in my heart. Because of the memory of what I'd learned last summer. That long-hidden secret that had taken away my father, given me another ... and then the ultimate treasonous act of the universe — made Rachel Jackson Crackpot Adams my sister.

I backed up — Rachel really wasn't a crackpot. At least not thirty-six percent of the time. She'd turned out to be a pretty good sister, texting regularly, making sure that I called our father often. Or, if I didn't initiate the calls, at least I accepted his.

I hadn't spoken to Simon this whole week while this was happening with Jefferson, so I did owe him a call. But right now, I didn't have time to think about my history or what had become my extended family.

I pressed the number for Mae Frances again, and like before, one ring, then voicemail.

"Ugh!"

I repeated the process, and so did she until the fifth time, she cried uncle and picked up.

"Jasmine Larson, somebody better be dead or you will be," she said.

"Why aren't you answering my calls?"

She huffed, then puffed, and said, "If I don't answer your call the first time," another huff, another puff, "that means I'm busy and I'll call you back."

"Why are you out of breath?" I asked. "What are you doing?"

Then, a voice that was so close, it sounded like he was speaking right into Mae Frances's cell phone, said, "Come to Daddy."

Oh, my God!

I couldn't unhear that. And that voice — that was Rachel's Uncle Bubba, which kinda meant that he was my uncle, too. Which kinda meant that whatever he and Mae Frances were doing was some kinda incest.

Oh, my God!

"I'm enjoying life." Mae Frances's sing-song voice broke through my mental machinations.

"Where are you?" I pressed my eyes closed because I never knew with Mae Frances. She would either tell me it was none-of-mine … or she would tell me the truth and describe how she was naked, in bed, with … my uncle.

Oh, my God!

Mae Frances said, "Are you my mama?" choosing the none-of-mine route. "I don't think so," she answered for me. "So don't ask me no questions."

"Well, wherever you are, when will you be back?"

She released an exasperated sigh. "Bubba and I are in DC. We're staying at Trump Tower."

I gasped. And then, gasped again. Like seriously, I thought I was going to start hyperventilating. "Mae Francis, how could you spend any money on that fool in the Oval Office?"

"You think I spent a nickel here? Girl, bye. I'm here 'cause I'm in one of these thousand dollar a night penthouse suites — for free."

"Free? Why?"

"Why you think? I got something on that man. Uh-huh," she hummed. "The Russians aren't the only ones. It'll come out soon, but until then …." She paused, then sang, "Hey … party over here!"

Oh, my God!

Actually, I was glad that Mae Frances didn't share the details of what she knew. Because not only did I not want to know, but there were more important, personal issues to handle right now. "Well, we have to work out something because I really need your help."

The music was gone from her voice and now she sighed as if my words were a burden. "You always need my help," she said. But then, in the next moment, she broke out in a fit of giggles. "Stop," she dragged out the word like she was a schoolgirl.

"Really, Mae Francis? Can you ask Bubba," I refused to call him uncle, "to give you a moment?"

"You know what, Jasmine Larson?" But before I could say anything, she granted my request. "Give me a minute, baby and I'll make it worth your while." A couple of seconds ticked by, then, she returned, speaking in her all-business tone. "Okay, what you need?"

"So, here's what's going on …." I inhaled, then exhaled a short version of what happened over the last week: from Jefferson's accident, to my reconnecting with Kyla, to the mystery hat lady and the blessing of finding her license plate.

"That's all I have," I said, finishing up. "Her license plate. So, can you find out who she is?"

For many moments, there was nothing but silence and I knew Mae Frances was rolling the conversation through her mind. Then, "Now, tell me again why this is any of your business? If the man wanted to get his freak on, that's no concern of yours. That's between him and his wife, right?"

"That's just it," I said. "I think there's something else going on. I can't tell you what it is, but I'm really concerned about this woman. I think she's up to something and I don't want her hurting Kyla."

"Well, that's not your responsibility. You didn't sleep with her husband."

If she had been right in front of me, I would have told Mae

Frances the whole story; in fact, over the years, I was almost sure that I had shared that part of my past with her. But I couldn't remind her of that now, not while she was in her double-king bed, on thousand-thread-count sheets, laying up with Bubba. I was well aware that my time was limited.

So all I said was, "Kyla is dealing with enough right now, just praying that her husband will survive. It's really sad, Mae Frances. He's been in a coma since after his operation and I don't want her to have to deal with anything else. Especially not another woman. That would break her heart; it might even kill her."

"Ugh! You're laying it on thick, but I get it." She sighed. "You know I'm a softie. So, all right. I'll come back home."

That was what I wanted, but still, I said, "You don't have to do that. Don't you think you can handle it from D.C.?"

"Do you want my help or not, Jasmine Larson? You know how I operate. I need to take care of these things in person." She didn't give me a chance to say anything. "So here's what we'll do. Text me the license plate and I'll call my connections."

"You know someone at the DMV, right?"

"The DMV? Why would I go there? I'm gonna go straight to the top. Gonna call the Cuomo brothers. Andrew or Chris. It doesn't matter. One of them will help me."

I shook my head. I didn't even know why I'd asked her about the DMV. I was talking about some clerk and Mae Frances was talking about the governor of New York or the CNN anchor.

"Yeah," she said. "You know their daddy, Mario, was one of my best friends, God rest his soul. So Andy or Chris would be glad to give me anything I need."

Now, the governor of New York was Andy?

"Not that they would do it themselves, 'cause you know they can't. But they know people, who know people, who …."

"I get it," I told her.

"Okay. So, I'll fly back home tomorrow."

With a smirk, I just had to say, "Oh, I'm glad you still call New York home."

"You know what, Jasmine Larson?"

"I'm sorry." I couldn't get the words out fast enough. "So, you'll fly back tomorrow and ...."

"And you'll pick me up from LaGuardia."

"Would it be okay if I sent a car? Tomorrow is my spa date with Hosea and you know we do everything never to miss that."

"Well, since I love Preacher Man," she said, calling Hosea by the only name she ever used for him, "you can send a car. I'll get on that two o'clock flight." She spoke as if she knew the schedule of every airline coming into New York from DC. "So I'll land between three, three-thirty."

"I got you."

"You'd better."

And then, she hung up. Without a goodbye, or see you tomorrow. I guess her attention was already back to Bubba.

That made me cringe.

But, at least Mae Frances was coming home.

That made me happy.

Because things were about to be handled. For real.

chapter 17

Kyla

My eyes fluttered open. How many days had it been? Four, no five because today was Saturday and I was just plain exhausted. But here, in this bed, on these sheets and under this bedding that made me feel like I was sleeping on clouds, I had some peace. Because of Pastor Hosea Bush, life with my husband in a coma was a little bit easier.

I didn't want to do it, but I knew I had to get up soon. Rolling over, I glanced at the clock on the Victorian-style nightstand. The digital numbers glowed: 8:11.

"Hmmm," I moaned and did one of those morning stretches to awaken my limbs. The only good thing about the time I'd spent in New York was that my body had finally adjusted to East coast time.

Pushing myself up, I planted my feet on the rug, then trekked into the oversized bathroom that was a big as a small New York apartment. The mosaic floor was cool under my feet and just as I turned on the faucet, the hotel phone rang.

I picked up the extension, already knowing who was on the other end. "Good morning, sweetheart," I said, my voice echoing through the bathroom.

"Morning, Mom. I'm back from the gym and I'm going to jump in the shower. You up?"

"I am," I said, surprised that Nicole hadn't knocked on my door this morning. She was right across the hall, and she usually checked on me most mornings before she went down for her hour workout. "I'm about to do the same. So, I'll meet you downstairs at our regular time?"

"Uh-huh. I'll be ready before then and I'm gonna walk over to Starbucks. Want me to get you the regular?"

"Yes and thank you."

"Okay." She blew me a kiss, then added, "Love you, Mommie," and if I didn't know for sure that my child was thirty, I would think that she was nine. She still held that same sweetness, that same innocence. That is, until she got up to Harlem Hospital. When she walked through those doors, she was a warrior, marching in wearing the full armor of God.

I paused for a moment and remembered those long-ago days. It was something that had started in children's church with Pastor Ford, something that Nicole brought home and wanted to do ev-ery day before she went to school.

"Ready, Mommie?" Nicole said, dumping her backpack on the floor as she came into the family room, dressed for school and ready for battle.

I nodded as my seven-year-old sat next to me on the sofa. And then another nod from her, and together we began, "Therefore put on the full armor of God so that when the day of evil comes, you may be able to stand your ground and after you have done everything, to stand."

Nicole and I stood up.

Then together, we continued, "Stand firm then, with the belt of truth buckled around your waist."

We paused and pretended to wrap belts around us.

"With the breastplate of righteousness in place."

More pantomiming.

"And with your feet fitted with the readiness that comes from the gospel of peace."

We continued with the scripture, acting it out as if we were putting on all the pieces of armor.

"In addition to all this, take up the shield of faith, with which you can extinguish all the flaming arrows of the evil one. Take the helmet of salvation and the sword of the Spirit which is the word of God."

Then, the last verse, Nicole recited alone: *"And pray in the Spirit on all occasions with all kinds of prayers and all requests. With this in mind, be alert and always keep on praying for all the Lord's people."*

Then, she paused and together we said, *"Amen."*

That had been our daily ritual, one that we'd kept until the day she'd left to attend Yale University. We'd had to stop then, though I was convinced that my child put on her armor every day the same way. It was clear that she wore it; it was in the way she walked, the way she talked, the way she demonstrated strength and commanded attention and respect. There'd been many times this week when she'd taken the lead away from me with the doctors. And because of who she was at her core, I was fine with that.

"Thank you, Lord," I whispered. There was much that I had to be grateful for, but the gift of my child was at the top of my list this morning.

As I brushed my teeth, my thoughts shifted from the past to the present, from my daughter to my husband. The doctors were using the word progress more and more. Jefferson hadn't yet awakened, but the doctors were pleased with the direction.

"As you know, our major concern has always been the swelling, which is improving every day."

I didn't need Dr. Reid to tell me that. It was apparent; Jefferson's eyes no longer looked like they were swollen shut.

"He's recovering well, and maybe tomorrow, but most likely Sunday, we'll begin to bring him out of the coma."

Dr. Reid had told me that last night.

That was good news.

That was scary news.

Because to this point, the doctors couldn't determine the extent of the damage to his brain. They were optimistic because of how quickly he'd been treated. But they had concerns: would he have his memory, would he be able to talk and walk, would he ever function again as Doctor Jefferson Blake? Those questions didn't matter. Whatever the answers, whatever his condition, I would be fine. It would all be for the better because just having Jefferson back would mean there could be no worse for me.

Under the two-headed shower, I thought about how magnificent it would be to stand under this pulsing rain for the rest of the day. But since that wasn't possible, I got in, took care of business, then got out. My next stumbling block came when I wrapped myself inside the chamois microfiber robe that felt like the duvet that covered me at night. Then, when I stepped back into the room, the king-sized bed and cloud-soft sheets cried out to me, but I ignored all of that and turned instead to the suitcase that Alexis had shipped to me.

I was grateful for more clothes and put together a jeans, white T-shirt and a camouflage jacket outfit that made me look like I was ready for the battle that would come with my husband's recovery. Then, I gathered my wallet, phone and tablet, dumped them into my purse and after tucking the room key into the back pocket of my jeans, I headed downstairs.

When the elevator doors parted, the grandeur of the Plaza's lobby greeted me as it did every morning and I strolled through the opulence as if it were ordinary. But no matter how long I stayed here, I would never grow accustom to the elegance of this national historic landmark. How could I? How could I ever walk below the five tier crystal chandeliers and not be in awe? Or step across the marble floor and not be amazed? Or how could I not smile at the millionaires and billionaires who huddled in the lobby making plans, setting meetings, all to shake up the world?

But the best part of each morning was seeing my daughter, standing by the gilded doors, waiting for me with a grande vanilla mocha. Compared to Nicole's latte macchiato with a double shot of espresso, mine was a kiddy drink. But it helped me get my day started.

I smiled as I made my way to her, but then, I was sure my smile widened and brightened when I realized that she stood next to

Hosea.

"Good morning." I first kissed Nicole, then gave Hosea a hug. To him, I said, "What are you doing here?"

"I thought I'd accompany you ladies this morning. I have a full schedule this afternoon, so I thought I'd ride in with you and we can pray with Jefferson before I leave to take care of business."

Looking up to him, I said, "I'd like that."

As we stepped through the lobby's door to the car that always waited for us two feet to the left, Nicole chatted.

"I don't think I will ever get used to the fact that the Hosea Bush is a friend of my family's." She fanned her face the way she'd done every day since she'd met Jasmine's husband.

The driver held the door for us as Nicole and I slipped into the back and Hosea sat in the passenger seat. Once the driver pulled away from the curb, Nicole started up again.

"Where's Auntie Jasmine? She didn't come by yesterday …." And then, she paused like she wasn't so sure of her statement. She said, "Or did she?"

I guessed her days were running together like mine.

He said, "She wanted to come this morning, but had a couple of things to take care of. Her best friend is coming back to New York today."

"Oh, where has she been?" Nicole asked.

Hosea laughed. "That's a long story for another time."

He still chuckled and his joy filled the car. No matter what was going on, I felt good, I felt safe when he was around.

Hosea Bush was a really good man. That was a simple statement that meant so much. But that was exactly what Alexis had told me when she'd first met him:

"I'm on my way home from having dinner with Hosea Bush," *Alexis said when she answered the phone.*

"Really, how did that go?"

"I asked him to come home with me and I wasn't talking about having tea."

I'd been so shocked at her words and I'd asked her how much wine she'd had. She'd told me it wasn't just the wine.

"It's true, I drank my dinner, but he's such a good guy, Ky. He really cared about me finding out that his wife had screwed my husband. And now ….they had a baby. He wanted to help me get through this. I don't know how he ended up with Jasmine."

That was what Alexis said then, and that was my question now. Hosea had been there for me every moment of this ordeal, at least the moments that mattered. I knew that Jasmine had tried to do the same, but my feelings for her were so different than my feelings for him.

From the back seat, I stared at Hosea. He wasn't your typical fine man if the definition of fine was: tall, dark and handsome. He wasn't tall, under six feet, I was sure of that. And while I just loved a tall glass of chocolate milk, Hosea was more coffee with lots and lots and lots of latte. And handsome? His features, while pleasant, were not model-worthy. He was cute, in a Pillsbury doughboy way. Really cute. Really cuddly.

But he was beyond special. Because what was inside of him, came out. It was that glow, that joy of the Lord that made him finer than any man. Because the one thing that was true — there was nothing sexier than a black man with his hands and heart raised to God.

With that thought, my mind began to wander and I began to daydream, then, the ringing of my cell shocked me back to my senses.

I didn't recognize the 212 number, but that didn't matter because any New York number had something to do with my husband.

"Mrs. Blake?" the male voice asked after I said hello.

"Yes."

"This is Detective Green. My partner and I spoke with you the other day."

"Yes, Detective Green, "I said and watched both Nicole and Hosea shift in their seats to face me.

"I was wondering if you had a moment to come to the station this morning."

"I'm on my way to the hospital now. What is this about, Detective?"

"We won't keep you too long," he said, speaking like those cops on Law & Order when they only asked questions, but never answered any. "We just have a few things we want to ask you and something we'd like to show you."

I sighed aloud and screamed inside my head. Of course, I wanted whoever had done this to Jefferson to suffer a long and agonizing prison sentence. But I wanted the cops to catch my husband's assailant without me.

Hosea said, "What do they want?"

"They want to speak to me," and then, without a thought, I handed my cell to Hosea.

He took it, turned back to the front, and began speaking. As he said, "This is Pastor Hosea Bush, I think we met the other day," Nicole took my hand.

There was silence and I imagined that the detective was telling Hosea what he'd said to me.

Finally, "Okay, Detective," Hosea said. "Can you give us about an hour? We're on our way to the hospital, but I'll bring Mrs. Blake there right around ten. Is that okay?" The way Hosea nodded, then said, "That's fine, we'll see you there," I knew the conversation was over.

He clicked off the phone, turned to me and said, "They just have a few more questions. It'll be in and out." He handed the phone back before he added, "So we'll go to the hospital, pray with Jefferson, get Nicole settled, then we'll head uptown to the police station." He faced the front again, but then, as an afterthought hit him, he twisted back around, grinned and said, "Is that okay?"

I didn't even respond. At least not out loud.

All I did was smile.

***

The hospital had been bad enough, but this was worse. Yes, I hated driving up to Harlem Hospital every day because inside, my husband was still in critical care. But now, driving up to this police precinct was worse. Because again, I had to speak to officers about the violence that had taken my husband down and brought me to New York.

When the car came to a complete stop, I peeked out the window. The gray building stood tall, looked old, and if it carried any kind of emotion, it was anger. As if nothing good ever happened in this place. In front, patrol cars were parked perpendicular to the curb, but the street was active. Civilians and officers moved in and out, around and about taking care of the business of crime, I supposed.

I didn't even realize the car door had been opened until I heard Hosea say, "Come on. It'll be okay."

His hand was out and I reached for him.

When I stood by Hosea, he said, "It's scary, I know. But you'll be all right." He gave instructions to the driver to stay close and then, he pressed his hand against the small of my back and led me to the building. "At least you're going in on your own accord. Last time I was here, they had to drag me inside." I laughed at his attempt to lighten the moment, until he added, "I'm not kidding." Another pause before he explained, "I shot a man."

I was sorry, but I had to stop moving. There was no way that my feet could guide me while I was trying to get my brain to compute those words. Looking up at him, I squinted. And the light that was always in his eyes dimmed a bit. "It's a long story that maybe I'll share with you later. But back in twenty-ten my daughter was kidnapped. And I took care of the man who … kidnapped her."

Inside, I let out a long, ohhhhhh. How could I have forgotten about that? Jacqueline had been kidnapped … and raped when she was only five. It had been the most horrific of times for everyone, Brian included, even though he hadn't been in his daughter's life.

But she had been found safe, rescued, and as far as I could see, she seemed well, thank God. And like everything that the devil meant for evil, God turned it to good because Hosea had been found guilty, but served no time … and Jacqueline's disappearance had been the impetus that brought Alexis and Brian back together. They had remarried right after Jacqueline had been found.

There was so many thoughts swirling in my mind as my feet

began moving again and Hosea led me into the building. This man, this gentle man had taken a gun and shot the man who'd raped his daughter — shot him right between his legs. Taken away the rapist/kidnapper's manhood. Made Hosea even more of a man in my eyes.

"Mrs. Blake, Pastor Bush."

We turned to the voice and Detective Green approached, his hand already extended to us. "Thank you for coming down," he said after we exchanged greetings. "Let's go talk in my office."

He led us down a hall to an office that was the size of most closets and was made even smaller with the desk, three chairs and file cabinets that were squeezed inside. Papers were piled so high atop the cabinets, I was convinced the digital age hadn't yet arrived at the 25th precinct.

He said, "Let me get Al in here," then, left us alone to figure out how to cram ourselves into the chairs.

Not enough time passed for me to fold my mind into my thoughts and I was glad about that. I had no time to speculate before both detectives returned. Five seconds for pleasantries, then the detectives led us to the point of this meeting.

"Like I told you on the phone, we're not going to take long," Detective Green said.

"I'm not sure what I can do to help you." I looked from one detective to the other. "I don't know anyone in New York," then, I paused, "except for Hosea ... Pastor Bush and his wife. So I know there isn't anything I can add to the investigation."

He nodded. "I understand, but you may know more than you think."

I frowned.

He said, "Were you and Doctor Blake having any problems?"

My eyes narrowed even more. "What do you mean?"

"You know," he bobbed his head a little from side to side, "married people sometimes go through things, they have problems ...."

Every part of my body hunched up. "No and I resent you even asking me that."

"I don't mean anything by it." The detective held up his hands.

"We just have to ask all the questions."

"Well, the answer to your question is no. My husband and I are very much in love. What happened to him wasn't about anything like that. He was at a conference, for God's sake."

"Well ...." The detective tilted his head and gave me a look that said a conference was the perfect opportunity for a husband who was having problems with his wife.

"Well," I mimicked him, "I've answered your question."

I didn't know why, but he had to press just one more time. "So no issues with infidelity in your marriage ...."

That flash: Jasmine ... naked ... in my bed ... naked.

Hosea rescued me. "Detectives," he began in that voice that could've disarmed Gideon's army, "I understand that you have to ask these questions because the spouse or partner is always the primary suspect, right?"

The detectives didn't nod, didn't say a word. Just stared at Hosea as if they were waiting to see where he was going with his line of questioning.

He leaned forward and continued, "But like Mrs. Blake has told you, she and her husband have a wonderful marriage. Everything is fine. She loves him and had nothing to do with this." He sat back. "What do you think? She hired a bunch of teenagers to rob that store just at the time that she knew her husband would be there?"

If I weren't so pissed, I would have jumped up and said, 'Bam!' But I stayed in place and let the glare of my glance speak for me.

"We're only asking these questions because we really need to find the witness. We need her to go through some photos and without her ...."

"I told you before, maybe the woman who was with my husband was a doctor from the convention. I don't know."

"Well, we've spoken to several of the doctors at the convention ...."

"See ...."

"And many did see your husband in the bar with a woman on Sunday, but she wasn't one of the doctors."

My stomach did three backflips.

"We didn't get a lot of descriptions because no one got a good look at her face."

That made me frown. What did that mean?

"But before we go back to the convention, we're hoping you might be able to tell us something about her." He opened a folder and began sliding a picture across the desk. "As you know, the security camera wasn't operating in the store, but the surveillance cameras on that block were."

Hosea and I leaned forward at the same time.

Detective Green said, "We got the images of everyone who entered the store a minute before your husband and a minute afterwards, before all those kids barged in. And only one was a woman."

Together Hosea and I stared at the picture.

"Now, you can't see her face because of her hat, but is there anything familiar about her?"

I gasped.

"You know her?" both detectives and Hosea said at the same time.

I took another moment to take in her image; it was a grainy picture, but so much of it was familiar. She was wearing a cream-colored dress, similar to the navy one she wore when I saw her — a dress that left no room to imagine what she'd look like with it off. And then, there was that hat that matched her dress ... just like the other day.

"Yes," I exclaimed. "I mean, no. I don't know her, but she's been at the hospital."

"With your husband?" Detective Green asked.

"Yes. I mean, no, I don't know. I saw her coming out of Jefferson's room the other day, but I was talking to Doctor Reid. But Jasmine," I turned to Hosea, "she knows her."

Now it was his turn to look confused. "What?"

"I mean, I don't know if she really knows her, but they were talking a lot." I decided to leave out that part about this woman being Dr. Reid's girlfriend. If that were true, the detectives would figure that out. And if it was another one of Jasmine's lies, I didn't want to send them chasing false leads. "So who is she?" I asked the detectives again. "What's her name? What was she doing with my husband?"

"You said, Pastor Bush's wife was talking to her. You didn't ask her name?"

"I did, but …." I paused. "I think we got interrupted and something happened and I forgot all about it. I didn't think at the time that it was any big deal. But now …."

"Well," he slid the photo back to his side of the desk and slipped it into the folder, "those are all questions that we're going to try to answer."

"What's her name?" I asked again, as if that would give me a clue to something.

"We don't know. We only have the photo." He took a breath. "But Pastor Bush, we may need to talk to your wife."

"That's fine, Detective. Just give me a call," Hosea pulled a card from his jacket, "and we'll come down here if you need us."

"Okay, well," Detective Green turned to me, "I told you we wouldn't keep you long."

If he were dismissing us now, he had made and kept that promise. But even though just minutes before I didn't want to come into this place, now, I didn't want to leave. I wanted to stay and learn more. I wanted to know everything that they knew. About that woman. And what happened to my husband.

When all three men stood, I hesitated for a moment, then did the same. But that was all I was capable of doing. Thank God, Hosea was with me. Because he shook their hands for me, said goodbye for me, led me through the door, down the hall, and into the street because surely, I wouldn't have found my way without him.

He called the driver, the moment we stepped outside and I paced a few steps to the left, then back to the right.

So … Jefferson had been with a woman that night. That woman. That night and the night before. That woman. She'd been in Jefferson's hospital room. That woman. And Jasmine had told me a lie.

Why?

Why had Jefferson been with her?

Why had Jasmine lied?

"Oh, God!" I moaned as I pressed my fingers to my temples.

I'd forgotten that Hosea was with me until he wrapped his arm around my shoulders. "The car will be here in two minutes and then, we'll talk."

I nodded and tried to hold on. And tried not to think about my husband having an affair.

Again.

And tried not to think that Jasmine had something to do with it.

Again.

chapter 18

Kyla

This time, Hosea sat in the back of the car with me and I wondered if it was because he could hear my thoughts. I wondered if he believed that, while this car was moving, I'd open the door and jump out into traffic.

Of course, I would never do that — even though that was what I was feeling. Or was it? I couldn't really say because in my mind, there was such a battle brewing:

The good angel: *Of course, Jefferson is not having an affair. After what the two of you went through twenty years ago, he would never bring that kind of pain and devastation into your lives again. He loves you and he's spent all these years proving it.*

The evil one: *Once a cheater always a cheater. And this probably isn't even the first time that Jefferson cheated. This is just the first time that he got caught ... again. 'Cause that's just what men do. For men, sex trumps love.*

"Oh, God!" I moaned.

It wasn't until Hosea covered my hand with his that I realized I'd said that aloud.

He said, "I was thinking that we should go back to the hospital first and then ...."

I shook my head. "No." I didn't want Nicole to see me this way. When she asked what happened at the police station, she'd know something was wrong right away. Not that she'd need lots of clues; it would be obvious from the break down that I was sure to have when I thought about her father and that woman as I was standing in front of her. I told Hosea, "I need a little time."

He squeezed my hand like he understood. "We can go somewhere. Have a late breakfast, early lunch."

Again, my head went back and forth. It wasn't just that I couldn't face my daughter, I didn't want to do anyplace classified as public right now. I didn't want to be any place where anyone could see me, because I just wasn't sure how long my sliver of strength would last.

Then, Hosea did what Hosea does. He heard my thoughts and answered my cries. Said to the driver, "Change of plans. We're going to City of Lights."

City of Lights. His church. The mega-congregation, mega-successful New York City icon that stood in the midst of Harlem.

That was a good choice, I thought. In the middle of this Saturday afternoon, the church would be empty, I'd be out of public view and only one person — and God would see my breakdown if it were to come.

Less than ten minutes later, the car slowed to a stop in front of the Gothic building with its twin towers that flanked several stain-glassed windows. Like the police precinct, the church was gray, stood tall and looked old, but unlike where we'd just been, this massive structure almost bowed, smiled and said: Welcome.

Hosea led me up the walkway toward the huge double-doors, then he made a left, and I was a little disappointed. I wanted to walk into the famed church and what so many had said was a spectacular sanctuary.

But then, as we walked along the side path, Hosea said, "I'll give you a tour of the church after I get you settled inside."

I looked at this man with wonder. And then, I looked for the cord that stretched from his heart to the sky because clearly, he had some kind of direct connection to God.

When Hosea had told the driver to bring us to the church, I'd been pleased with that suggestion, thinking that no one would see my breakdown. But when we walked inside, I had been wrong about that. In front of us was a full office and although it was Saturday, it felt like everyone was in the middle of a workday operation.

One, two, three, four … I counted nine people in total, who greeted Hosea, smiled at me, and then, kept it moving. Hosea led me through the activity of the church's business, then, he stopped at one of the desks where a short, stout, gray-haired woman, stood as she spoke into the phone.

"Okay, I'll give Reverend Bush, Senior your message; he'll be back next Tuesday. Thank you." She hung up the phone, then glanced at us over gold-rimmed glasses that were set low on her nose. "Well, I didn't expect to see you here today," the woman said, eyeing Hosea first, then she turned that stern glance toward me. "Don't you have an appointment with your wife?"

"Oh." With the heel of his hand, Hosea tapped his forehead as if that would knock his memory into place. "I need to call Jasmine. I'm going to have to cancel." Facing me, he added, "Mrs. Whittingham, this is Jasmine's friend. I told you about her, Kyla Blake."

The stern stare softened. "Oh, your husband was the one who was shot." She reached for my hand. "I'm so sorry." Then, she came around her desk and hugged me. "We're all praying here and you and your husband are on our intercessory prayer list."

I thanked her before Hosea and I turned away. But right before we stepped into his office, Mrs. Whittingham called out, "Pastor Bush … do you need me," she gave me a quick glance, "to join you?"

Hosea looked at me … and blinked. Mrs. Whittingham, looked at me … and stared. My glance skipped between the two, knowing what this was about. This was something that Pastor Ford did in her church as well. Hosea probably never spoke to women (and there may have been a few men who feel in this category, too) alone.

But after a long, studious moment, he said, "No, I think we'll be all right."

His words made her face soften and she smiled her approval, then after we stepped into Hosea's massive office, she closed the door behind us.

Walking into this space, lifted my mood in an instant. How could I be sad when I was surrounded by God and everything that was right with Him? Hosea (and maybe even Jasmine) had decorated the office in the masculine, yet warm tones of burgundy and beige and then, they'd stuffed the space with bookshelves that held Bibles of every translation and concordances, some short, others exhaustive. Then, there were the framed scriptures on each of the walls, some of my favorites: Jeremiah 29:11, Isaiah 43:2, James 1:3.

But it was the photos that were everywhere — on the bookshelves, on his desk, on the tables — that made my smile wide — pictures of Jacqueline and Zaya that chronicled their lives. Some photos were of each child, most were of the two together, and there were even ones, that I suspected, were the most recent, that were selfies.

I marveled at the number of photographs, but even more, I was in awe of the fact that there were as many (if not more) pictures of Jacqueline as Zaya. Hosea made no difference between his children.

The measure of this man.

"Have a seat," Hosea said as he motioned toward the leather sofa. I sank into the softness as he rounded his desk. I figured that he was going to sit down, check a couple of emails and then, get back to me and my issues.

I welcomed the silent seconds that I would have, maybe enough time to get my emotional-self together. That was why I closed my eyes.

But then, I heard, "Hey, Darlin'."

My eyes snapped open. Hosea had his phone pressed to his ear. After a pause, he continued, "That's why I'm calling. I'm not going to be able to make it." Another pause. "Something came up with Kyla that I have to handle, but if you're on your way, go ahead. Make a whole day of it." More passing seconds. "No," he glanced at me, but then blinked away our eye contact and returned this gaze to his desk. "I got this. We're cool. No need for you to change your plans." Another pause. "You know I'll make it up to you." Then finally, "Thanks for understanding. I love you. Call me when you get home." When he lowered his phone, he kept his glance on his cell.

I said, "You know what? I didn't know you had something to do with Jasmine until Mrs. Whittingham mentioned it. We can talk later. Really. I can go to the hospital now and check in with you this evening ... or whenever."

When I stood up, Hosea looked up and gave me a glare that said, 'Sit-your-ass-down,' though I had a feeling he'd never spoken those words aloud. But his look sure said it and I did what I was told.

The moment I sat, he stood, walked over, and settled in the chair across from me. He leaned forward, resting his elbows on his legs before he said, "Jasmine's fine. She wants me to help you with anything that you need."

I nodded, not believing him. She'd probably just cursed him out — or maybe I was the one she cursed.

Continuing, he said, "And what you need to do now is talk to me." He paused. "Tell me what happened back there at the police station."

I tilted my head and squinted, trying to figure out what he was talking about.

He explained, "You said that Jasmine knows the woman in the photo, yet you didn't know her name."

I parted my lips to begin my story, but Hosea held up his hands.

"And don't give me that line about you and Jasmine got interrupted. If you saw a woman coming out of Jefferson's room and you didn't know who she was and Jasmine did, I know you wouldn't let that slide. Jasmine would have lots of explaining to do. So talk to me."

And that's what I did. I started at the beginning and recalled how I'd been talking to Dr. Reid, when the woman walked out. I told Hosea that while she seemed to be trying to sneak around, she stood out with that big hat and fitted dress, just like the one in the picture. I told him how Jasmine had rushed after her, how they had talked for long minutes and how at first, Jasmine denied any knowledge of the woman. Then, I told him how Jasmine had come back and told me about Dr. Reid and that woman's relationship.

"So, that's all I know." I finally took a breath. "I really don't know her name because before I could prove too much further, Nicole came."

"Ah, the interruption."

"Yeah, it was real."

His nod was slow, steady and went on for a couple of seconds before he asked, "Do you believe Jasmine?"

It took me a moment to respond only because he was a good guy, so I didn't want to tell him that his wife was a lying liar and could never be believed or trusted. But he asked, so I said, "No." And then, with my eyes right on his, I said, "Your wife hasn't always been the most honest person in my life."

"Are you talking about when she had an affair with your husband?" Shock must have been all over my face, because he added, "She told me about that."

"I'm surprised."

"We have no secrets between us." He paused. "Let me take that back. I don't keep any secrets from my wife and she tries not to lie and keep secrets from me."

I liked him too much to laugh right in his face, so I pressed my chuckles down. "And you don't have a problem with that?"

He shook his head as if my question was one of the most ridiculous ones that he'd ever heard. "Not only do I love my wife because she was the woman that God made especially for me, but I accept people for who they are — the good and the bad within them." Then, he went on to preach what felt like a three sentence serious sermon. "God created Jasmine. She's His work. He's still working on her, and using me to do that, but I can only love God's creation."

I wondered how many microphones they had in this church. Because if Hosea spoke like that on Sundays, he'd have to drop the mic a couple of dozen times. Surely he'd broken several by now.

"Wow!"

He grinned. "You say that as if what I just told you was special."

"Uh ... it is."

"It shouldn't be."

"You say that like Jasmine could do almost anything and you'd be okay."

He paused as if he had to think about my words. "I wouldn't say anything, but since I've looked into her eyes and I've seen her heart, it would take something massive for me to leave. But you know what, I'm not special. If we truly understood God's plan for the union between a man and a woman, we'd fight harder. People give up on the husband or wife God has chosen for them too easily. Anyone can walk away, the courage comes in staying and fighting. And if God is in the mix, staying is worth it. Like I said, we just have to understand marriage."

That made me look away. That made me sigh. "Understanding marriage."

He let me sit in the silence of the words I'd spoken for a moment before he once again said, "Talk to me."

Where would I begin? "There seems to be so much going on and all I'm trying to do is help Jefferson fight for his life."

"That's a great thing. That's what a wife, a praying wife should do."

"But now I find out that he may have been cheating on me."

"Well, you don't know that, but even if he were, would you stop fighting for him to live?"

"No, of course not," I exclaimed as if I were insulted by the question. But then, I slowed my roll. "At least, I don't think so." Hosea's eyes were steady on me. "I mean, I think I wouldn't want him to die ... if he ... were having an affair." Then, I ended right where I'd started. "No, of course not. I want Jefferson to be well, even if it turns out that he's a cheating dog."

My words were meant to make him grin and he did. He leaned back. "Now that we have that out of the way, I think what you have to do next is forget about that woman. Let the police handle her and you handle your husband."

I shook my head at that impossible task. "How can I forget her? And suppose she has something to do with my husband?"

"She doesn't have anything to do with him being well. She doesn't have anything to do with him being awakened from his coma or the recovery that will follow. She doesn't have anything to do with the fact that Jefferson needs you."

It must have been the way I bit my lip and shook my head that made him say, "Anything that you conjure up in your mind about her is just that — conjecture. People spend all of this time coming up with scenarios that aren't facts. Scenarios aren't the truth, facts are. Let's wait for the facts and in the meantime, let's help Jefferson get well."

This man had been given a gift and he knew how to use his. He'd just softened my hardening heart and he'd done it with that soothing voice that cloaked me with comfort. Made me believe that I didn't have anything to worry about when it came to Jefferson and this woman.

But still.

"And there's something else I want you to consider."

I tilted my head.

He said, "My wife is a different person from the woman you knew. She's told me not only about you and Jefferson, but so many other things and … I'm sure there's lots that she's yet to tell. But Kyla, I've watched her mature and grow into someone I am proud to call my wife. And I really want you to consider this about Jasmine or anyone else that you've cut out of your life: No one is as bad as the worst thing that they've ever done."

I did what he asked, I considered his words and that led me to say, "If that's true, if Jasmine is a better person than she was twenty years ago, then, you've been really good for her."

He shrugged. "When people are growing — and we should all be growing till the day we die — we are not who we were last year, let alone twenty years ago. I believe that we're all just trying to get this life right."

I nodded.

"And my wife? We've been good for each other," Hosea said.

"So, think about this, maybe somewhere, somehow in your heart, you can forgive her. And that's not me asking, but what Christ demands."

"Actually, I have forgiven Jasmine."

He stared and me and only smiled.

"What? Really I have. If I hadn't there would've been no way that I could've spent these last couple of days with her."

"Well, if you have …."

My eyes narrowed. "You sound like you don't believe me."

He shrugged. "I'm not the one you have to convince." He slapped his hands on his legs. "But anyway … what we're going to do now is I'm going to have Mrs. Whittingham order us something for lunch, anything you want. While I do that, you should call Nicole and let her know that the police are not holding you against your will."

"Oh, my God," I said, digging into my purse for my cell. "I've got to make sure she's all right. She's probably going nuts."

"She's fine," Hosea said as if he were so sure. "She's a strong woman of God."

"And I'm not."

"You're a strong woman of God who needed a little refueling. We all do sometimes." Then, he continued, "And after we eat, I'll give you a tour of the church before we head back up to the hospital and talk to the doctors about the next steps."

"That all sounds good. Thank you for everything."

"Oh, and one last thing — right after you forgive my wife, you're going to forget about that other woman."

"What other woman?"

He laughed. "That's what I'm talking 'bout." Leaning over, he entwined my fingers with his and squeezed my hand, before pushed himself from the chair. "Let me get these menus from Mrs. Whittingham."

When he left me alone, I sat in the quiet for a moment, not believing how I felt — so much better than I'd felt an hour before when we walked out of that precinct. Yes, he'd challenged me about not forming conclusions without having facts, really forgiving Jasmine, and forgetting about the mystery woman.

I would be okay.

Jefferson and I would be okay.

I planted those words in my mind, then pressed repeat.

But no matter how many times they played, I couldn't get my heart to believe my thoughts.

Because of that woman. And Jasmine.

I couldn't just toss that woman to the side the way Hosea told me to do. And about forgiving Jasmine, maybe I would be able to do it if I didn't think she was lying now.

I thought about going to her one more time, telling her about what we'd found out from the police and asking her again about the woman. But after two seconds, I knew that would be a wasted effort — no matter who Hosea thought Jasmine was, I would never get the answers from her. So, I would have to get them from the only person who would tell me the truth.

Pressing Nicole's number, I had only two questions for my daughter: Was she okay, and when did the doctors say they were going to wake up her father?

Because no matter what it was, Jefferson would tell me the truth.

chapter 19

Jasmine

I stared at my phone as if the blame belonged to my cell. I'd been stood up.

For almost five years, Hosea and I had been doing these spa dates, the second Saturday of every month. We had a standing appointment: a couple's massage, then time together in either the private Jacuzzi or steam room, depending on our mood. It had been Hosea's idea to have these Saturdays together.

"Darlin', the kids are getting older and are more demanding of our time, Pops is stepping back from his responsibility and dumping it all on me ...."

I cracked up at his choice of words. His father, Samuel Bush had been the lead pastor for City of Lights for more than fifty years. Now that his son had stepped into his calling, my father-in-law had stepped into semi-retirement with the greatest of ease.

"And, I don't want us to ever lose each other. We may only get one day a month, but that day needs to be all about us, just you and me, together. Always."

"That is so sweet, baby."

"I mean it. We need to make time for each other. This has to be a priority because life can mess up relationships, and that's never going to happen to us. I love you way too much."

I had to wipe away a couple of tears.

"Plus, you need me, Darlin', you need me so much."

That was when my tears mixed with laughter. I cried because I still couldn't believe how much God had blessed me with this man after all the dirt I'd done in my life with other men who didn't belong to me. And, I laughed because ... well, Hosea always made me laugh. And his words were true. I did need him ... and I needed our second Saturdays. That was why I did everything to never miss a date, even scheduling my out-of-town trips around these days that were meant for us alone.

And Hosea did the same — he had never canceled once.

Never!

Before today.

I sighed now, as I finally tucked my phone back into my purse. There was no need to keep staring at it, as if that would change the fact that Hosea had canceled ... because of Kyla. What was going on with her that was so important? That took precedence over me?

As soon as I asked myself those questions, I snatched them back. Really? I was asking that when her husband had been shot in the head? When, while his chances of surviving were improving, he was still in the most critical of conditions?

Those had to have been the dumbest questions I'd ever asked because the doctors still had no idea how much damage had been done to Jefferson's brain. No one knew what Jefferson would look like, what he would be like when he was finally awakened.

So, how could I ask what was going on?

Except ... it felt like I needed to ask that question. It felt like there was so much more going on than what I knew. It felt like Hosea knew something that he didn't want to share — like there was some secret between just him and Kyla.

"Stop it, Jasmine," I whispered.

But my self-scolding did no good. Inside, I still went back and forth:

Of course Hosea would be there for Kyla, and I was all kinds of out of order for even feeling some kind of way about it.

But shame the devil 'cause the truth was, I did feel some kind of way. Especially after Hosea told me that he had to cancel and I told him that I would join them so that I could be there for Kyla, too. We always ministered together.

But my husband didn't want or seem to need my assistance today: *I got this. We're cool. No need for you to change your plans.*

Translation: Kyla doesn't really want you here, and because she doesn't want you, neither do I.

"Okay, Jasmine, you're really taking this too far."

"Excuse me?"

When I looked up, I had to blink a couple of times. Where was I?

"Did you say something?" the Uber driver spoke to me through the rear view mirror.

"No." Glancing out the window, I realized that the driver was still zooming toward Oasis, the spa where we had our appointment. He didn't know that I'd been stood up and had no desire to indulge in a couple's massage alone.

"Uh … I'm not going out to Long Island, anymore. My husband … just called …."

He frowned at me with a glare that said I-don't-know-where-you're-going-but-you're-gonna-pay-for-this-trip.

"Listen, whatever you have to do; can we stop this trip and start a new one?" I glanced at my watch. I still had several hours before Mae Frances came in, but I could find somewhere to eat, maybe read, and definitely think before I picked her up. "Can you take me to LaGuardia?"

"Okay." He spoke with a grin. I guessed he'd done the calculations and this was gonna work out just fine for him. Whatever worked for him, worked for me, and after he told me what to do through the app, he made a U-turn, and then, we were on our way to the airport.

If I couldn't hang out with my husband, at least I could see my friend who I'd missed so much. And Mae Frances would give me something to focus on besides Kyla and Hosea. Really, I was looking forward to hearing about her antics in Smackover and wherever else she'd been since I'd seen her last.

But not even thoughts of hanging with Mae Frances could keep my brain from shifting back to my husband ... and Kyla. I couldn't explain why I was tripping. Of course, Kyla needed someone. Of course, she would gravitate to my husband who was strength and power personified. Of course, my husband would be there for her. Hadn't her husband been there for me? After my divorce, I counted on Jefferson to help me with everything: from carrying heavy packages into my home to fixing my garage door.

It was my garage that started my plan to trap him all those years ago. Knowing that Kyla was away for the weekend, I'd asked him to come over, then met him at the door wearing nothing but the tiniest of slips. Even though I'd kissed him, he hadn't fallen then, but it was easy to see that he was ready to be plucked. It was in the way his eyes had lingered on me, the way his voice had filled with lust ... and the way, that he had kissed me, tongue-to-tongue. But even though he was more than attracted, he was tempted ... he'd run away, telling me he was sorry about the kiss and that I'd have to find someone else to help with the garage door.

I'd followed him to his house. There, I'd apologized, made some excuse about being out of my mind because of my divorce, then appealed to his Christian heart.

It was because of that heart, that he had opened up the door to his home and let me in. Mistake number one. At first, it had been innocent enough...

Sitting on opposite ends of the couch, we watched a movie together. But the whole time, I seduced him. I kept my focus on the TV screen, but from the corner of my eye, I saw him watching me as I ate the popcorn one kernel at a time. And each time after I swallowed, my tongue lingered on my lips, sliding across the skin as I licked off every grain of salt that remained from the popcorn. For the whole ninety minutes of the movie, I teased him without ever looking his way. I teased him with my tongue, taunted him with my laughter, and by the time the movie was over, Jefferson was so ready.

"That was really good," Jefferson said, then stretched into a yawn. "I can't believe this, but I'm really tired. I'm going to take a rain check on the rest of these movies."

"You're not going to watch them? I was looking forward to The Sky Below."

"Well, I don't have to return them to Blockbuster until tomor-row if you want to take it with you."

"Okay . . ." I hesitated, then was careful to keep my eyes away from his. "Jefferson, I have a favor to ask." I paused, for effect. "Would you mind . . . if I stayed here tonight . . . please?" His frown was so deep; it almost gave me a headache. I added as quickly as I could, "Please don't think I'm going to try anything. Believe me, I've learned my lesson. The only reason I'm even asking is because my house . . . it's so scary sometimes. I hate being there alone."

My words did not move him. "I'm sorry, but since Kyla's not here . . ."

"I don't know if Kyla has told you, but recently . . ." I bit my lip . . . that effects thing again, "I've been getting calls . . ."

"What kind of calls?"

I sniffed. "Threatening calls. From a man saying he knows that I live alone. And I've been so afraid. That's why Kyla lets me stay here with you guys so much." I tilted my head. "I can't believe she hasn't told you."

"Have you called the police?"

"Yes, but they said there's nothing they can do until he tries something . . . like breaking in or attacking me . . ."

Jefferson winced.

"I'm having an alarm installed when I get the money."

In the silence that followed, I could almost hear Jefferson's brain turning and churning. I heard his questions: how could he let me stay while Kyla was away? But on the other hand, how could he turn me away with that threat out there?

It was time for me to push him to the edge. "I wouldn't ask if I weren't scared," my voice trembled. "I wouldn't ask if I had anyone else I could depend on."

That was it, that was what took him out. He wouldn't be able to live with himself if anything happened to me. He said, "Okay, the guest room is yours . . . ."

That had been mistake number two. Jefferson never had any kind of chance once I was in that house with him. The rest of the night had been too easy. Now, I closed my eyes. Twenty years had passed, but I remembered every moment. I remembered the way I had slipped into Jefferson's bed. The way he'd taken me into his arms and made love to me like I was his wife.

Even now, I could feel him, smell him. I could see our faces ....

My eyes popped open.

The faces.

Not our faces.

Those sheets in my mind were being heated by Kyla and Hosea.

"Really, Jasmine?"

The smile that the Uber driver had been wearing faded fast and in its place was the deepest of frowns. He looked concerned — as if he had never had a passenger in the back of his car talking to herself.

Please. This was New York. What woman didn't talk to herself?

I returned his frown with the fakest of smiles and went back into my world where Kyla was stealing my husband. Except it was such a make-believe place. In no part of this universe would Hosea betray me. And no way in this world would Kyla do that, despite what I'd done to her. She loved her husband as much as I loved mine.

But then, as I thought about that night, I knew revenge was not only powerful, it was tempting. So powerful and tempting that God had even sent us a warning through His word.

Revenge is mine.

Maybe Kyla was remembering that night, too. Maybe revenge was too tempting for her to walk away from this chance to make me pay for every transgression.

I leaned back in the seat, but this time, I wasn't going to close my eyes. There was no way I wanted to revisit that image. So instead, I kept my eyes on the cars that rolled along the Van Wyck Expressway with us.

And I told myself, "You're being silly, Jasmine. You're being silly."

That became my mantra. But I didn't feel silly, I felt sure. Something was going on. Maybe it hadn't happened yet, but Hosea and Kyla were on their way.

Now, the real question I needed to ask was: How was I going to stop them?

chapter 20

Jasmine

I had a couple of hours between the time I arrived at LaGuardia and Mae Frances's plane landing. So after the Uber driver dropped me off, I'd spent the time running into the little coffee shop, scanning my timelines on Facebook and Twitter, and then, ordering a sedan because after all … I was picking up Mae Frances. And well, she only traveled one kind of way.

The thought of that made me shake my head and chuckle a bit. Back in 2006 when we'd met, I didn't know what to make of the woman who caked her face with the thickest of make-up, wore a thirty-five year old mink coat that swept the floor — in the summertime — and who'd laughed in my face the first time I told her that I was a Christian, and then went on to tell me that she didn't believe in God.

That was the most shocking of all the shocking things she'd ever told me. A black atheist? I didn't think that was genetically possible. But the shocker of all shockers — the way that she lived. Unbeknownst to anyone in the exclusive apartment building, Mae Frances lived behind her doors in abject poverty with empty cupboards and an emptier wallet.

But talking about a come up … life had truly changed for Mae Frances. Her cupboards were no longer bare, thanks to the job she'd been given back then at City of Lights. There was more method than madness when Hosea's dad had brought Mae Frances into the church. He wanted to make sure God became anchored in Mae Frances's heart. And He had.

And then, being Jacqueline and Zaya's 'grandmother came with lots of privileges since Hosea and I loved showering Mae Frances with the same love that she gave so openly, unselfishly, and unconditionally to our children. She didn't want for anything these days, and she let everyone know it.

So that was the reason why I'd had to trade in the Uber for a black stretch sedan. Because ordinary would never do for Mae Frances.

My cell phone vibrated and I looked down at the incoming text:
JL: *where the hell is my car?*
I grinned. Mae Frances was home.
I said to the driver, "You can pull up now, she's coming out."
As we rolled up to the door for the Delta shuttle, I saw Mae Frances's luggage before I saw her — three oversized Crocodile suitcases that she told me were a gift from Al Sharpton in the 70's or 80's … she couldn't exactly remember when.

"You know we used to call him Big Al back then," she said, tell-ing me another one of what I called her fantastic stories. "Yup, that was all the way back in the day when he was always trying to court me. He was a cool cat and everything, but I had to cut him loose. I kept telling him, ain't nobody had time for all of those protests and marches. I had a different kind of life that I wanted to live."

I rolled down the window and waved as Mae Francis plopped some oversized sunglasses on, looked around, and then pointed toward our car. The porter nodded and rolled the cart to us.

As the driver jumped out to open the trunk, Mae Frances slid into the back seat next to me.

"Did you give the porter a tip?" I asked.

She did one of those lean-back moves and looked down her nose at me. "Is that the first thing that you have to say to me?"

"I just want to make sure, Mae Frances," I said, already digging into my purse because I just never knew with my friend. "Tips are how they make their money."

As I grabbed a twenty from my wallet, Mae Frances slapped my hand. "Put your money away. I gave him a tip."

I breathed.

"I told him when Aqueduct reopens next month, to put one hundred on Petty Betty."

"Huh?"

"Yeah, Bubba and I are thinking about buying a horse and if we do, we're gonna name her Petty Betty and race her at Aqueduct. They still race horses out there, don't they?"

"What in the world are you talking about?"

She slowed down her speech like I was a little slow. "Aqueduct is a racetrack, right?" Mae Frances didn't give me a chance to respond. "Well, Bubba raises all kinds of animals on his farm, so we were thinking why not a horse? We can train him how to run a race."

I rolled my eyes. "First, Mae Frances, I don't think that's how it works. And second," I waved the bill in her face, "do I need to give that man this money?"

"I told you; put that away. You know I got class now. I gave him a tip. A real one and that one hundred dollars is probably gonna be the biggest tip he gets all month."

One hundred dollars? But I didn't say anything; I just put my twenty back in my wallet. Mae Frances giving away money was way better than what she used to do.

When the driver slipped back into the car and then eased away from the curb, I twisted in the back seat and faced my friend.

But before I could say hello, she asked, "What are you doing here? Aren't you supposed to be laid up somewhere with Preacher Man?"

"He canceled on me."

"What?"

"It's a long story that I don't want to talk about. I wanna talk about you and DC." I leaned back in the seat. "Your trip, to DC, it went well?"

She giggled. Yes. Mae Frances actually giggled.

That made me frown and want to give myself one of those

donkey kicks for even bringing up the subject. Though I had to admit that if black people glowed, then, Mae Frances was radiant.

She was still having a serious fit of giggles when she said, "That Bubba ... whew." And then, what was worse than the giggles — she fanned herself. "I wanted to bring my boo to New York with me, but he had to get home to the farm. You know, to take care of the pigs and the goats and the cows."

Boo? Did she call that man who was sixty seconds from being a centenarian her boo? I couldn't believe it. Mae Frances was more cosmopolitan than I could ever be, yet here she was acting like living in a place called Smackover with pigs and goats and cows was equivalent to Paris.

When she started giggling again and when she said, "The memory of these last few weeks will last me for a lifetime," I knew I needed something else to talk about. Because I was in no ways interested in hearing anymore about her ... and my uncle ... Bubba. Just admitting that (even only on the inside) made me throw up (a couple of times) in my mouth.

But before I could change the subject, Mae Frances leaned back, snuggled in the seat, and closed her eyes like she was about to take a power nap. Nuh-uh ... we had business to handle. Just because she hadn't gotten much sleep with Bubba didn't mean that I was going to let her sleep on my watch.

"Were you able to find out anything?"

Her eyes were still closed when she said, "You just sent it to me yesterday."

Dang. My hope had been that Mae Frances would have hung up the phone from me and handled life the way she always did. With what I'd been thinking about Hosea and Kyla today, I really needed to get this going. "Oh. Sorry." My friend didn't open her eyes. "I just thought ...."

"And you thought correctly." Her eyes snapped open, she fumbled through her purse, then pulled out a couple of pieces of paper stapled together. "Bam!"

She shoved the pages into my hand. "The woman's name is Lola Lewis. Can't tell you where she's from, at least not yet. But, she's been in New York for the last eleven years. The car, which she keeps in a garage on Seventy-Seventh Street, is registered in her name, but it was paid for by some anonymous benefactor, which isn't a good sign. Anonymous benefactors don't just buy random women cars. So that means she's up to some shifty kind of business."

As Mae Frances talked, my eyes scanned each of the pages. It was a dossier of the woman, including everything that Mae Frances was saying and even included a Google Earth photo of the brownstone where she lived.

"She lives on Seventy-Third Street? That's not far from you."

"Uh … no. She lives on the west side and I'm an east side sophisticated kind of girl."

"Whatever, those brownstones cost millions."

"Exactly." She once again leaned back and closed her eyes.

"So does she own the brownstone or does she rent an apartment inside?" I shifted through the pages.

"Jasmine Larson, I've had two minutes to find out this much. Give me five."

Still I asked, "Since someone paid for her car, do you think someone paid for her brownstone? Or at least they're paying her rent or mortgage?"

She opened her eyes and glared at me. "Didn't I just tell you that I needed five minutes?"

"But you can make an educated guess. What do you think? Is she really living this high? And if she is, who's paying for it? Do you think she was involved with Jefferson? Like, he was her sugar daddy or something?"

Her eyes were wide and then, she just shook her head. "Well, you don't even need me if you're gonna come up with the whole story."

"I do need you. It's just that I'm trying to figure all of this out."

"Well I gave you what I know and I can't answer any more questions. I don't like to speculate; I make my moves on facts and you know that. So, I'm gonna make some more calls, ask some more questions, get some more answers and then get back to you on this Lola chick."

I sighed.

"But at least you have a name and an address."

I nodded.

She asked, "So what's your next move?"

It was hard to believe that Mae Frances was asking me that. Like she'd just said, I had a name. I had an address. What did she think I would do?

Mae Francis shook her head. "I see those wheels turning in your head. That means you're about to do something you don't have any business doing."

"I'm just going to talk to her. I don't have all the questions in my head, but I know she needs to tell me something. Explain what happened Monday night. What was she doing with Jefferson. At least she needs to tell me that."

"You need to wait until I get the rest of my information? Because if you go to her now, she can tell you anything. Tell you all kinds of lies and make up all kinds of stories."

"I'm thinking I have enough — at least to start."

"You don't have squat and it's always been my experience that you shouldn't start something you can't finish. Just wait … let's see what else I find out and then, we can come up with a plan." When, I was silent, Mae Frances added, "Don't make me sorry that I gave you what I had." She paused. "Okay?"

"Okay," I said.

"You're a liar."

It was my turn to do a lean-back. "Mae Frances!"

"I'm just telling you what I know and I know you, Jasmine Larson. All you want to do is run over to that Lola girl's house. Just let me finish my work and we'll figure it out together."

"Okay."

"Liar," she said again.

But this time, I didn't challenge her. Because I didn't know if I was lying or not. I really wanted to do what Mae Frances said, but her name and address was already burning a hole in my hand.

"You know me, Jasmine Larson," Mae Frances said. "It won't take me long to find out more."

"Okay."

"You better listen to me."

"Don't I always?"

"No. You never do."

"Well, maybe I'll start now."

"You better because you don't need to go searching for anything that you're not prepared to find."

"Okay." I had no idea what she meant by that, but her words felt as if they were weighted with a foreboding.

I would try to wait. I really would. I just wasn't sure that I could.

chapter 21

Kyla

"Are you sure you don't want me to go in with you?"

I didn't turn my head from the window as the Uber rolled up the boulevard. Not that I was upset or anything; I was so far from that. It was just that I wanted to relish these last few minutes. I wanted to take in the sights and sounds of New York that defined this city — the yellow cabs that zigged in and zoomed out of traffic, the buses that groaned as they edged from the curbs, the sidewalks filled with people strolling past street vendors who sang out about their wares. It was a melody that belonged to New York alone.

I'd always been one of those people who, though I lived far away, claimed some kind of connection to this city. I certainly used to say — I Heart New York.

But after what happened to Jefferson, I was sure that I'd never speak nor sing about New York again.

That was what I thought — until today.

"Kyla?"

This time I turned and faced Hosea.

He said, "Did you hear what I said?"

"I did. But don't you think you've spent enough time with me today?"

He glanced at his watch. "It's not even six and it's still light

outside." His expression stayed straight until he looked up and
then, he gave me another one of his heart-reaching smiles.
"Anything else you want to do?"

My smile turned into a chuckle as I nodded. "Yes, I want to see
my husband and I'm sure you want to go see your wife."

He shrugged a little. "If you say so." His words were designed
to keep me smiling, but I could tell by the way he'd kept glancing
at his watch throughout the afternoon, and then reaching for his
phone several other times, that he really did want to go home to
Jasmine. But he wasn't going to leave until his assignment with me
was complete.

I needed to let him know that he could tell God his part in res-
cuing Kyla was done. "I will never be able to thank you for today."

Another shrug. "I didn't do anything, not really. Nothing that I
wouldn't do on any other Saturday."

"Oh really?" I laughed. "So, you always spend your Saturdays
having a magnificent soul food lunch catered in your office?"

"Melba is great, isn't she?"

"And then, every Saturday you stroll through Central Park?"

"Gotta get my steps in." He held up his wrist revealing his
Fitbit.

"Oh, so that's why you took me to the Empire State Building.
So that you could more steps?"

He shook his head. "Nope. I had enough steps. But how can
anyone come to New York and not see what used to be the world's
tallest building?"

"You know I'd been there before."

He nodded. "I know. But you needed to be there today."

This time, my smile was more in my heart than on my lips because that was where Hosea reached me. Today, he had ministered
to my soul.

This morning, I'd left that police station in such despair, filled
with so many questions. And though one part of me felt hopeful
when I called Nicole and she told me the doctors were definitely
going to wake Jefferson up tomorrow, so much of me was simmer-
ing in confusion. What was going to happen once Jefferson was

conscious? Would Jefferson wake up to tell me that he'd been with someone else? That he loved someone else?

I'd been on the verge of a breakdown, but because of Hosea, I'd had a breakthrough. And he'd done it all without us speaking about Jefferson and that woman again.

He'd done it by making me smile as we talked about Nicole over our lunch of catfish strips, and then the best chicken and waffles I'd ever had. He'd done it by making me remember as we walked along Central Park West and I shared with him how Jefferson and I had built the African American Wellness Center over the last twenty years.

But the best part, what touched me the most was when he took me to the Empire State Building. There, we hadn't spoken. Just went up to the Observation Deck and there, I remembered.

I didn't even ask Hosea how he knew what this place meant to me. I was sure that Jasmine had told him since I'd often shared with everyone the story of how Jefferson and I became engaged. Or maybe Jasmine hadn't told him. Maybe the message had come to him from God. Hosea had that kind of connection to the Lord.

However he found out, he'd taken me to the one place in New York where I needed to be. On top of the Empire State Building, I'd closed my eyes and felt it. I felt all of the love. Jefferson's love. Standing there, just feet away from where Jefferson had slid the ring on my finger, I knew … I knew that Jefferson hadn't cheated on me — not again. I knew it with everything inside of me.

My belief in our marriage had been fortified high above the streets of New York and by the time we jumped into this Uber, I'd never felt so sure about me and Jefferson. I didn't know the story of what happened to Jefferson on Monday night — not yet, but I was now willing to bet on my husband … because of Jasmine's husband.

As the car eased to a stop in front of Harlem Hospital, I glanced up at the building and for the first time since I'd arrived in New York, I didn't feel that overwhelming sinking feeling. Instead, I was filled with a new hope.

Turning to Hosea once again, I said, "You were right. I did need to visit the Empire State Building today."

"See, I'm a genius."

I laughed. "Yeah, you probably are." Then, I got serious. "But what you are even more … is a god-send." Leaning over, I pressed my lips against his cheek. "Thank you, once again," I said.

When I leaned away, he asked, "So, church tomorrow?"

"I really want to be here as they're waking up Jefferson, but if we can make it to the eight o'clock service …."

"Whatever is best for you. You can have the car bring you to church or bring you here."

I nodded, then, slipped out of the car and waved before I rushed into the hospital. I couldn't believe I'd been away all day, but Hosea had been right. After four days of only leaving this place to sleep, he gave me a break I hadn't even known that I needed. He gave me this break that gave me a new perspective.

But now, I wanted to see my husband, I needed to see my daughter.

I rushed into the lobby, then into the elevator and to the fourth floor. I waved at the nurses who I'd spent so much time with, they were becoming my friends, and then pushed the door open to Jefferson's room.

The vision in front of me made me stop.

Jefferson was still sleeping; I knew he would be. But it was Nicole who brought tears to my eyes. She was going to have an awful crook in her neck or her back tomorrow with the way she was leaning over the side of the bed with her head resting on her father's chest.

My lips trembled and with my fingertips, I pressed my sobs back as I traveled in a time-capsule to twenty-eight years, twenty-nine years ago. To Nicole's toddler days when I battled with her to sleep. But what I couldn't do, Jefferson could. He would lay down with her and rest her head on his chest. And every time, in minutes, she slept. It was as if she had to connect to his heart before she could close her eyes. That connection allowed her to rest.

Nothing had changed.

It took a few moments, but I was able to turn my sobs into a big ole smile. How could I not be filled with joy as I took in the sight of the loves of my life? I wished that they could stay this way until Jefferson awakened. But I had to get Nicole up.

Stepping over to her, I rubbed her back, not wanting to startle her from her sleep.

After a few moments, she lifted her head, blinked, then turned to me.

"Hi, sweetie." I moved a couple of stray curls from hiding her eyes.

She moaned her hello before she sat up and stretched. "Hey, Mom. Hmmm," she hummed. "You've been out all day."

"I know. And I'm sorry."

"What are you talking about? I told you that I thought it was a good idea to hang with Pastor Hosea for a little while. What did you do?"

I thought about my afternoon once again and with a smile, I said, "I'll tell you later. But get up. Come on. Walk with me. Have you eaten?" She shook her head and before she got the words out, I said, "We'll go down to the cafeteria."

"I'm not ...."

Again, I didn't let her finish. "I know."

She did as she was told, even though I didn't really tell her a thing — at least not with words. She just followed me into the elevator and down to the first floor.

Together, we roamed through the hospital's cafeteria that had just opened for the dinner hours. But even though there were lots of hot dishes to choose from, Nicole grabbed a tuna sandwich wrapped in plastic and a bottle of water. I couldn't even convince her to add a bag of chips.

We found two seats and even though I didn't have anything in front of me, I bowed my head when Nicole blessed her food.

The first thing she said after her, "Amen," was, "The doctors are really optimistic, Mom. "

I nodded. "So am I. I prayed a couple of times today with Pastor Hosea."

"I know you did." She chuckled, even though her mouth was

stuffed with a good bite of her sandwich. "He is one praying dude. I didn't think I'd ever meet anyone who prayed as much as Daddy, but Pastor Hosea," she shook her head, "he might have my dad beat."

That made me smile. Nicole was right. Jefferson and Hosea shared the same heart for God. "Well, it's a good thing it's not a contest. Just two men who love to talk to the Lord."

She nodded. "What about Auntie Jasmine? Did she join you?"

The mention of Jasmine's name wiped that smile right off my face, and I had to press down the little bit of petty rising inside of me. The petty that reveled in my spending the day with Hosea so that he wasn't home with her.

But I shook that thought away. Had I ever been petty? Yes. But, I'd never been passive-aggressive with it. No, if I was going to do something to Jasmine, I'd come right out and do it — the same way she'd done it to me.

"No," I finally said to my daughter. "Jasmine wasn't there. Hosea went with me to the police station and then, after that, we did a couple of things, but Jasmine … I guess she was home with her children."

"Hmmmm."

"What does that mean?"

"Nothing. Just hmmmm."

"Okay, so are you going to tell me what you mean, or are you going to keep it to yourself?"

"I can ask you the same thing, Mom."

I frowned.

"You know how you used to say 'I know my child?'" She didn't give me a chance to respond. "Well, I know my mother. So tell me, what's going on with you and Auntie Jasmine?"

I cringed every single time she gave Jasmine that honor. "First of all, she's not your aunt. And secondly, I don't know what you're talking about. Nothing's going on with us."

"Okay." She put down her sandwich. "See, that's what I'm talking about. Aunt Alexis isn't my aunt either, but you don't have a problem because she's always treated me that way, just like Auntie

Jasmine."

Her words made me fold my arms and I had to fight hard not to glare at her.

She said, "We're gonna play this game? Come on, Mom, just talk about whatever it is. The tension between you two is thicker than my roots." With her fingers, she combed through her honey-brown natural curls. "So are you going to talk to me?"

I managed to toss her a weak smile and then, hoped that my words would be more convincing. "There's no tension. It's just that we haven't seen each other in a long time so, you know, it takes a minute to get back into that friendship space."

Her blank stare lasted longer than a moment. "You know what? Just tell me, 'It's none of your business, Nic,' or 'You're too young to understand, Nic,' or 'It's too much to handle, Nic,' or ...."

I held up my hand. "Okay, okay. I surrender." But even though I'd said that, once Nicole sat back, ready to listen, I couldn't find the right thing to say. What was I supposed to tell my daughter? Because anything I said about her 'Auntie Jasmine' would blow the feet off that pedestal that held her father.

When I stayed quiet for too long, she said, "I know she did something bad, something that you think is unforgivable."

Her words sent my heart pounding.

"And I can only think of two things that you would consider unforgivable sins."

My heart rate slowed a bit. She said 'two things'. So, she was on the wrong track.

She kept on, "It would be unforgivable if she did something to me, and I don't remember Auntie Jasmine doing anything to me. So ...."

Now, it was my head that was pounding.

"Did she have an affair with Dad?"

"Wha ...."

"And before you answer that, Mom, remember that I was a really smart kid. Sensitive and intuitive. I felt things and I knew things. And, I kinda felt it before, but watching you with her since I got here, I think I know it now ... no matter what you say."

I wanted to open up to Nicole, tell her everything, all that I'd been feeling for all these years, and what I felt now seeing Jasmine again. But my lips wouldn't move because my heart still didn't want her to know the truth about her father's failings. Yes, she thought she knew, but once I affirmed her words, it would be out there. Complete certainty.

She inhaled a deep breath, then took just as long to release it.

"Wow, I can't believe it." She shook her head. "Dad and Auntie Jasmine. Wow. That's a lot to handle."

I wanted to tell my daughter that she was right. It was too much, it had been too much and I wanted to ask if now she understood why my heart had no love for that woman.

She said, "It's really something that you worked it out with Dad. Because, I mean, that was a whole lot to forgive." She paused and I still couldn't say anything. "I don't know, Mom. I don't know if I could have done what you did. I don't know if I could have forgiven Dad."

Those words made me find my voice. "Oh, no, Nicole. It was tough and it was rough for your father and me," I said, finally admitting what I'd never wanted my child to know. But I had to say something. I had to explain the process of forgiveness to her so that she wouldn't hold this against Jefferson. When he woke up, I wanted her love for him to be the same, so I had to convince her that he deserved to be forgiven. "But your father and I worked really hard. Especially your father — he did everything that he could to not only earn my forgiveness, but earn my trust. He loved me enough to put in the work."

She nodded.

"And when you think about it, Nic, I didn't do anything special. I just did what God does for you and me every single day. No matter our transgressions, He forgives us and He asks that we do the same."

She nodded, but I still felt like she needed a little more. "I never wanted to tell you because I never wanted you to look at your dad differently. He's a good man, Nicole. A good man, who did a bad thing. A very good man, who deserved to be forgiven."

Her nod was more forceful this time and I could tell that she truly agreed. "You're right. I'm really proud that you're my mom. I'm proud that you allowed God to work it out with Dad."

I leaned back and though, I didn't smile, I did breathe, filled with relief.

Until she said, "So why haven't you let God work it out with Auntie Jasmine?"

I gasped, I blinked, I didn't understand.

"You've forgiven Dad, and he was the one who made the promises and vows to you. But you're having a hard time forgiving your friend, I don't get that."

The words were out of my mouth before she even finished. "Because if she did that with your father, then, she was no friend to me."

Through the corner of her eye, she glanced upwards as if she were trying to get my words to compute. "Well, by that logic, Dad was no husband to you, either."

Sometimes truth came wrapped in a punch to the gut.

I guess because she didn't want to see me cry, she covered my hand with her own. "Mom, I understand, I really do. Because if it happened to me, I don't know if I could have been as forgiving as you. I mean, I would like to believe that I would be, but no one knows what they'll do until they walk in those shoes. So believe me when I say that I understand.

"But it just kinda feels like you did all of this work to forgive, but in God's eyes you're gonna get half credit. There were two people who needed forgiveness, but you only closed fifty percent of the deal. And if forgiveness is for you and not the other person anyway, then you're only half healed." She shook her head. "That's not what I want for you. I want my mom to have complete healing and after … how many years has it been?"

I didn't have to do any kind of mental calculation. I knew when it happened, down to the year, the month, the week, the day, and if I glanced at my watch … the minute ….

I gulped and said, "Twenty."

Her eyes stretched wide, but then, she pulled her surprise back.

"Well ... after ... twenty years, you deserve the freedom because that is a long time to carry the burden of unforgiveness. And trust, I'm not thinking about your husband, or your friend ... I'm thinking about you. So forgive her. The same way you forgave Dad."

I blinked, I nodded, and this time, I did understand. While there were still plenty of tears in my eyes, there was so much pride inside of me. Isn't this what we all hoped for with our children? That they would grow into mature, intelligent, wise adults. "When did you get to be so smart?"

"Oh, I came out of your womb this way, didn't you know? I was ready for college at three, but you and Dad wouldn't allow me to be great."

I laughed and wiped a tear from my cheek.

"Mom, I hope you don't feel like I'm judging you."

"Oh, no, sweetheart, I don't."

"And I hope you don't think I've overstepped my bounds."

"I'm your mom, but you're grown now. So I can be your friend, too. And friends tell friends the truth."

That made her grin. "And I'm grateful. Because to me, that's the best kind of relationship. I wanted to help you the way I know that you would help me if I were ever in the same situation."

I sniffed, then said. "So ... are you saying that you're finally in a relationship?"

"Mom ...." She turned that single syllable into six.

"I'm just asking because if you can get in my business ...."

"Ugh ... you know that it's all about work for me right now. I really want an ambassadorship in a few years."

"And you'll get it. But you can still get married and have grandbabies for me."

"Really, Mom?" She rolled her eyes. "How did we end up talking about me and grandbabies?"

I shrugged. "I don't know. Maybe I'm trying to help you be great."

We laughed together, and then, we stood together. And we held each other for seconds and seconds and seconds.

Until Nicole said, "Okay, Mom. Let's go upstairs and see the man who makes us both great."

As I followed her, I raised my eyes to the ceiling and imagined that I could see right through it to the throne of God. And then, I thanked Him for the young genius that He had gifted to me. Because my child had blossomed into one brilliant woman.

chapter 22

Jasmine

I'd been waiting. And thinking. And pacing.

My mind was on overload. Lola Lewis. I had a name, I had an address. That was all I needed to take the first step. But at the same time, I had Mae Frances and her warning.

You don't need to go searching for anything you're not prepared to find.

What did Mae Frances mean?

It had to be serious because she really wanted me to wait, but I couldn't. I was itching to run right over to that address. There was one thing stopping me, though — my thoughts. I was trying to come up with a plan of what I'd say to Lola, but my thoughts kept drifting to my husband. And Kyla. And my husband and Kyla.

I plopped down onto the chaise in my bedroom, ready to chastise myself for trippin' about Hosea spending time with Kyla. What was this about?

Uh … maybe it's about you sleeping with her husband?

Yeah, well, she would never do that to me.

Uh … you don't know that girl anymore.

I know Kyla Carrington Blake and she's a good-girl from way back.

She told you she was different now.

I jumped up from the chaise. "Would you just shut up!"

"Mama." I swung toward the voice. "Who are you talking to?"

My son stood in the door jamb, with his legs slightly parted and his hands stuffed deep inside his pockets. Hosea's stance.

"Oh, nobody, baby. I was … just making a list of things I had to do." I waved for him to come in. "Did you want something?"

He shook his head. "Nah, I was just looking for Dad. He's not home yet."

I know, right? "He'll be home soon."

"Where is he?"

That's what I want to know. "I don't know, but he'll be here, probably around seven or so."

"It's after seven now, Mama."

What! "Oh, really?"

"Yeah, I was gonna text him, but I didn't want to do it if he was in a private session with someone."

He'd better not be in anything private with Kyla. "Why don't you do that, Zaya? Text your, Dad. Go on. Text him over and over until he responds."

He nodded and then shrugged, a move that I didn't quite understand. "Okay," he finally said.

My son strolled toward the door with so much cool. Hosea's swagger.

At the door, he glanced over his shoulder, gave me a little nod, then disappeared into the hallway.

As soon as he was out of my sight, I rushed to the bed and grabbed my purse in search of my phone. I checked my messages thinking that maybe there was one missing, one that may have gotten by me.

But the last one from him had come in just a bit after three: *I'm out with Kyla. Getting her on track mentally. Will get back with you. Love you.*

I'd read this earlier, but now, I read it again. Then, studied it some more. And analyzed it so that I could read all the words that weren't on the screen. What did this text really mean?

I'm out with Kyla: Okay, that was a good thing because that meant if they were out, they couldn't be in somewhere.

Getting her on track mentally: Okay, another good thing — no mention of anything physical.

Will get back with you: What did that mean? That he was coming home … eventually?

Love you: Did he really?

I tossed my phone onto my bed. "You're being ridiculous." This time, I whispered my chastisement. I was acting like I thought Hosea was cheating on me. As if he ever would.

Well ....except for that time when he almost did.

Sighing, I sank back onto the chaise and remembered those days back in 2008 when I was sure that I'd lost my husband. It had been my fault. In those early years of our marriage, I'd hidden so much from Hosea, though if I were telling the truth, hidden was the wrong word — I'd lied. I'd lied to my husband about everything — from being married before to lying about in which decade I was born. The discovery had been too much for Hosea and he'd left me for...*Oh, God,* how long had he stayed away? I closed my eyes and remembered the worst part of that time:

I'd tricked Hosea's assistant, Brittany into telling me where Natasia was staying — at the Rendezvous. I couldn't believe that I was really in this place, competing with Hosea's ex-fiancée, a woman he told me he hadn't married because she wasn't the one God had chosen for him. How many times had Hosea told me that I was the one?

But now everything, my marriage, my life, my all was on the line because I had lied.

I swerved my car into the circular driveway of the hotel, jumped out before I even put the car in park, and tossed my keys to the va-let, not giving him a chance to ask if I were a guest or just visiting.

If Brittany had told me that Natasia's suite was on the fourth instead of the fourteenth floor, I would've climbed the stairs. But even though I felt like I had enough rage inside of me to scale Mount Everest, I wanted to reserve it all for Natasia. Because if she had my husband in her suite, I was going to do to her what I'd dreamed about doing since she'd come into our lives two months ago. She'd made it clear — she wanted Hosea back and she was willing to do whatever. Well, tonight she was gonna learn — I was going to fight for my husband in every way.

Once inside the elevator, I punched the 14 button like it was Natasia's face, then watched the numbers ascend until the cham-ber stopped. I stomped out of that elevator, found her suite, then banged on the door like I was the CIA, FBI, IRS, DOJ and all the other alphabet agencies that I couldn't quite remember through the red fog in my brain. I banged and banged until Natasia finally swung the door open and then, I busted inside like a keg of dyna-mite, all of my rage on the verge.

I barreled over the threshold and then stopped, taking in the sight in front of me. First, I glared at a stone-still Natasia, and then I turned my fury to Hosea, who was just as unmoving as Natasia in his shock. He sat with his pants undone.

My stillness lasted only about three seconds because when I turned back to that trick, my fists were flying. I didn't fight like a girl; I was more like a pit bull, plunging forward and landing my first strike — the center of Natasia's eye.

Natasia shrieked. Fell back. But I had just started. I was that pit bull with a single command in my mind — kill!

Hosea jumped from the couch and corralled me from behind before I could land the knock-out punch.

"Jasmine!" That was what Hosea called me.
And I called her, "You stank ho!" I fought as hard as I could to get loose from Hosea's arms, but his grasp was like a leash.

"Jasmine! Stop it!" He squeezed me, held me, and kept whispering, "Please, please, please," over and over until I could do nothing but settle down.

But I kept my glare on Natasia, because if I had half-a-second that would be enough to give me half-a-chance to put that skank into the ground.

When Natasia stayed in place, I twisted in Hosea's arms until I faced him. "How could you do this?" My question came through tears.

"I haven't done anything, Jasmine."
I fought harder to get away, but the more I fought, the tighter

his grasp.

"Listen to me," he demanded. "I haven't done anything, I promise."

"Then what are you doing here?"

He looked at Natasia. "I needed a place ... that's all. Nothing happened ... I just got caught up ...."

Sighing, I opened my eyes and walked over to the window. Usually, standing at this window as the day bowed to night, calmed me. But not now. All I could think about was my husband and those days with Natasia and these days with Kyla. He'd almost left me for another woman once ... could it happen again?

Kyla's married.

So what?

Hosea's married, too. And he loves you.

"I come bearing gifts."

For a moment, I wondered if that was the voice in my head. I swung around and faced the door. Though I'd heard his voice, I didn't see Hosea, at least, not all of him. Only his arm that was attached to his hand, that held one of my favorite things — a blue Tiffany's bag.

I squealed, though I stayed in place and I guess that sound was the signal to my husband that it was safe to enter.

He stepped into our bedroom, still holding the bag high, and wearing the biggest of grins. "The strangest thing happened." He took a couple of steps toward me. "I was walking past Tiffany's, and this silver and diamond necklace that happened to look like the one you showed me after our last spa date," more steps, "hopped out the door and into my pocket."

I folded my arms. "Oh, really?" I asked without a bit of the delight that was in my heart.

"Yeah, and the box and the bag followed, begging me to bring them home so they could be yours."

Now, he stood in front of me and I hated that I was so superficial that I could be bought with a twenty-five hundred dollar necklace. But by the time the bag was under my nose, I sniffed those diamonds and I was done. Playfully, I snatched the bag, hugged him, then sat on the edge of our bed as I opened the box and once again, swooned at the sight of the necklace that was inspired by the majesty of waterfalls.

"Oh, baby," I turned to him, and then, remembered my day and all of my anxiety. I pulled back my glee. "So, is this supposed to make up for missing our spa date?"

He took the necklace from me, then wrapped his hand in mine and helped me up. Standing behind me, he circled the jewelry around my neck. "This is to make up for missing our date and all the hours after." He clasped the closure and turned me to face him. "I'm sorry, Darlin'."

How was I supposed to stay mad with this? With this man giving me puppy-dog eyes and this gift. It was like magic, the way my anger faded.

But then, he said, "I just got caught up."

There went the magic. And in its place were thoughts of Natasia ... I mean, Kyla. I glared at him. "Caught up? With what?" I asked, remembering how he'd said the same exact thing about being with Natasia.

He frowned as if he didn't expect that question. "With Kyla. You didn't get my texts?"

"Yeah, but the last one came hours ago." I glared up at him. "So what were you doing all the rest of the time?"

There were deep lines carved into his forehead, but then, the lines softened and in their place was a smile, no a grin. A big ole grin, like my husband was on the verge of bowling over with laughter.

"Seriously, Hosea? You're laughing at me?"

"Seriously, Jasmine. You're jealous of me ... being with your friend. A woman who you keep saying used to be your best friend."

"Well, if I'm jealous it's because you're right — she used to be my best friend and because of the reason that she's not anymore, I don't trust her."

"Wow! You don't trust her?" Then, he had the audacity to let it loose — and he did laugh. Like laughed right in my face. "That's rich, Jasmine. Because of what you did, you don't trust her."

"You know what I mean."

He nodded. "Yeah, I do. And that's why I don't get why you're upset. Because I was only with Kyla because she's spent the last four days in the hospital by her husband's side. Her husband, who by the way, was shot in the head and hasn't been conscious since his brain surgery. Her husband, who's missing half his skull. You remember that, don't you?"

I bit my lip because when he put it like that ....

After shaking his head for a few moments, he wrapped his arms around me, continuing his assault on my anger. "I'm really sorry, Darlin', that I missed our date, but you don't have a thing to be jealous about. Not today, not ever. I took the time with Kyla because she was in a bad way and I thought she needed some space away from the hospital and even from Jefferson ... for just a little while after what she went through this morning."

I looked up at him. "What happened?"

He sighed and led me back to the bed. When we both sat, he said, "This morning, I met her and Nicole at the hotel because I knew I'd be away all day with you, so I wanted to pray with them and see if the doctors had determined a definite day to begin waking Jefferson. But then, the detectives called and wanted to see her."

"Why?"

"Well, first, they wanted to know if Jefferson was having an affair."

"What?" I shouted, shocked that someone else shared my thoughts. "Why in the world would they ask her that when her husband is laying up in the hospital?"

"Because they're detectives, not doctors. Not that they don't care about Jefferson's recovery, but their first priority is solving this case."

"Well, his recovery might help them solve the case."

"True, but I guess they can't wait, which honestly, makes me feel good. They're on their jobs and you know, many times shootings like this might not get a lot of attention."

I shook my head, trying to imagine Kyla sitting through those questions. "Poor Kyla. I know she lost it when they asked her that."

"Pretty much."

"What did she do? Did she stomp out of there?"

"I think that was her first instinct. That's why I spent the day with her because those questions messed her up."

"Oh, my God." I pressed my hand against my lips. "So, they brought her down there just to harass her?"

"It's not harassment. These are questions they have to ask, things they need to know. And they had another purpose; they wanted her to take a look at a picture."

My question was in my frown and Hosea continued.

"Turns out they did have surveillance video from one of the city's cameras on that block."

I inhaled and hoped that Hosea didn't notice. Did they have video of Jefferson and Lola? Did they show it to Kyla?

"They caught Jefferson and a woman on tape."

Hosea's expression hadn't changed and I wasn't sure how I should play this. Wasn't sure if I should feign surprise or not. He gave me a little pause, but I stayed silent.

"They got an image of a woman, the only woman who was in the store during the time Jefferson was there."

"Um, did ... they show ... you and Kyla the picture?"

He nodded again and with the same straight face, he told me, "And she said you knew the woman."

In the passing seconds, I tried to make a quick calculation. What did I want to tell Hosea? How much of this did I want him to know?

"Jasmine."

Hosea hardly used my name, always preferring his term of endearment. But when he called me by the name that my mother had given to me, that was code for: Don't lie. So, I decided to tell him the truth.

"I don't know her."

He turned his head slightly. Body language read: he didn't believe me.

I held up my hands. "No, I really don't know her. Actually, you've seen her before."

He frowned.

"When we were at the hospital on Tuesday, she was in the waiting room with us. She was wearing this hat, a fascinator. That's what made her stand out to me."

Now, a tilt of his head accompanied his frown as if he were trying to remember.

I said, "She seemed out of place. And then, when we were talking to Doctor Knight, she came out to the hallway and was eavesdropping."

"I didn't notice any of this."

"Well, I did. I even followed her when she tried to leave, but she got away. Then, she came back the next day."

"Is that when Kyla saw her?"

I nodded. "While Kyla was talking to Doctor Reid, I cornered the woman, but ...." I hesitated. This was where I wondered if I should part from the truth. Should I tell Hosea what Lola said, or should I share the made-up story? If I told him the truth, Hosea would make me go to the police and I was sure that somehow, she would find a way to, at best, think that I was involved somehow ... or at worst, blame me for everything.

And then, they would pull Kyla back in, and tell her that her husband was having an affair. While she was trying to deal with her husband's fight for his life, she'd have to fight for her heart.

And she'd go through all of that for what? I doubted that what Lola had told me was completely true. But whatever, I needed to know more first. I needed something concrete before I ripped Kyla's heart and world apart.

"Jasmine."

Code for: Don't lie.

I said, "She told me some story ...." I shook my head. "Something about she was involved with Doctor Reid and they got into a fight and she found him in Jefferson's room and he told her to get herself together." I waved my hands. "I didn't believe a word she said, but that's what she told me."

Hosea gave me one of those long, penetrating, lie-detector

stares. And I held his gaze, until he began nodding. "Kyla told me that story."

"It's not a story. That's what Lola told me."

"Lola?" He paused. "Is that her name?"

Crap! I should have thought this through. Of course, the cops didn't have a name. All they had was a video and unless she had looked up at the lens and stated her name, they wouldn't know who she was. "That's the name she gave me." I did that waving thing again, trying to minimize what I'd just said. "But it's probably not real."

After a couple of nods, Hosea said, "Yeah, well, you're probably right. But the detectives need to know this." He glanced at his watch. "It's too late now, but you need to speak to Detective Green on Monday."

"Really? But I don't know anything."

"I know you think you don't, but you may know her name. Just tell him what you know and let them figure it out."

"Are you sure? Because I don't want to get Doctor Reid caught up in anything."

"I doubt if her story is the truth, but whether it is or not, the police need to know everything to solve this. You've got to do this for Jefferson."

I nodded.

"I'll call Detective Green."

"No, that's okay. I'll call him. I don't know how this will help, but if you think it will, then I'll do it."

"Okay." He pulled me into his arms. "So, do you want to model this necklace for me?"

I smoothed out the collar of my blouse.

He said, "I think it would look better if you highlighted the necklace."

"Huh?"

"You know, if you made sure the necklace was all that I could see. If you were wearing the necklace and nothing else, then, I could appreciate … the necklace even more."

I laughed. "Pastor Bush, don't you have church in the morning?"

"Exactly! How do you think pastors get ready for Sunday morning? They get turnt up on Saturday night."

I cracked up. "No. You did not just say that."

"It's the truth. Now, stop stalling and model that necklace, woman."

Backing away from him, I began to unbutton my blouse. Slowly. Hosea leaned back on the bed and prepared for my show.

I put myself on automatic, going back to my stripper days, when I commanded the stage at Foxtails Hostess Club as Pepper Pulaski. Back then when I was in college, I rocked and rolled my hips, dipped into splits, swirled upside down and around on the pole. I'd done it for cash then, but it was only for the man who had my heart now.

And oh, how I loved Hosea. Which was why I really hated lying to him. But even though my lying days were truly behind me, there were times when I just had to do it. For the good of everyone.

I just prayed that this would turn out for the good of me, too.

chapter 23

Jasmine

"I'm sorry I missed church this morning," Kyla said as we stood outside of Jefferson's room. "It's just that I wanted to be here when they woke Jefferson up."

"Are you kidding?" Hosea said. "Of course we understand." My husband paused and squeezed my hand that he'd been holding since we'd arrived at the hospital. "And what's most important is that God understands, too," he continued. "This is where you were supposed to be."

She nodded and then, the way she blinked, I could tell she was in a battle with tears. I wanted to embrace her and hold her for as long as it would take for her to feel some kind of peace. I just couldn't imagine going through something like this with Hosea. But, I stood back and instead thought about how she'd spent yesterday with my husband.

"I don't know what I was thinking," Kyla said. "When they told me they were going to start waking him up, I thought he was going to do that — wake up."

"I did, too," Hosea said. "But now that I think about it, you know, it makes sense. Jefferson's been heavily sedated for almost a week; it would take time for him to come from under all of those drugs."

"I guess." Kyla wiped her eyes as if she were trying to rub her weariness away.

I asked, "So, what are the doctors saying?"

She slapped her hands on her legs as if my question annoyed her. "Not much of anything."

I wasn't quite sure if she meant to snap at me, but her tone made me take a step back. Really, she made me want to cut and run. But I stood steadfast, holding my husband's hand.

She said, "They started today at about ten and they didn't tell me until then that it could take twenty-four, even forty-eight hours for Jefferson to be completely awake."

Hosea and I nodded together.

"So, all I can do is wait."

"Well, do you want to go out and grab something to eat?"

Hosea hadn't even finished his question before Kyla shook her head. "No, thank you. Even though we don't know when it's going to happen, I'm not going to leave until Jefferson opens his eyes."

Hosea blew out a long breath.

She responded to his sigh. "I know. You're going to say that I'll need to rest, but I know for sure I won't be able to sleep until my husband wakes up." It must have been Hosea's expression that made Kyla add, "Maybe Nicole and I will do this in shifts if we begin to get too tired."

With his chin, Hosea motioned toward the door. "Nicole's in there now?"

"Yup. Praying with her dad."

"She's a special girl."

For the first time, Kyla's lips spread into something that could be considered a smile. "Yeah, she is." But then, she glanced at me and her expression reverted back to her pain.

Looking at me, made her say, "Listen, I really want to get back in there."

Hosea held up his hand. "Go on. We just wanted to stop by and make sure all three of you were okay. I'll give you a call later."

Her smile was back and when she reached for Hosea, I dropped his hand and gave them room to hug. It was an awkward moment for me, though I wasn't sure why. My husband had given many of those Sunday church-hugs to women where they stood almost two feet apart. But watching Hosea and Kyla, it looked like the only space between them was physical.

I looked down at the floor, up at the ceiling, down the hall, then repeated. I finally turned my glance back to them and just when I was about to shout take-your-hands-off-my-man, Kyla stepped away from my husband.

She spoke to Hosea, "I'll give you a call if anything changes with Jefferson." It was as if I wasn't even there.

Hosea nodded, once again took my hand, and we both turned away. But we hadn't moved more than ten feet when Kyla called out.

"Jasmine."

We swiveled and faced her. At first, Kyla stood in place, and then she took a couple of quick. She stopped right in front of me and pulled me into a hug that left me surprised and stiff with my arms at my side.

"Thank you," she whispered into my ear. "Thank you for everything."

When she stepped back, I was the one blinking back tears. Because she'd only uttered six words, but they felt like the most sincere words that she'd spoken to me all week.

She gave us a small smile before she pivoted and walked back to Jefferson's room.

I probably would have still be standing there in shock if Hosea hadn't taken my hand again. This time, he pulled me closer to him as we made our way out of the hospital.

***

I was a liar. And while that gift had served me well over the years, it didn't make me feel good now. But I was good at it because last night, Hosea had believed the story I'd told him about Lola and now, I'd gotten away from him — with another lie.

When we jumped in the Uber leaving Harlem Hospital, I told him, "You know what? I'm gonna run over real quick to see Mae

Frances."

"Nama's back?" he had asked, calling Mae Frances by the name that Jacqueline had chosen for her when she first began to talk.

"Yeah, I guess I forgot to tell you since," I eyed the driver, "you were checking out my necklace last night."

He laughed, then leaned over and whispered, "Maybe I should buy you a matching bracelet."

"Why don't you? And I'll … model it … after I get back from Mae Frances."

"Bet," he said. "So, you go hang out with her and I'll see what the kids want to do. We might hang out in the park since it's a gorgeous day."

"Okay, I'll just be an hour or so. I'll text you."

The driver had dropped Hosea off first and now, as we continued to my destination, I texted Mae Frances:

Don't have time to explain, but don't call my house because I'm with you.

After just a moment, she texted back:

What you lying about now, JL?

I shook my head, dumped my cell into my purse, then peeked through the window as the driver slowed the car on the other side of Columbus.

It'd been about twenty-four hours since I picked Mae Frances up from the airport and she'd given me this information. But I still didn't know what I was going to say to this Lola chick; I was just going to knock on her door, hope she was home, and let it ride.

I thanked the driver when he stopped in front of the brownstone, then hopped out. The east and west sides of Manhattan always felt so different to me. The east was swanky, while the west side was just fly. What they had in common, though, was their exclusivity, especially in this part of the island. Swanky or fly, these were high-rent districts, housing multi-million dollar brownstones if you could even find one for sale.

It wasn't until I walked up the steps of the brownstone that I realized that I wouldn't be able to just walk in. I wouldn't be able to just knock on her door.

I hadn't thought of this.

Still, I moved to the double doors and looked at the buzzer —
there were two. One had a name above it: Johansson. I rang the
other bell. After five seconds, I rang it again. And then again.

No answer.

Ugh! Just like Mae Frances had said, I should have waited for
her because I wasn't sure if Lola was inside, peeking at me through
some hidden camera and now she knew that I had found her, or if
she really wasn't home.

Still, I wasn't ready to give up, though I wasn't sure what to do.
Think, Jasmine, think.

I descended the steps, moving slowly. It was time to call Mae
Frances.

Pulling open my purse, I grabbed my cell phone, but when I
looked up, I couldn't believe it. The car that stopped in front of the
brownstone had delivered a gift to me.

She was still wearing a hat, a black one. Today, though a short
veil still covered her eyes, her hat was more refined and retro —
one of those Jacqueline Kennedy pillbox hats. And when she slid
out of the passenger seat of the car, she wore the same style dress
that she'd worn the other times that I'd seen her. Only today, it
was black.

She gathered her clutch in her hand, slammed the door, turned,
and then saw me.

Though she paused and took a little stutter-step, she was good.
Those were the only signs; her face showed no surprise and I could
tell right then that this woman played a good game of poker.

When she stepped up onto the sidewalk next to me, she said,
"What are you doing here?"

I moved closer to her. "I need to talk to you."

She looked over my shoulder, then the other way before she
faced me again. "This could be called stalking."

"You would know. It seems like you're stalking Jefferson Blake."
I folded my arms across my chest, my stance meant to send my
message: I wasn't going anywhere.

This wasn't a major throughway, but still, there was enough

traffic for Lola to not want to handle this in public view, I was sure of that.

I said, "This won't take long. I only have a few questions." Then, I glanced up at her brownstone and she did the same.

With the way she'd reacted when she saw me, I wasn't surprised that she didn't question me about how I found her. I was beginning to get a measure of this woman. She wasn't moved, she didn't crack easily.

Her eyes roamed up and down my body, not in a gay sort of way, but as if she were reading me.

When her eyes met mine again, she said, "Carolina Herrera?" motioning to the purple pencil-skirt suit that I wore. Before I could tell her that she was correct, she added, "Good taste," as if she already knew that she was right.

I was surprised that she knew this designer, since she seemed to have a penchant for only one style. Always body-hugging, showing the smooth lines of every one of her bends and every one of her curves. "Thank you, but I'm sure you realize that I don't want to talk about fashion."

"What do you want?"

"I don't want to talk about it out here like this." Again, I glanced at the brownstone. "Can we go inside?"

"I don't know you like that."

"And, I don't know you. So we'll be even, Lola."

It was the first time that I'd spoken her name and the first time that she gave a little hint of surprise on her face. Her eyebrows rose, just a smidgen. I saw the reaction only because I stood so close.

She gave me a long stare before she spun and moved to the stairs. Then, she did a serious model stroll up the steps. I mean, the way she swung her hips was almost obscene, certainly profane. I lowered my eyes, a bit embarrassed and embarrassing me took a lot since I'd spent a few years on a pole.

But once she'd unlocked the outer door and we stepped through the vestibule, by the time we got to her apartment, my focus was back to why I was there.

The moment we stepped over her apartment's threshold, I said, "Were you having an affair with Jefferson?"

She chuckled.

I didn't.

She dropped her purse onto the coffee table and I took that moment to look around. Whoever Lola Lewis was, she didn't buy her furniture at IKEA. No, this was upper east side furnishings that didn't seem to match her. I'd put Lola at thirty-five, maybe forty-years-old, though that never cracking gene that most of us possessed, always threw me. But still, I could tell, she was a little younger than me.

So her taste in furniture surprised me. Really, we could have exchanged many pieces, from my apartment to hers, and no one would know. She seemed to fancy the Victorian period, as did I, which showed that she had some kind of class.

Then without a word, she turned and began walking away. I followed her, our steps in sync across the polished parquet floors. First, we passed through her dining room (and a preset table for ten covered with what I was sure was Wedgewood china) and finally into a kitchen that was straight out of Architectural Digest where the refrigerator and other appliances blended into the cabinetry.

Hosea and I had priced that and we hadn't even done this to our kitchen. This chick had either inherited some major money or she was the CEO of Apple.

Or the third option — she had a major benefactor and I wanted to know if that man was Jefferson.

"How do you know Jefferson? What were you doing with him on Monday night?"

She reached into a cabinet and pulled out a wine glass. Just one.

When she didn't answer me, I said, "Look, you can either talk to me, or we can go to the police station because they're looking for you."

She didn't flinch.

She was reaching for the handle on her refrigerator when I added, "They're showing your picture around."

Again, she was good — there was only a slight moment of

hesitation before she opened the refrigerator and pulled out a bottle of wine. I waited as she popped the cork, filled her glass, then took a sip. Finally, she looked up at me.

Like I said, she knew how to handle hers because there was no stress on her face from what I'd said so far, though I began to wonder if maybe that was a facade. Maybe my showing up and my questions were why she needed a glass of wine at just a little after three on a Sunday afternoon.

After taking a few sips, she set her glass on the limestone countertop. "What do you want to know?"

Her question took me aback a bit. I'd been prepared to fight for every answer to my questions. "I already told you. I want to know what was your relationship with Jefferson?"

"And, I already told you … he's a … friend."

"That's what you said … a friend, with benefits."

"That's right."

"I don't believe you," I said.

She chuckled and picked up her glass. "And I care what you believe … why?"

"So, if you're a friend of his, why did you leave when he was shot? If you're his friend, why didn't you stay?"

I'd only asked that question because it seemed the most natural thing for me to ask at this point. But it seemed like I'd pinched a nerve or something because for the first time, she stiffened.

What was that about?

Had she been involved with Jefferson's shooting? Had she set him up?

She said, "Look, I was sorry that Doctor Blake was shot, but I had nothing to do with it."

At first, I was going to follow the lead of the way she tensed when I asked about the shooting. But then, she'd just said something that sent my antenna amok. "Doctor Blake? Are you always so formal with the men you screw for benefits?"

She lifted her wine glass as if she were saluting me and laughed. "You're not even his wife, but you're here playing twenty questions with me. Why is that?"

I wasn't about to give too much information away, but I wanted Lola to know this truth. "Because his wife is my best friend. And she's been through enough; the last thing she needs is some side piece coming in and bringing her more grief."

The smile that crossed her face spread slowly and widely. "Side piece? Oh trust, I was far more than that." She sat on one of her bar stools at the counter and wiggled her hips across the leather cushions until her butt fit.

I squinted, hoping that would activate my lie-detection capabilities. But, I couldn't tell. I just didn't know if this trick was lying or not. "So, you really want me to believe that you were having an affair with Jefferson?"

"Maybe I didn't make it clear … I don't care what you believe. I'm telling you the truth."

"So what? You were his New York side piece?"

"You have that half-right. I was his New York woman."

I raised my eyebrows. "That doesn't make sense; he lives in Los Angeles, but he was having an affair with you?"

"You say that like distance matters. In fact, distance is better because when he was in New York, we never had to worry about running into anyone he knew."

I folded my arms, getting a bit concerned that she had a good answer for every one of my questions. "And so you also want me to believe that he came to New York to see you?"

"I keep telling you, what you believe is a non-factor."

I shook my head. "No. This doesn't make sense. Jefferson wouldn't cheat on Kyla."

I had to push back the flash in my mind — of Jefferson … in bed … with me.

I said, "And if he were that man, there are thousands of women in California who would do his bidding. Why would he travel all the way to New York to see you?"

Slowly, her eyes left mine and she looked down at her body before she returned her gaze to me. "You want to ask me that question again?"

She. Was. Good. But not good enough to convert me to a

complete believer. "You're lying. So why don't you tell me what you're really up to."

She gave me a one-shoulder shrug. "I keep telling you, what you believe doesn't matter." She paused and held up her forefinger. "But his wife ... that's another story. Or at least, Doctor Blake thought so."

I frowned and she lifted her glass to her lips once again.

"That's right. I decided that it was time for his wife to know about us."

"You told Jefferson that?"

She nodded. "Yup. And of course, he was just like any other man. He wanted his wife and my cake, too." She sighed. "But I didn't want to share him anymore."

"Share him?" I was trying my best to play this game of poker, but her words made me indignant. "You weren't his wife."

"He promised me that I would be his next wife and then when he reneged," she one-shoulder shrugged again, "I decided he had to pay."

Now, I really didn't believe her. Jefferson wouldn't leave Kyla. Not for her. Still, I asked, "Pay?"

She tilted her head and looked at me as if she wondered if I had any kind of sense at all.

I said, "Were you blackmailing him?"

"Are you recording me?"

I had to blink a couple of times. "What?" Where did that question come from?

"In today's times, you can't be too careful." She wagged her finger. "So answer my question if you want me to continue with the truth."

I paused. Dang! That would have been a good idea. To record her on my cell. But since I hadn't thought of that, I grabbed my phone from my purse and placed it on the counter. "I'm not recording anything."

"You could have another device, but it won't matter. Now that I've asked the question, if you lied, you won't be able to use this in court."

Dang! Who was this woman? Mae Frances's child?

She took another sip of wine. "Anyway, where were we? Ah! Yes, you accused me of blackmailing Doctor Blake." She shuddered as if she were cold, but I knew it was all a performance. "Blackmailing is such a dirty word. Let's just say I gave him a bill for services rendered."

"You were blackmailing him."

"And the fee for my services — twenty-five thousand dollars."

That was it. Game over. No more poker. Because my body language gave it all away. I gasped, my eyes widened, I pressed my hand over my mouth. When I finally gathered my non-poker-playing self together, I said, "I know he wasn't going to pay you twenty-five thousand dollars."

"Oh, you are so wrong. We were on our way to get the money when he got shot."

"Why would he pay you?"

She sighed. "Haven't you been listening? You may want to use your ObamaCare and get that checked out." Then, she slowed her cadence as if she were breaking it down for me. "I was having an affair with a married man. He didn't want his wife to know."

That was such a simple explanation that sounded like the truth, but could easily be a lie.

She continued, "And, I'm sure you don't want his wife to know either, right? At least, that's what you said."

I stepped closer to where she sat. "Stay away from Kyla."

She did that eye roaming thing over my body again. "And how are you going to make me do that?"

"There's no way she's going to believe you."

"Really?" She shrugged. "You may be right, but I say you're wrong. We can do a test, go there together and see who she believes."

All I wanted to do at this moment was beat this woman down. And then, I had another flash: Of Alexis saying almost the same thing to me when she found out what I'd done with Jefferson.

Lola interrupted my memory. "Or, since Doctor Blake and I were never able to close the deal, you can close it for him and we can save his wife this grief."

That brought my focus all the way back to her. "What?"

"You seem to have difficulty understanding me. So, I'll spell out all the specifics. You pay me ... twenty-five thousand dollars ... and I'll walk away. From Doctor Blake, from his wife, from everything. None of you will ever hear from me again."

"I'm not paying you a cent."

"Well, that's good because I asked for dollars. Cash." Then, she stood and sauntered over to the counter near her phone. She jotted down something on a pad, tore the paper off and handed it to me. It was only reflex that made me take the paper from her.

She said, "You probably already have it, but just in case your private investigator didn't get everything, here's my cell. I need to hear from you within twenty-four hours. Call me and we'll set up a time to meet."

Looking straight into her eyes, I tore that paper into the tiniest pieces possible, then let them flutter onto her sparkling kitchen floor.

Her gaze followed the floating pieces, then, her eyes returned to me. "Twenty four hours, twenty-five thousand dollars," she said. "Or I'm going to his wife." There were long moments of silence as we stood there in a battle of glares. She spoke first, "I'm sure you don't need me to show you out." She swiveled, grabbed the bottle of wine and poured herself another glass.

I stood still for only a moment longer before I snatched my cell from the counter. Inside, I growled, but I didn't want Lola to think that I was fazed in any kind of way. So, I did my own spinning and marched from her kitchen.

"Remember, twenty-four hours," she called out. "Or it won't be good. Not at all." And then, after a pause, she said, "Jasmine."

Though I was a little surprised that she knew my name, I didn't turn around. I didn't stop moving (though I was tempted to break every piece of expensive china on her dining room table) until I stomped out her front door.

It was only then that I breathed. Lola Lewis had really shaken me and now, I wondered ... what the hell was I going to do?

chapter 24

Kyla

Thank God for Tuesday night Bible study. Because I needed church tonight.

It was hard to believe that a week had passed and really, today should have been the most hopeful of days. Jefferson was waking up. But in a way, it was even harder than before because more than forty-eight hours had passed and Jefferson still had not opened his eyes. Color me naive, but I thought that by now, he'd be sitting up, chatting just a little. Maybe not quite ready to go home, but I could at least begin packing our bags.

But no, so far, all we had were a few squeezes of our hands. Dr. Reid said that it was all good because Jefferson responded to commands. That meant that he could hear us. I wouldn't be dancing, though, until he could see us. That was my prayer.

So when Hosea called this morning and told me and Nicole to come to church tonight, I was so grateful.

"You won't be away long," he'd said. "But there are so many people at City of Lights who want to pray with you, who want to encourage you."

That was what I needed — a whole bunch of encouraging prayer.

When the car slowed to a stop, Nicole and I said together, "Thank you, Maurice," before we slid out.

"Just text me when you're ready," he said.

Our driver was becoming our friend. We'd spent as much time with him as anyone in this last week and every evening, before he dropped us off, he prayed with us — one of the highlights of each day.

I held my daughter's hand as we walked up the path to the front doors of City of Lights. This was only my second time here, but it felt so familiar. Maybe it was because like on Saturday, this church felt so welcoming. Even in the dusk of this September evening, I could see the building bowing its greeting.

Nicole pulled open the heavy doors and the moment we stepped inside, she gasped. I hadn't warned her of the majesty of City of Lights. Even from where we stood at the expansive entryway, she got a glimpse into the sanctuary and the stain-glassed domed ceiling that rained a rainbow of color streaks onto the seats below. This really was a spectacular place.

"Kyla," Jasmine called out. "I'm so sorry." She moved toward us with such grace, almost as if she'd gone to a First Lady's school that taught her everything from how to walk, how to stand, how to speak and certainly, how to dress.

Nicole and I'd worn jeans — Hosea had told us to come as we were, that it was that kind of church.

But while Jasmine wore pants, it was far from jeans. Like when I saw her on Sunday, she was straight designer in her navy pinstriped suit and a magnificent white blouse with a huge bow tied at her neck. The outfit was perfect for the bun she wore atop her head. This was the first time I saw her with her hair tied back. So refined.

She said, "I'd wanted to greet you at the door."

"Uh … this is good enough, Auntie Jasmine," Nicole said as she hugged Jasmine. "You look fabulous. And this place." She stopped and did one of those Dorothy-in-the-land-of-Oz spin-and-stares. "My goodness. This place … no words."

I was in awe of my daughter and I checked out the way she interacted with Jasmine. I hadn't been sure how my daughter would react to Jasmine once she knew the whole truth (and not her conjecture) about Jasmine and Jefferson.

But just like when Jasmine had stayed with us practically all day yesterday this little girl that I'd had the blessing to raise and love showed no signs of any trauma. She didn't show a bit of difference from knowing what Jasmine had done. I guessed she felt that I carried enough unforgiveness for both of us.

When Jasmine turned to me, I saw her hesitation. "How are you?" That was the question she asked, but I could tell that she had an unspoken one — is it all right to hug you?

I answered her by pulling her into my arms.

She said, "It's good to have you here."

"And, I'm glad to be here," I said when I stepped back.

From the corner of my eye, I saw my daughter beaming as bright as this afternoon's sun. But I didn't look at her. Because I didn't want her to think that I was totally there. I was on my way — but I hadn't reached the destination.

Jasmine asked me, "How's Jefferson?"

"It's a slow process, but he's waking up."

"Yeah," Nicole jumped in. "No one is concerned except for us. The doctors keep saying that he's doing well."

"Well, let me get you inside." Jasmine took my hand, but it had to be a reflex because a second later, she dropped it as if she remembered that we weren't friends and at any moment, I might scream out and remind her of that.

I could tell Jasmine was getting ready to introduce me, but before she could say a word, the woman said, "Oh, I know who you are. You're the Bush's friend." She pulled me into a hug. "We are all praying for you and your husband."

"Thank you so much." I had to choke out the words because she had me in one of those death-grip-bear-hugs where I gasped for air when I was finally released. Then, I introduced her to Nicole and she greeted her the same way.

Sister Patterson said, "What's your name, baby?"

"Nicole."

And then, she turned to me.

I told her, "My name is Kyla."

My name seemed to shock her, but then a smile filled her whole face. "So, that's where it came from, Lady Jasmine."

My brow furrowed.

Then, as if she knew that I needed some kind of explanation, Sister Patterson said to me, "My great-grandbaby." Her smile faded in an instant. "My granddaughter was lost to the world ten years ago, only eighteen years old and working at one of those," she lowered her voice, "gentlemen's clubs, though they are no gentlemen." She shook her head. "But Lady Jasmine," she grabbed Jasmine's hand and her voice was back with the light in her eyes, "she helped our baby find her way back home. Got her out of that business, even though she came home pregnant." Another shake of her head and now her smile burst back like the sun busting through rain clouds. "But that little baby is what makes our hearts beat every single day. When she was born, we gave Lady Jasmine the honor of naming her."

"Wow," I said to Sister Patterson and Jasmine. "So, what's the baby's name?" Before they answered, I added, "Let me guess — Jasmine."

Jasmine shook her head and chuckled, while Sister Patterson shook her head and frowned. "Her name is the same as yours, baby. Her name is Kyla."

I felt a jab in my heart. Or maybe that was just the stab from the stare that I felt in my side coming from Nicole. Why had I said that? I remembered the way this story began, but I guess I'd forgotten because I was thinking — this was Jasmine. At least the Jasmine I used to know.

"That's a beautiful story," I said to Sister Patterson, though I spoke to Jasmine, too.

"Well, you have a beautiful name and now, my great grandbaby has a beautiful name, too."

Before the floor swallowed me whole, Jasmine said, "We're going to take our seats, Sister Patterson." And then, she sauntered down the aisle, greeting people along the way.

It was amazing to watch Jasmine in this role, totally open, seemingly honest, apparently loved, definitely respected. When we got to the first row, she stood in front of the first seat, then directed me and Nicole to sit on the other side of her.

It was perfect timing. A group of men and women walked in — the praise team, I was sure.

Jasmine leaned over to me. "Don't worry. They only sing one song at Bible Study. Like Hosea promised, we'll get you in and out."

The music had already started and I closed my eyes, clapped my hands, swayed and sang along:

Perpetual praise and continual prayer
Take the joy of the Lord with you everywhere
Perpetual prayer and continual praise
Acknowledge Him in all of your ways ...

It wasn't until I started singing that I realized just how much I needed to be here. Though I did pray continually and tried to praise perpetually, I needed to be in this midst. I needed to stand shoulder-to-shoulder with God's people in agreement this way.

That thought made me open my eyes. I was standing shoulder-to-shoulder with Nicole on one side ... and Jasmine on the other.

Jasmine.

God's people.

That was the thought that remained in my mind until Hosea came through a side door and walked to the altar. He smiled down at me and Nicole, but then, blew a kiss to his wife and again, I paused, thinking how different this Jasmine was from the one I knew. Maybe I didn't have hate, but I had a very strong dislike for a person who didn't seem to exist anymore.

"Let the church say Amen."

"Amen," rang throughout the sanctuary.

"How is everyone on this blessed Tuesday evening?"

All kinds of responses poured out from the people.

"Well, I am blessed, too. And the beauty of life is that we get to experience new blessings every day."

"Amen!"

"You know, we've been studying the book of Genesis and I don't know about you, but I really enjoyed last week's lesson."

I was a little surprised when the congregation broke out into applause.

"Yes, cheer for the Lord."

And that's what the people did. They roared like the crowd in a stadium that'd just watched their team score the winning touchdown in the Super Bowl.

When the people settled down, Hosea said, "I know how you feel 'cause when we talk about Joseph, we can see how the devil is defeated."

"Yes!"

"How God flipped the devil's script. Because all bad became good, all negative became positive, all weeping became joy."

"Amen," so many said through the cheers that rose up once again.

"Well that's what I want to talk about tonight. Usually, Bible study is just that — we study from the Bible because you see, if you go to a church where they don't open up the Word of God, then what you need to do is put on a pair of Nike's and run."

Now there was laughter.

"You don't never need to be interested in the preacher's words alone — the only words that matter are the ones that are coming from Him," Hosea pointed to the ceiling, then added, "through him." He pressed his forefinger against his chest.

"Amen!"

"However, tonight, I don't want to talk about a particular scripture. I want to talk about a question that many of us ask — and the answer is on every page in the Bible."

I pulled my phone from my purse, ready to open my Bible app, ready to read along.

Then, Hosea said, "Why does God allow bad things to happen to good people?"

Oh, my God! How many times had I asked myself that question over this last week? And my question wasn't about Jefferson alone. It was about all that I was going through — from the fear of losing my husband, from the pain that rose from seeing and having to deal with Jasmine, to the new doubt that came from the question of whether Jefferson had been unfaithful once again.

He said, "That is the universal question and ... I sure wish I had an answer."

It took everything not to throw my hands up in the air and shout out, 'Really?'

He continued, "But I do know a few things about this question. A few things that I can say about why bad things happen to good people. First, our faith never guarantees a perfect life, only a perfect eternity."

Hosea had to pause for longer than a moment with all of the hallelujahs that were shouted.

When the congregation returned to their seats, he continued," What's going on here in this place, on this earth, is preparation for the real game, the everlasting one and so sometimes, I have to wonder if these bad things are not really good things."

"Preach!"

"Maybe these bad things are good things because they build our faith for what is to come."

"Tell it, Pastor."

"These bad things awaken us to God when you think about it. Sometimes that's the only time when we truly depend on Him. It's when we have no choice, that He becomes number one. It shouldn't be that way, but ...."

I lowered my head and thought about my own faith. I had always been a talk-to-God-every-day kind of girl. But there was something to be said about struggles. Because those were the times when I didn't talk, I cried out. Those were the times when I didn't walk to the altar, I ran. Those were the times when I went to that prayer closet and settled in.

Hosea said, "But the real answer to our question about why bad things happen to good people ... I think God would say, it's none of our business."

The congregation chuckled.

Hosea said, "I'm serious. Because what happens to us here on earth is all up to God." He held up his hands. "Now, I'm not saying that the bad things are all God's will. Nothing irks me more than when Christians blame all of this stuff on God saying — it's His will, He's in control."

"You better preach that word!"

Hosea said, "He is in control, but He will give us what we ask for. If all of this was God's will, then we wouldn't have to pray for His will to be done."

"Amen!"

"So don't get it twisted; everything in this world isn't happening the way God wants it to. *He allows it*, but it's not always going the way He wants it. If that were the case, we could all sit back every day, not work and just tell the bill collectors, 'Hey, this is God's will. Deal with it.'"

Even I had to laugh at that and I sat up in my seat. I'd only seen Hosea Bush on television a few times, and never for a full sermon. But now, my plan was to watch him every Sunday, before we left for our own church. Because though, Pastor Ford would always be the best spiritual teacher to me, Pastor Bush was sure up there, too.

I loved his voice, his tone, his cadence. I loved the way he sang some of his words and the way his hands were the punctuation for his words.

"But seriously," his voice came down a couple of decibels, so low that I imagined the people behind us leaning forward to hear him better. "I get the question, I understand why I hear it so often. But instead of asking why things happen, I go with: how can I use this to make my faith and other's faith stronger? What can I learn, and how can I turn this test into my testimony?"

I expected the sanctuary to ring out once again with shouts, but it was quiet, as if the people followed their pastor. His voice was low and I guess everyone understood that meant they should be quiet, too.

Folding my hands, I lowered my head, thinking about his words — test into testimony. To this point, the biggest test I'd had in my life was what happened with Jefferson and Jasmine. I hated that the memory of that time had been dug up and felt almost as fresh as

October of 1997.

But Jefferson and I had done just what Hosea said. We'd turned that test into a testimony. We'd stood up with Pastor Ford and testified about the snake who'd slept with my husband.

As I had that thought, Jasmine reached for me. She was facing forward, her eyes on her husband, but still she held my hand and then squeezed it, making me feel all kinds of guilty about just having called her a snake.

But I kept my head lowered because I wanted to reflect on Hosea's teaching. And what Nicole had tried to teach me, too. I was battling with my unforgiveness and I didn't want to fight this war anymore. I really needed to pray because with what I'd been holding onto for twenty years, the only way to get it out of my heart was through prayer.

I didn't know how long I was in my meditation, but suddenly, Jasmine pulled away from me. Looking up, I leaned forward a little, to see a woman kneeling in the aisle next to Jasmine. They whispered back and forth, only for a couple of seconds before the woman handed Jasmine an oversized yellow envelope.

Even though I was sitting on the side of her, I saw Jasmine's frown. She waited a beat, opened the envelope, then slipped something out. Because of the angle, I couldn't see what it was — a picture? Maybe?

Jasmine gasped and stuffed whatever she'd taken out back into the envelope. She was trembling when she laid it across her lap, though she grasped it as if it held the winning lottery ticket.

I'd seen that look on Jasmine's face before — when she was talking to that woman in the hall. Complete mortification. Like before, if Jasmine were not black, she'd be totally white right now.

"What wrong?" I whispered.

She shook her head and when she finally looked at me, there were tears in her eyes.

"Jasmine?"

She said nothing, just slipped out of her seat, and almost ran up the aisle. I wasn't the only one who followed her with my eyes. Everyone behind me did, too. When I finally turned back to the front of the sanctuary, Hosea stood at the altar with the deepest of frowns on his face. It felt like the sanctuary was filled with the same question — what had just happened?

I had no answer to that question, but what I had were flutters, inside. I felt squeamish, a foreboding, like something really bad was about to happen. Was that because of Jasmine ... or Jefferson? What was God trying to tell me?

Closing my eyes, I went straight into prayer: Please, Lord. Please, Lord. Please, Lord.

But no matter how much I prayed, it didn't stop the sickening feeling that had spread inside of me.

chapter 26

Jasmine

How long had it been? An hour? Maybe two. I wasn't sure because all I had done from the moment I ran from the sanctuary and into my office, to grab my purse, before I hailed a cab (I couldn't even wait for an Uber) was stare at these photos.

I stared at them while I was in the cab: Jefferson (with his wedding ring in view) holding Lola in his arms.

I stared at them while I was on the elevator: Lola with her mouth all over Jefferson (with his wedding ring in view).

I stared at them while I sat in my office: Jefferson (with his wedding ring in view) with his mouth all over Lola.

That was all that I'd done — just stared at these five pictures — eight by ten glossy photos. And every one showed Lola and Jefferson in their natural glory. They were butt-bare; nothing covered them at all.

I'd stared at the pictures, checking for any sign of photoshopping, or any indication that maybe Jefferson hadn't been conscious. But while his eyes were closed in some of the photos, they were open in others. He was aware, and that meant these photos were real.

Looking up, I whispered, "Oh, God," and I said that not for the first time.

That call out to the Lord came from so many places. Yes, these pictures, but also from the place where I now knew that I'd been so wrong.

When I'd left Lola's apartment on Sunday, I'd done a complete analysis. While Hosea and the kids were at the park, I'd sat down and thought the whole conversation with Lola through. In the end, I'd come to one conclusion: though she'd been cool and thorough, she was a liar. I knew that because of one thing she'd said: *He promised me that I would be his next wife ....*

Even now, just remembering, I shook my head. Everything else she'd said could have been the truth, but not that. That was why I was a non-believer. Because ninety-nine percent truth was still one-hundred percent a lie.

But these pictures showed that my equation was wrong.

I slammed my fist atop the pictures, not really sure who I was more angered by. Jefferson: because in all the years that I'd been married, I'd never cheated and I was sure Jefferson was a better man than I was a woman.

Lola: because that trick knew Jefferson was married.

Or me: because how could I have the audacity to call her a trick when I'd done the same thing with the same man?

Pushing myself away from the desk, I staggered to my favorite spot — the window. The night's blackness blanketed Central Park, though even if there had been light, I wouldn't have seen anything. Because I was obsessed with my thoughts. How could I have been so wrong after I'd been so sure that I was so right? Especially once the twenty-four hours that she had given me had ticked by and then ticked on.

Not a thing had happened yesterday when I'd called her bluff, though I hadn't taken any chances. I'd spent all day at the hospital with Kyla and Nicole, pretending to be there in Hosea's place — though, that part was true. My husband had a gig in New Jersey, so, I'd gone to the hospital to do what Hosea would normally do — to pray with Kyla and Nicole. And then, I did what I do — I stayed to block that heifer. Because if Lola had shown up at any time and any kind of way, the only blessing for her would have been that she was already at the hospital.

Being there, I'd protected Kyla in two ways: I blocked Lola from getting to her and I didn't have to go and talk to Detective Green like Hosea had asked me to.

But not understanding my mission, Kyla had eyed me with suspicion the whole day, though Nicole didn't seem to notice my attempt to be omnipresent. She was thrilled to have me there.

I'd stayed focused on my goal, though, my eyes on the door, on the elevator, on the hall. I'd stayed until I walked out of the hospital with Kyla and Nicole. It was well past ten and well past Lola's twenty-four hour threat of doom.

The victory was mine.

But tonight I discovered that I hadn't won a thing. Lola Lewis played a major game of poker and she had the winning hand. Five pictures — a royal flush.

Her story wasn't a story. Her story was the truth.

"Damn, Jefferson," I whispered. "I just never thought …."

Not for the first time tonight, or today, or this week, month or year, I lifted my eyes to the heavens and said, "God, thank you so much for the blessing of Hosea Samuel Bush."

But though usually speaking my husband's name made my heart swell with love, right now, it ached with pain. This was going to kill Kyla. That was a fact. This was going to end their marriage. Another fact. Because once Kyla found out about Lola, there was a good chance that she'd leave Jefferson right there at Harlem Hospital. She might tell the doctors to never wake him up. Hell, she might pull a plug or two herself.

"No, that would be me," I said, then chuckled (though it was bitterly) as I realized that I was having a full-out conversation with myself.

Still, it was the truth; Kyla would walk away, she would just do it would grace. Because she'd given Jefferson his one chance already and he'd blown that one chance with me.

The thought of that brought tears to my eyes again and I wondered, not for the first time, why I cared so much. And then, I asked, why wouldn't I care?

I had always loved Kyla and what I realized since I'd seen the report of the Jefferson's shooting was that I'd never stopped loving her. Yes, we'd been estranged, but that hadn't changed the soul connection that we'd had since we were five. Kyla Carrington Blake had never done a single bad thing to me, so why would I ever be angry with her? What kind of grudge could I hold? Based on what?

And with all of that, why wouldn't I want to help the woman whose only crime had been excommunicating me from her life because of my sin?

Returning to the desk, I picked up the one picture that had carried a message beyond the photo. Lola had sent me a note … written in lipstick … on the photo that was the most explicit … her mouth filled with Jefferson's ….

I closed my eyes, but the image and the words she'd written were etched behind my lids:

Your twenty four hours has passed. As a favor, I'll start the clock again. NOW!

Those fourteen words could send Lola to prison for twenty years. But while Lola would suffer those years beyond bars, Kyla would be sentenced to a lifetime of misery.

The beep of the alarm startled me and I froze for just a second. The front door. Hosea. Normally, my husband would go into the children's rooms first before he searched the apartment for me. But with the way I'd left the church, his mission would be singular tonight — to find me. Once he didn't see the light in our bedroom, he would come into our office.

I stuffed the photos back into the envelope, then pushed it under a stack of papers. Then, I counted down the seconds and right when I got to 'one', Hosea stepped into the space where I'd been for the last hours.

He stared, studying me as I stood behind the desk. His eyes were filled with concern and I wondered if he saw the sorrow in mine.

"I got your text," he said.

I nodded. I'd texted him from the cab: I have to go home, no worries, the kids are fine. "I'm sorry I had to leave."

It was like he never blinked as he moved toward me. And I kept my gaze on him.

When we were just inches apart, he cupped my face in his hands. He stared like he could see through me, then he kissed my forehead. "Talk to me."

There were so many reasons to tell him everything and only one reason not to. And that single reason outweighed all the others — he would make me go to the police. Because he would want Lola to be arrested and he would say that Kyla and Jefferson would work this out, that they would recover from this.

The thing was, I knew for sure that they would not. It still stunned me sometimes that they'd recovered twenty years ago.

"Jasmine."

Code for: Don't lie.

I told my husband the only thing that I could. I said, "I can't tell you."

His concern faded and in its place was surprise. "What?" he asked, though he still held me.

"I can't tell you," I repeated, this time with more conviction. "Really, Hosea, I don't want to lie to you. I don't. But if you force me to say anything about this … it will be a lie."

He stood still, just staring, taking in my words.

"This is something I have to handle," I told him. "It's something I have to do … by myself."

After a moment, he nodded, then took my hand and led me to the sofa across the room. We both sat, on the edge, our hands folded in front of us. As he looked down at his hands, I studied him. In all the years of our marriage, I'd never said anything like this. Usually, I would just lie. But I didn't want to this time.

Finally, he cocked his head toward me. "Does this have anything to do with the children? Are they in any kind of danger?"

"No! Of course not." I rested my hand on his shoulder.

He nodded again. "Does this have anything to do with you? Are you in danger?"

This time, I took his hands into mine. "No. I'm not. I'm not in any danger at all. I ... I just have to do something for a friend."

Again, he nodded. "It's not Mae Frances, is it?" He didn't give me a chance to say a word. "Because she's not a friend, she's family. And if she's in any danger ...."

"It's not Mae Frances, but really, if it were, do you think she would need you with all the people she knows?"

He smiled, exactly the way I'd wanted him to.

"No one is in danger, Hosea. If I thought anyone could be hurt physically, I would tell you for sure."

He waited a moment before he said, "Physically." A pause. "But someone ... that you care about ... could be hurt in another way."

It wasn't a question, but still I said, "Yes."

He nodded and that was when I knew he understood. He said, "There are ways to hurt people that cut deeper than any physical pain."

"I know." I squeezed his hands in mine. "This is why I have to do what I have to do."

I could feel his thoughts, his concern in all the moments he let go by. "Are you sure?"

"Yes," and I left it right there.

My husband must have received the message because he didn't ask another question. I guess he knew this was where I got off the truth train and my lies would begin.

He leaned back and pulled me into his arms and held me for a while before he said, "I'm glad that you and the kids are safe. That's all that matters to me."

I stayed silent because I'd told all the truth that I could.

He said, "Just promise me that if what you're handling, if that block gets too hot, you'll come to me."

I nodded, but he leaned away and twisted my body so that I had to look up at him. "Promise me, Jasmine."

Code for: I'm serious.

Hosea looked at me the way the flight attendants did when I sat in the Exit row on an airplane. They wanted a verbal agreement and so did my husband. "Yes," I said. "I promise."

He stared into my eyes and I didn't break away. That was my

way of sealing my words.

When he was satisfied that I'd told the truth to this point, he leaned back once again and just held me.

And I wanted to cry. Because I had it so good with this man and my gratefulness stretched beyond the heavens. What I had, I knew Kyla and Jefferson had too — at least they once had this and I wanted them to have this again.

Maybe Jefferson's sudden brush with death would change him. Maybe he would leave Lola ... and any other woman in his life ... alone. Maybe when he awakened, he'd be so grateful that he would want only his wife.

I knew he still loved Kyla; he'd been willing to pay twenty-five thousand dollars to keep his indiscretion hidden from her.

So that was what I had to do. I had to work to keep this away from Kyla, too, and I knew exactly how.

I'd never used the money that I'd received from the reality show that I'd done with Rachel back in 2012. That show with First Ladies had turned out to be just another one of those reality shows disasters with women battling each other. The money I'd earned had just been sitting in a mutual fund, earning interest, waiting for a good reason for me to spend it.

Well, I guess that reason had come.

I had worked out the plan in my head already. I was going to do my best to save the marriage that I once tried to destroy. I was going to do everything to save Kyla and Jefferson Blake.

This would be my penance.

chapter 27

Kyla

I covered Nicole with the blanket and she snuggled into the chair, sleeping as if she were in her bed at the Plaza. Since my first night in New York, I hadn't stayed overnight at the hospital. There had been nights when we'd left after midnight, but we had always returned to the hotel, even these last couple of nights when Jefferson was being awakened from his coma.

But after we'd left City of Lights tonight, this was something that both Nicole and I had agreed we wanted to do.

Nicole had brought it up when we first returned to the hospital a few hours ago. Our plan had been to come here after Bible study and kiss Jefferson goodnight, but as we stood over his bed, my daughter said, "Mom, I don't know what it was about Pastor Hosea's words, but I really want to stay with Daddy tonight."

"Wow. I'd been thinking the same thing."

I didn't add that it wasn't just Hosea's words that had led me to this. It was everything — especially what happened with Jasmine. The way she had jumped out of the pew and ran down the aisle, never to be seen again. I'd wanted to ask Hosea if he knew what was going on, but I could tell by his expression that he was as clueless as the rest of the people in the sanctuary.

Once again, I replayed the scene in my mind — the woman kneeling beside Jasmine, handing her the envelope, Jasmine opening it and then, the look on her face. I shook my head. Something happened that was pretty bad, but what I couldn't figure out was why did I have the feeling that had anything to do with me?

Still, what happened had left me so queasy that all I'd wanted to do was come back to the hospital and not leave again until I could roll Jefferson out of here with me.

But I hadn't told Nicole any of that. We'd just come back here and prayed and read scriptures and talked to Jefferson as if he could hear us, because we knew that he could.

I glanced at my watch: 3:20, then looked at Nicole. She would get a couple of hours in and what I needed to do was find a way to get a little bit of rest, too. Pulling the chair from the wall, I moved slowly so the scraping sound against the linoleum wouldn't awaken Nicole. Then, I lowered the rail on Jefferson's bed, and after staring at him for a moment, I rested my head on him, almost the way Nicole had done the other day. When I finally closed my eyes, I twined my fingers with his.

It was an awkward position, but didn't really feel that way. Maybe it was because I was leaning against my husband, comforted by his heartbeat. Maybe it was because I was holding him and it felt like he was holding me.

I began to drift, drift, drift toward that peaceful state of unconsciousness and it felt good. But just when I was about to enter that zone of complete rest, I was kinda awakened. It was so annoying the way Jefferson kept squeezing my hand.

My eyes popped open right as he squeezed my hand again.

For a moment, I sat frozen, still holding my husband's hand and staring straight at him — and he stared right back at me.

"Baby," I whispered.

He smiled, though it looked more like a grimace. He licked his lips. "Water."

"Oh, my God!" I jumped from the chair so fast, it fell back and fell over. "Okay, baby. I'll get you some water." And then, I screamed, "Nurse. Nurse. Nurse."

"Mom! What's wrong?" The room wasn't very big, but still

Nicole was on the other side. That didn't matter, though; in two hops, she was right next to me.

I didn't have to say a word, didn't have to explain a thing. Because she looked down and into the eyes of her father. "Daddy," she cried.

"Here." I put Nicole's hand into her father's. "Hold him until I get back." I rushed around the bed and had almost made it to the door before I stopped, swiveled, and mad-dashed back to my husband. I leaned over and kissed him. My lips lingered and I wondered if that was why it felt like a first kiss.

When I brought my lips away from his, he blinked and blinked and blinked. He blinked like one hundred times. That was a good sign — he could feel.

Nicole laughed. "Oh, Daddy is back!"

I was in my sprinter-mode again when I went into the hallway. The moment I stepped out of the room, I called out, "Nurse." The one sitting at the nurses station looked up. "It's my husband. He's awake."

A grin, almost as wide as mine, filled her face before she leapt from her chair and then together, we raced back into the room.

"Well, Doctor Blake," she said as we entered.

He turned his head to face us and I knew that was another good sign — he could hear.

She checked the monitors, nodded, then went back to Jefferson.

"Water," he mumbled, sounding like his mouth was stuffed with a pound of cotton.

"And I have some right here for you because that was the first thing you were supposed to say when you woke up. Good job."

I hadn't even noticed the pink container with the straw on the nightstand. The nurse pressed the button on the side of the bed, raising Jefferson to a half sitting position and then, she pressed the straw against his lips. "Not so fast," she told him. "Just small sips."

Another good sign — he could swallow, such an important reflex that everyone took for granted.

I moved to Nicole's side and grabbed her hand. All Jefferson was doing was sipping water, but we both cried as we watched this first accomplishment. My husband might as well have been climbing Mount Everest … that was the way it felt to me.

After a few sips, the nurse lowered his bed. "Okay, Doctor Jefferson. I'm going to call Doctor Reid. He's not on duty, but I have a feeling he'll be here in a few minutes."

As she began to walk out of the room, I stopped her. "Wait. Is there anything we should do?"

She frowned.

"I mean," I glanced at Jefferson, "I don't know what to do."

She smiled. "Just talk to him. Love on him. He's awake now. Do whatever you would do when he was awake before." She paused, and then thought about what she said. "Well not everything." Her laughter followed her right out of the room.

There was not a bit of hesitation in my daughter. She was already by Jefferson's bedside, but she stepped aside for me. I looked down at Jefferson and this man that I had loved for so long — I didn't know what to say.

He murmured, "Don't … cry."

I laughed. Another good sign — he could see, he could understand. I wiped the tears from my cheek. "Oh, you're better all right. Already telling me what to do."

For the next minutes, we talked to Jefferson, told him that we were in New York and at the hospital, but that he was going to be all right. We didn't mention the shooting — there was no need. It would come back to him, I was afraid, soon enough.

Like the nurse had said, just about fifteen minutes later, Dr. Reid came strolling into our room as if it were noon and not at least two hours before dawn.

He was already grinning as if he had no cares when he said, "Doctor Blake, I hear you wanted to see me?"

Nicole and I laughed again, and in that moment, I noted that we'd done that more in the last seven minutes than we'd had in the last seven days. We stepped away from the bed to make room for Dr. Reid, who just like the nurse, headed straight for the machines.

I asked, "Doctor Reid, would you like us to step out of the room?"

He didn't even face us, his eyes were on the green machine when he said, "If you don't mind."

Nicole had heard the doctor, but still I had to drag her away. Once we were in the hallway though, she hugged me and let loose her tears. "Oh, my God, Mom. I just knew it. I just knew we needed to be here tonight." She didn't give me a chance to say anything. "Suppose we weren't here? Suppose he had opened his eyes and he was alone?"

"Well, God made sure that didn't happen."

Then, I wondered if that was why I'd had that queasy feeling. Was it just anxiety, my subconscious anticipation of Jefferson's awakening?

Nicole said, "You know what? We have to call somebody. Actually, we have to call a lot of people. We have to call Grandma, and Aunt Alexis and Uncle Brian ... oh, and definitely, Pastor Hosea and Auntie Jasmine. Oh, and did you ever call Pastor Ford? You know she would want to know. She'll probably fly here in the morning. We have to call them now."

"Well, we have to call everyone for sure, but ummm ... do you know what time it is?"

She glanced down at her watch. "It's four-twenty." When her eyes returned to me, she had a so-what expression on her face.

"Oh, no." I shook my head. "We don't need to wake anyone. They'll all have plenty of time to celebrate after the sun comes up."

"I bet they would want to know now, even in the middle of the night. This is huge. This is epic."

"Well, when they yell at you for not calling them right away, blame it on me," I said. "Because you're not calling anyone."

She crossed her arms and pouted, a pretend temper tantrum that looked so similar to the ones she used to throw. But the act didn't last for a dozen seconds. It was difficult to feign anger when all you wanted to do was dance.

Six minutes later — I'd been eyeing my watch — Dr. Reid called us back into the room. He had Jefferson sitting up at the same angle that the nurse had him before.

"Well," he drew out that word. "There are lots of tests that we have to run, and we'll begin those in the morning. And it's still going to be some time before Doctor Blake will be up and walking, but ... " He shook his head. "I think we're looking at one of God's miracles right here."

I pressed my hands against my face, hoping that would hold back my tears, even though I wanted to bust out into one of those Oprah-Winfrey-ugly wails. What I really wanted to do was drop to my knees and just give thanks right here.

But while I held back, my child did not. The heart she had for God made her kneel and bow her head, right there at the foot of her father's bed.

"Thank you, Jesus. Thank you, God. Thank you, Jesus. Thank you, God."

It became a praise song that I sang with my daughter when I joined her on my knees, too.

Through many of the words that Dr. Reid had spoken to me over the past week, I believed that he was a praying man. But now, I knew that he was. Because though he didn't join us physically, he did bow his head and close his eyes and stood still, listening as we sent our praises up.

It was only a minute or maybe three, but I felt totally spent when Nicole and I helped each other to stand. When we faced the doctor, he spoke through his smile, "There is nothing like a praying family."

Nicole and I looked at each other and nodded.

The doctor turned to Jefferson. "Doctor Blake, do you have anything to say?"

Jefferson moved his head, just a little, like he was trying to nod. And then he licked his lips. They trembled a little, before he whispered, "Lola."

***

It was only because Hosea showed up that Nicole agreed to leave.

"But I'm only going to the hotel to shower and change. And

then, it will be your turn," Nicole said before she kissed me, hugged Hosea, then scurried away.

We watched her run — yes, actually run — to the elevators before I turned to Hosea.

"Thank you for getting here so quickly."

"No problem," he said. "I couldn't get here fast enough. And I'm so glad you called early because I have to catch a flight at noon."

I prayed that my expression didn't drop the way my heart had. Hosea was leaving town? No! He'd been my rod, helping to hold me up. He'd been my compass, helping me navigate through these horrible days. How was I supposed to do this without him, especially now that Jefferson had awakened?

"How ... how long will you be gone?"

He waved his hand. "Just overnight."

Now I hoped he didn't notice the way I released a breath of relief.

"But if you need anything, just call Jasmine. She wanted to come, but there was something important she had to handle this morning."

I nodded, not telling him that I was grateful that he'd come alone. I said, "Can we talk in here?" With my chin, I motioned toward the door closest to us. I didn't even hesitate; I wasn't afraid of the Quiet Room anymore. I didn't yet know when, but I would soon be taking my husband home.

Hosea followed me inside, closed the door behind us, and waited until we sat down before he asked, "So, how long has he been awake?"

I glanced at my watch. "Just about three hours."

Hosea leaned back in the chair and unbuttoned his suit jacket. "I wish you had called me."

"Nicole wanted to, but I didn't want to call in the middle of the night."

He raised a finger as if he were scolding me. "I told you, I would be here for you through this. No matter the time of day."

I nodded. "Well, that's why I called you now." I paused, leaned forward and rested my hands against the small conference table.

"Hosea, it's so bizarre. But when the doctor asked Jefferson if he had anything to say, he said 'Lola.'"

Hosea flinched, then frowned and for a moment I wondered if the name meant something to him.

But I shook that thought away and added, "And then, he kept saying that name. In fact, that's all he's been saying whenever he speaks."

"That's all he says?"

"Well, when he first woke up, he asked for water, and then, he told me not to cry. But when Doctor Reid asked him, he said 'Lola' and then, got really agitated before he fell asleep."

Hosea's frown deepened.

"Doctor Reid said that he could just be thinking about the last thing that he saw before he was shot — maybe a movie or a song he heard with that name."

Hosea waited a couple of long moments before he asked, "What do you think?"

I shook my head. "I don't know. That's why I called you. Because ... I wondered ... if this had anything to do with Jefferson being shot and with ... that woman?"

As I said the words, I thought about all that I'd imagined in the last three hours. Was it just some random utterance that Dr. Reid said often happened with comatose patients waking up from a fog? Or did this mean something?

I said, "I was wondering if I should call Detective Green and maybe tell him what's going on with Jefferson."

It took him a moment to nod, as if he were in deep thought. "You may want to talk to him, but I'm thinking, let's wait a day or two. For Jefferson to get a little stronger. If you call Detective Green now, he'll be right here with his questions."

"No." I shook my head, not worried about that at all. "I don't think Doctor Reid will let him get anywhere near Jefferson right now."

"That's what I mean. If you call him, he'll be down here questioning you." He paused and then, as if he were more sure of his words, he said, "We'll call Detective Green when I get back because we definitely have to tell him this news, but let's see what's going on with Jefferson today."

"Okay." This was why I'd called Hosea. When Jefferson had first called out that name, I'd almost run out of the room and called the detective. But I'd called Hosea instead, knowing he'd talk me down from this cliff the way he'd saved me from jumping off all the other ones I'd encountered this week.

Hosea was right and Dr. Reid was probably right. I was making this into something that was really nothing.

We sat, both of us contemplating my words. We were in such a state of seriousness, so appropriate for this room. And then, Hosea leaned forward and grabbed my hands. "Wow, your husband is awake."

My grin was instant. "Yes. And the doctor thinks there was minimal damage to his brain. They won't know for sure until after all the tests and he begins physical therapy, but so far, it's looking good."

"Praise Jesus."

"Oh, you know I did that already."

He laughed. "I know that's right. Let's get back in there and do some more praising. And, I want to pray with him, too."

"I'd like that."

We stood at the same time and faced each other for a moment, as if neither one of us knew exactly what to do. I moved first — I pulled Hosea into a hug. "I don't know what I would have done without you this week. I'm so grateful for you, Hosea. Just so grateful."

When I leaned back, my head moved to the left and he did the same. That was the only reason our lips were right there, so close.

It was something that happened often between two people, an accident. But what most did was step back and laugh it off. I didn't do that. Instead, I leaned in closer and pressed my lips against his. That was all.

No tongue, no anything except for the meeting of our lips.

My eyes were closed, but I was sure that his weren't. I was self-aware enough to know that this was all about me. This was my way of showing this man my true gratitude. Letting him know that at another time, in another place ... things may have been different. If we weren't both so totally in love with other people, who knows.

It was just a couple of seconds, but enough time to fill Hosea's face with surprise. But I didn't want him to read more into what was there.

So, I smiled, took his hand and said, "I can't wait for Jefferson to wake up. I can't wait for you to meet my husband."

chapter 28

Jasmine

I never carried cash and now, I knew why. Because there were so many reasons to just live life through plastic.

First, I never knew how difficult it was to get your own money out of your bank. It seemed like if you wanted anything more than your ATM limit, that created a situation.

At least, that was the way they'd made me feel this morning. As I tapped my fingers against the banker's desk, all I could think was — this is ridiculous. Not only had Hosea and I been banking at this branch of New York Financial Services forever, but they handled most of our City of Lights investments, too.

So why did the branch manager — Felix Winsome — who was a member of City of Lights make me feel like I was robbing the bank instead of taking out just a small portion of my own money?

"Are you sure everything is all right, Lady Jasmine?" Felix asked me.

I wanted to tell him that his asking the question a dozen times wasn't going to change my answer.

"Yes, everything is fine. Why do you keep asking me that?"

"It's just that twenty-five thousand dollars," he shook his head, "is a lot of money."

"And?" I gave him a stare that was meant to shut him up. It didn't.

"And you want it in cash."

"Yes, I told you that." I paused and let my eyes roam around this Fifth Avenue branch of one of the largest banks in the world. "And you have that kind of cash here, right?"

It was as if this man just couldn't hear me. "Are you sure? A cashier's check is much safer."

"Mr. Winsome." I hadn't shut him up, but now I said his name in a tone that let him know I was shutting him down. I wasn't going to talk to him about this any further. I glanced at my watch. "I really don't have a lot of time. I have an appointment at ten."

But even with that, the banker blinked at me, as if he were trying to give me a code. Finally, he stood and I shook my head. Taking out twenty-five thousand dollars was definitely not as easy as putting it in. It still took another thirty minutes (at least) before I was given the stacks of cash. I piled them into the clichéd attaché case, then locked it.

"Thank you," I said to Felix.

He nodded and asked, "How's Pastor Bush?"

My eyes narrowed. "My husband is fine. He's on his way to an event in Philly."

"Oh that's nice." His words were normal, but the way he still stared at me was not. He studied me as if he were trying to see through me, but I needed him to understand that one: there was nothing to see here and two: what had just happened in this bank had better stay in this bank.

I told him, "I would appreciate your complete discretion about this. This is my money. No one needs to know."

He nodded, then stood when I stood. And even though I didn't look back, I knew he watched me as I stepped through his door, then walked through the lobby that had few customers at this early hour on a Wednesday morning. He watched me until I spun through the revolving doors and walked into the madness of Fifth Avenue.

But once I was outside the bank and Felix Winsome's eyes were no longer on me, I panicked.

I was walking around the streets of New York with twenty-five thousand dollars. I gripped the handle of the briefcase like all the answers to life were inside. Moving to the curb, it only took about fifteen seconds for a cab to pull over. I jumped in, gave the driver Mae Frances's address and now, I cradled the briefcase like it was a newborn baby.

Still, I wasn't sure how safe I was. Supposed the cab driver had found out that I had this money and he had a grand scheme to kidnap me and take me to his home … in Nigeria. Or maybe someone in the bank had seen me and they were following me and planned to snatch the bag the moment I got out of the car.

"Really, Jasmine," I said to myself, shaking my head as I looked out the window. "It's only twenty-five thousand dollars."

The moment the words were out of my mouth, I pressed my lips together. I couldn't believe I'd said that out loud. Glancing at the rear view mirror, the taxi driver's eyes stared straight back at me.

Dang! I was on my way to Nigeria for sure.

By the time the car rolled to a stop in front of Mae Frances's apartment building, I was in the middle of a full-fledge panic attack. Not that I'd ever had one, but surely, this was how that kind of breakdown felt.

When I finally knocked on her front door, all I could do was stumble inside when she let me in.

"Jasmine Larson, what is wrong with you?"

I didn't say anything at first. I just lurched toward her grand dining room table and placed the case on top of it.

"What are you doing?" She grabbed the briefcase from the table. "Do you know how expensive that Cherrywood is?"

"Just … look … inside."

She eyed me like she thought it was some kind of trick before she returned the briefcase to where I'd laid it. In true Mae Frances fashion, she took her time, dramatically, unhooking the locks then slowly lifting the cover.

At first, I thought the sight of all of that money had done something that no one had ever done to Mae Frances — frozen her vocal cords. But once she gathered herself, every curse word known to man, and a few new ones that she'd made up, came out of her mouth. She finally settled on, "What the hell is this, Jasmine Larson?"

I plopped onto her cashmere sofa. Yes … cashmere. This was what she'd done with her money from the reality show. She wasn't even one of the stars of First Ladies since she wasn't married to any kind of pastor. But she was one of those scene stealers and the producers kept encouraging Mae Frances to become a regular, finally paying her, and even thinking about offering her a solo show.

So with the money she'd earned, she'd taken all the new furniture that Hosea and I had brought for her (okay, it was about twelve years ago, but that was still new in furniture-life) and given every piece … to the Salvation Army!

There was still a little bit of pissivity inside of me about that. But I couldn't think about the cashmere sofa nor the real Persian rug nor any of the other fabulous pieces in her apartment right now.

"Jasmine Larson," Mae Frances called, bringing me out of my thoughts, "don't mess with me. You'd better start talking."

But I didn't say a word. Like with the money, I could show her better than tell her. So, I reached into my purse, pulled out the envelope and handed it to Mae Frances.

"Look, I'm getting tired of opening stuff," she said, even as she unfastened the envelope. "Why don't you just tell me what's …." And then, that slew of curses spewed from her mouth again as she glanced at the first picture of Lola and Jefferson.

The only problem was — Mae Frances's moans of shock had too much glee. She didn't seem disgusted at all. Nowhere near where I wanted her to be. She seemed like — she kinda liked what she was looking at.

"Is that your friend?" she asked with a grin that was much too wide on her face. "Damn."

When she started turning the pictures to the left and to the right and then upside down, I stood, snatched the photos from her and stuffed them back into the envelope.

"Really?" I tossed the envelope onto the couch, out of Mae Frances's reach.

"What?"

That big ole grin was still spread across her face and I wanted to smack her. The problem was, Mae Frances would smack me back. "I'm coming to you with a major problem, probably the biggest one that I've ever needed your help with, and you're ogling my friend?"

"Oh no, Jasmine Larson." She held up her hands and sat down in her traditional Queen Anne chair. "You don't need my help. You have this all worked out."

"I don't have a thing worked out." I plopped back down on the sofa.

When she raised her eyebrows at me, I wasn't sure if it was because I'd raised my voice or because she knew that I'd done something with the information she'd given to me.

We were both quiet for a moment and then, she said, "So, do you want to tell me what's going on?"

Sitting back, I sighed. Then, I started talking, telling her everything, from going over to see Lola, to not believing Lola and calling her bluff, to receiving the pictures last night.

"I'm telling you, Mae Frances, when I got those pictures, I couldn't sit there in that church."

"Well, I can understand that." She leaned forward to grab the envelope, but I got to it before she did and shoved those pictures back into my bag.

"Are you even listening to me?"

"Yes, I am, Jasmine Larson." She eyed my purse as if she were going to snatch it away from me.

"I was talking about Bible study. And how I ran out of there."

Her eyes finally left my bag and returned to me. "Dang, I wish I'd been there to see that."

My eyes narrowed. Was she really making fun of me in my hour of need?

"I was supposed to be there, you know I never miss Bible study. But Bubba called and ...."

I rolled my eyes. "Can you just try ....just focus on me for a second."

"Focus on you?" She gave me a blank stare. "And what can you do for me?"

"Mae Frances," I whined her name, "I really need you."

She gestured with her hands. "Okay, okay, go on."

I blew out a long breath. "Well, that's the whole story. Now that I know she wasn't lying and she was having an affair with Jefferson, I'm going to pay her off."

My friend's eyes went from me to the money on the table, then back to me. "Wow, you're a good friend."

"Let's just say that I owe Kyla and Jefferson this. And since I have the money …."

"So tell me again, why you need me? 'Cause it seems to me that you have it all worked out. You went to see her, she's blackmailing you, you went to get the money." She shrugged. "You don't need me at all."

"That's not true." When she folded her arms, I said, "Look, I'm so sorry that I didn't wait for you, but I couldn't. Once I had her name and address, what was I supposed to do? Just sit there? You know me; if you'd wanted me to wait, you shouldn't have given me the information."

Mae Frances leaned back as far as she could in her chair. "Are you kidding me? The way you begged me, interrupting my time with Bubba. I had to give you something or you wouldn't have shut up."

I didn't like what she said — even if it was the truth. I wanted to argue her down, but since I needed her help, I pressed my lips together and forced everything I wanted to say back inside.

She lectured on, "I thought you had more self-control, Jasmine Larson. I thought that was one thing you'd gleaned from me over the years."

Gleaned? When had Mae Frances started talking like that? Did that come from hanging out in Smackover?

When she remained silent, I realized she wanted an answer. "Well, I didn't wait … and I'm sorry for that. But now, I really need you."

"Why?" She shrugged. "You're gonna pay her the money, right?"

"I don't have a choice."

"Well, you need to be careful with that because a blackmailer is just like a cheating man. They keep doing it, again and again. She'll be back for more."

"Exactly." I slapped my hands against my lap. She had finally gotten to the point that I was trying to make. "And that's why I need you," I told my friend. "I know that she'll be back for more, but I can't figure out a way to stop her from doing that. But," I gave her a smile, "I'm sure you can."

She did that eye-brow raising thing again; my words hadn't hit their mark ... she was not impressed.

"Look, I'm sorry." I drew out those three words into so many syllables, I sounded like Jacqueline when she was trying to get me to submit to her will. "I don't know what else to say except that I've really learned my lesson."

She folded her arms. "Have you?"

I held up my right hand as if I were about to take an oath. "I will never go ahead of you again. I will always wait for you."

She nodded as if she at least accepted my promise. But then, she said, "How about we just close this chapter here? How about you don't get into anymore messes where I have to come behind you and clean it up. Because I have a new life, Jasmine Larson, and I ain't gonna have time to be running back to New York every time you call with another one of your disasters."

"Okay. We have a deal."

"I don't believe you." She shook her head.

"It's not like I'm trying to get into trouble; I just can't help it. But it's almost like it's not my fault. It's like there's some person out there writing my life story and he ... or she ... keeps writing these awful situations that I can't get out of."

"Well if that's the case, let's hope this is the last book on the life of Jasmine Larson. Because I'm telling you, I'm not letting anything come between me and Bubba. It's not like he has that much time left, and the way we go at each other ...."

She smiled, I grimaced, sickened by that image. I was beginning to think that Mae Frances was just playing with me, enjoying making me squirm.

"Well, can you help me out this one last time?"

"This is what I'm talking about." She looked at her watch. "Time. I was expecting a call from Bubba. He called me at nine and he always calls back."

"Mae Frances, it's ten. Was he calling you back this soon?"

"Yeah, girl," she said as if she were nineteen years old. "We try not to let an hour go by without checking up on each other."

Now, they were acting like they were nineteen. Really?

With a sigh, she pushed herself up from the chair. "But if you need me, I guess, I can text Bubba and tell him that I'll talk to him later." Then, she paused. "I have an idea."

My eyes brightened until she said, "Let's go to the police."

"No!" Mae Frances stepped back like she was shocked at my tone, but I knew it was an act. With all that she'd seen, with everything that she knew, nothing shocked this woman. "I thought about going to the police, but if we do that, then, they'll go to Kyla and my whole purpose for doing this is so she won't find out."

She glanced at me through the corner of her eye. "You care an awful lot about this woman."

"Yeah, I do."

Her eyes narrowed with suspicion. "A friend you never mentioned to me."

"Actually, I did. A long time ago. But you don't remember."

A beat passed, and then, "Oh, I remember, Jasmine Larson. You know I remember everything. And what I don't remember, I find out from the dossier I keep on you."

I laughed, she didn't.

She said, "This was the chick that you met in kindergarten, but then, got jealous of her life and slept with her husband."

I frowned. Even if I had told her about Kyla and Jefferson and me, I wouldn't have said it like that. Where had she heard that? Or had she gleaned that information some other kind of way?

She waved her hand. "I'm just kidding. You told me. You're the one who forgot." Now, she chuckled. "Okay, Jasmine Larson, let me get my purse, and my phone, 'cause I don't want to miss a call, and then, we'll get going."

She was still chuckling when she walked out of the room, but I wasn't laughing anymore. Had Mae Frances really been checking out my background? I mean, she did that to everyone else — but me?

"Nah," I said, and then sat back. "She wouldn't do that."

But then I remembered this woman that I called my friend, and I knew for sure that with her, all things were possible.

I couldn't worry about that now, though. I had to focus on getting this money to Lola Lewis and ending this nightmare for Kyla and Jefferson.

chapter 29

Jasmine

I still held onto this briefcase as if it contained all the gold the world possessed, though I wasn't so concerned this time. Mae Frances stood just a breath behind me as we walked up the steps to Lola's brownstone. And even though I didn't know her age (I put her somewhere between seventy, eighty, ninety and one hundred) having her with me felt like Secret Service protection.

"I think this is her buzzer," I said to Mae Frances as I pointed to the first bell.

She nodded. "It is."

I gave her a backwards glance over my shoulder before I pressed it. "I hope she's home."

Again, she nodded. "She is."

Now, I did a full turn and faced Mae Frances. But she didn't look at me. "Turn around, Jasmine Larson," she said. "Face the door. Never turn your back on a snake."

The moment I did what she told me, Lola opened the door. And for the first time, she wasn't wearing one of those spandex-blend body huggers nor one of her signature hats. Today, she wore a robe, at least, that's what I guessed she called it, although the hem of the satin barely covered her butt and did nothing to hide her cleavage.

She didn't look a bit surprised to see me. "I guess you got my message." With a smile, she held up a glass of wine, once again, toasting me ... and it wasn't even noon.

"If you're talking about the photos that you sent to my husband's church last night ...."

"Oh, I'm sorry about that." She pouted before she took a sip of wine. "But I didn't have any other way to reach you. And it was like you were ignoring me and I refused to be ignored, so I just had to have that package delivered to City of Lights. I've always loved that church."

When she'd called my name on Sunday, I'd known then that she'd done her intel on me. She knew about City of Lights and I had no doubt that she knew even more — including where I lived — which was another reason why I wanted this done. I didn't want Lola Lewis coming anywhere near my children because if that happened, this would go to a whole different level and by the time the police got involved, it would be a whole 'nother case.

In the moments that I'd had those thoughts, the ends of Lola's lips drooped a bit when she got a glimpse of Mae Frances. "Who is she?" With her glass, she motioned toward my friend, but spoke to me.

"She's my insurance agent." I held up the briefcase. "I'm sure you don't want to handle this business out here in the open with all of this money and you dressed ... or not dressed ... like that."

She made no move to cover herself, just opened the door wider so that we could step inside. We followed her, as she sauntered into her apartment, and Mae Frances closed the door behind us.

"So," Lola began as she settled on her sofa, "you have my money." It was a statement more than a question, but still, I wanted to respond to call this just what it was. "It's actually *my* money, but you're *blackmailing* my friend about your affair."

She shook her head. "I keep telling you, this isn't blackmail. This is payment for my services rendered. It's not my fault Doctor Blake came after me." She paused. "So ... my payment is in there?" She pointed to the briefcase.

Without saying a word, I handed her the attaché.

She placed it on her lap, clicked the locks open.

Now, twenty-five thousand dollars in cash was a lot of money.

But when Lola glanced at the stacks, it was like she was flipping through a magazine — she didn't even blink.

"Looks like it's all here." She fingered through a couple of the bundles, then nodded as if she knew what twenty-five thousand dollars looked like. "I'm sure I can trust you, right?" She glanced up. "Because if you try to cheat me ...."

Mae Frances laughed. "If she cheated you, what?" my friend asked her. "You gonna go to the police?"

Lola cocked her head. "And again ... who are you?"

"I'm her banker."

She chuckled. "I thought you were her insurance agent."

"Well, if you knew who I was, why you asking?"

Lola snapped the briefcase shut, then stood up. "I think we're done."

I said, "We are, as long as you understand that this is it. I don't want you coming back for more."

She placed her hand over her chest, though her hand didn't cover a bit of her cleavage that was busting out of the teddy she wore. "What? You don't trust me?"

I folded my arms. "Just know this is the end."

She one-shoulder shrugged. "This is all that I asked Doctor Blake for. This is enough."

I nodded.

When neither one of us spoke for a few moments, Lola said, "Well, I would offer you a seat, but I'm sure you really don't want to stay and chat."

She was right about that. I pivoted, but when I turned, Mae Frances was still standing behind me, her feet planted like she had no intentions of moving.

I whispered to her, "Let's go."

"You know what?" Mae Frances circled me and plopped down on the sofa. "I do want to chat."

Both Lola and I frowned.

"That sure is a lot of money." Mae Frances grabbed the briefcase. She had it locked and closed before Lola took a single breath.

"Excuse me." Lola reached around Mae Frances. "Please get

your hands off my money."

Mae Frances moved the briefcase away from Lola's grasp. "Oh, it's not your money, sweetheart. This belongs to my friend."

"What are you talking about?"

Really, I couldn't tell you if I said that or if Lola had spoken those words. Because I had no idea where Mae Frances was going with this. I'd told her why I was paying Lola — if she played games with this chick, I had no doubt Lola would have no problem going to Kyla and exposing Jefferson's affair.

"I'm talking about why don't we all sit down and you tell my friend, Jasmine Larson, the real story."

Lola crossed her arms. "I'm not sitting down with you. You need to leave now, go on your way and we never have to see each other again."

"Oh, we're gonna leave," Mae Frances said, "and we'll never see you again. But Jasmine Larson is taking this money right back to her bank."

"Mae Frances." I hissed her name with all kinds of images in my mind of how this was going to play out and not one was good. "It's okay."

"No, it's not. Because I don't like being just another one of Lucy Levin's marks."

For a moment, I wondered if this was it — the point where Mae Frances's age was revealed through this onset of dementia. Because she'd called Lola by the wrong name.

Except.

Lola hadn't objected. She hadn't done anything — just stood there like she'd turned to ice.

That was when I realized this was no dementia; this was Mae Frances.

Mae Frances said, "Or maybe it wasn't Lucy the last time you pulled one of these things. Maybe it was Laverne Lockley."

Lola was no longer frozen. Those last words had thawed her and made her melt right down onto the sofa.

That didn't shut Mae Frances up, though. "You know," she paused to pull something from her purse and when I saw the yellow envelope (like the one that Lola had delivered to me), I wondered how Mae Frances had gotten into my purse. In an instant, I checked, but my envelope was still in my possession.

She said to Lola, "I do have to admit that you're really good." Mae Frances removed what looked like photos to me, but I couldn't see. She said, "These here pictures of you and the assemblyman must've gotten you a lot more than twenty-five-thousand dollars."

The way Mae Frances looked at the photos, the same way she'd done earlier, turning them from side-to-side and upside down, made me want to see them, too. Had Lola done this before?

As if she'd heard my thoughts, Mae Frances said, "How many times have you done this, Lola/Lucy/Laverne?"

Though she'd been a little shaken, her game-face was back. Lola sat like she was a hard rock.

"You can't answer that?" Mae Frances pulled another sheet from her purse. "Let me see if I can help you out." She scanned the paper she held. "I have seventeen here. Seventeen times — that I know of — where you've blackmailed men. And that's just in the last two years."

I gasped. "Seventeen?" When Mae Frances and Lola both glared at me, I held up my hand. "I'm sorry. Go 'head, Mae Frances." I was giving her permission to proceed, but at the same time, my words were meant to give her a verbal high-five.

Mae Frances kept her eyes on me for only a moment longer before she turned back to Lola. "Like I was saying, you are so good. Clearly these men were drugged, right?"

Lola didn't move, her eyes so still on Mae Frances.

"But what I can't figure out is how you get the dudes to look so natural? Like, how did you get their eyes open sometimes and closed other times?" She paused. "You're good, girl. 'Cause at one point, I believed these pictures. And if I believed them, then anyone else would for sure."

In a move that I was sure shocked Mae Frances, too, Lola snatched the paper from her hand. But then, I wondered, if my friend really had been surprised because she said, "Oh, that's your copy." She pulled another piece of paper from her purse. "I have the original right here."

Lola did the same thing, yanked it from her again.

Mae Frances said, "Oh, did I say that was the original?" When she removed a stack of papers from her bag, I couldn't help but laugh. "Here, you can have all of these."

As Lola glanced through the pages, Mae Frances kept talking, "So this is what I know … you've been doing this for a long time, Laverne."

Whatever this woman's name was, she looked up.

"You seem to favor professional men, those conventions are your specialty, huh?"

Again, she hardly moved, and even from where I stood, I could see that her eyes darkened. I wasn't fazed, though. Mae Frances — whatever her age — could take Lola. I knew that for sure.

"So what do you do?" Mae Frances asked. "Meet them in the bar? Slip them a roofie? Then go to work?"

Now, Lola squinted.

Mae Frances spoke as if she were asking questions, but I knew what she stated were facts.

She said, "And then, by the time you go to the men with these pictures, they're not so sure themselves, huh?" She paused. "They certainly don't want to bring their wives any grief or any issues with their careers."

Lola took a deep breath — at least, it was deep for her.

"I guess twenty-five thousand dollars is a small price for them to pay 'cause you only choose men who can afford it."

When she paused, I waited for Lola to say something, react in some kind of way — deny, deny, deny at least. But she said nothing.

My friend kept on, "I guess it's a good gig, if you can't get any other kind of work. And it seems to pay well." She stopped for a moment and looked around the living room taking in the furniture the way I'd done on Sunday. Turning back to Lola, she said, "But, it's a dangerous gig, isn't it, Laverne?"

Lola still didn't part her lips.

"All we have to do is ask your mama."

I didn't know this woman, so I certainly didn't know her mama.

But the way Mae Frances had just stated that, scared me. I wasn't the only one, though. In all of my encounters with Lola Lewis, she had that poker-face poise on lock — until this moment. It seemed Mae Frances had the key that broke this woman down.

Because every part of Lola's body reacted. First, there were tears, then, her shoulders shook and her hands trembled. I didn't have x-ray vision, but I would've bet that her organs were doing all kinds of somersaults and backflips.

"My mother," she whispered. There was shock in her tone.

"Oh, yeah. Your mama. What's her name? Gisele George?" Before Lola could respond, Mae Frances continued, "Or is that the name she gave when she was arrested. She was also Genine Givens and Gloria Gray." She paused and rolled her finger around in the air. "At first, I thought your best trick was always wearing a hat. Better that the police were looking for a hat than a face, right?"

That made me open my mouth wide.

"But I think what I love best is how you and your mama both use those alliterations with your names. Is that something she taught you? So that you remember all the names you have to use when you change up?"

"My mother … is dead," she whispered.

Mae Frances held her forefinger to her head. "Ah … no … your mama is in prison. Bedford Hills, if I'm not mistaken." And then, Mae Frances laughed. "What am I talking about? I'm never mistaken."

"No," Lola protested. "She's dead."

I didn't know a bit of this story, but even I could tell that Lola was lying.

Mae Frances said, "Girl, stop playing. You went to see her three weeks ago and you always make sure she has money on her books." But then, her laughter left just like that and Mae France's own game face was back. "Look Lola/Lucy/Laverne. I'm not even gonna go to the police. I mean, I want to so that you can see your mama more often … like every day. But Jasmine Larson," they both glanced up at me before Mae Frances continued, "has a good heart. And she told me she really likes you."

I wanted to raise my hand and rebuff all those words, but I was enjoying this (except for what she'd just said about me) way too much to stop her.

Mae Frances sighed. "Jasmine Larson might not like you as much, though, if she realized how you set her up."

"What?"

Mae Frances ssshhh'd me with her hand before she said to Lola, "Go on, tell her. Tell her how you set her up, showing up at the hospital knowing that one of Jefferson's friends — whoever was there — would do anything to save his poor wife from finding out about you. Makes me believe that you've done this part before, too."

My eyes narrowed. I'd been set up ... just like Jefferson.

I was growling when Mae Frances continued, "Oops. Maybe I shouldn't have told Jasmine Larson that." She chuckled. "Maybe I should have just kept that between us." She pointed her finger back and forth. "But still, I'm not gonna turn you in. I'm just gonna take this money and deposit it right back in the bank."

She paused when her phone vibrated and as Mae Frances glanced down for a moment, I glared at Lola/Lucy/Laverne. Ooohhh, how I wanted to take her right there. Just one good uppercut to that chiseled nose and her too-thin-to-be-a-black-girl lips.

But I'd already messed up, so I had to ride this the way Mae Frances wanted.

My friend nodded, looked up from her phone, then stood. "Now, this meeting is over." She grabbed the briefcase and when she moved toward the door, I scurried behind her. But right before she put her hand on the knob, she turned and said, "Oh, and you will never contact my friends again because you like the idea of your mama being safe in that prison, right?"

Lola blinked back what I was sure was a deluge of tears.

Then, Mae Frances did something that I'd never heard her do in the twelve years that I'd known her. "Right," she exclaimed, raising her voice.

Her tone made me stand up straighter.

Lola nodded.

"I hope you've learned a couple of things about me today. One, I know people and I can make things happen. Things that you won't like."

She paused as if she wanted those words to settle in for Lola.

Then, she added, "And two, no one messes with my friends."

Another pause.

Then, more, "So you can keep scamming all the people you want in New York. Just make sure that none of them are my friends. Before you drop that drug in their drinks, you may wanna ask, 'Do you know Mae Frances?'" She laughed, but then straightened up real quick and real good. "I'm not kidding. If you don't want to see my face again, stay away from anyone that I care about."

Mae Frances opened the door, and then walked out as if she hadn't just threatened this woman's mother's life. Before I stepped over the threshold, I turned back.

Lola/Lucy/Laverne sat on her sofa, her head down, her shoulders quaking from her sobs. In a few seconds, what Mae Frances had revealed rolled through my mind. This woman was a grifter, seemingly educated by her mama. It was a sad, sad song that almost made me feel sorry for her.

But that was the thing about the word almost.

Almost didn't matter. Almost never counted.

I walked through the door, not even bothering to close it behind me.

chapter 30

Kyla

Every doubt that I'd had about my husband, had been worked out. It was because of Hosea, helping me to remember who Jefferson and I were. And, I had remembered. And I *had* believed.

But now, I just didn't know.

Because of one word.

Lola.

I opened my eyes, though I kept my hands still clasped; my heart continued in prayer mode as I focused on the gold cross above the altar. I wondered, not for the first time, why I was always alone in this place? Except when Hosea had brought me here, and when I'd come in with Nicole, I'd never seen anyone else in the ICU chapel. Couldn't figure out why since this place was filled with God's peace.

That was why I'd come here. That was what I needed — God's peace. Because right now, what was going on inside of me was anything but peace.

Anxiety, unrest, even turmoil. All because of ... Lola.

I shook my head. What I should have been doing was rejoicing, giving God nothing but thanks for how Jefferson had opened his eyes just about thirty hours ago. From that moment, it had all been good, according to the doctors.

"Your husband truly is a blessed man."

That was what Dr. Reid had told me last night after a day full of tests. But I already knew that God's grace and His mercy was all around Jefferson. Because of all of the spoken prayers and ones that had been stored up.

There was no doubt anywhere inside of me — Jefferson waking up and being able to speak was a miracle. What I couldn't figure out, though, was why had that miracle included him speaking another woman's name?

Dr. Reid tried to explain it to me.

"Being shot in the brain is the most traumatic event the body can experience. Even with all that we know, there is so little that we know about the operating center of our bodies. Again, Doctor Blake may just be speaking about a movie or a song ... we just don't know. What I do know is that with speech and physical therapy, your husband's prognosis is very good. I'm cautious, but very optimistic. Really, Mrs. Blake, there is no need for you to be concerned about your husband's utterances after coming out of a coma."

But I was concerned. He wouldn't keep repeating that name unless it meant something. And then, when I put that together with Jefferson being with some mysterious woman that night ....

Unclasping my hands, I sighed. I felt like I was trying to put together a gigantic puzzle, yet, I'd only been given two pieces: Lola ... and that woman. Two pieces that I knew were connected. Like the corners of a puzzle ... once you get those pieces, any good puzzler could fill in the rest.

That was what I needed to do — fill in this puzzle. And with a few more pieces, I could.

With a final, "Amen," I pushed up from the bench and rushed from the chapel, passing the nurses (who felt almost like family now) and then, I peeked into Jefferson's room before I stepped fully inside.

Nicole must have still been on the phone and for just a moment, my thoughts turned to my daughter. She'd gotten a call from one of her colleagues right when we arrived at the hospital this morn-ing and with the time difference, I was concerned. It was after eight in the evening in Beijing when the call had been made and I wondered if the embassy wanted Nicole to return to work. That would be an issue because I knew my daughter; she'd quit her job before she'd leave her father.

Her father. My anxiety was back as I moved to my husband's bedside, and I stood there for a while. Even with all I was feeling, there was nothing I could do except smile as I looked at him becoming himself again as the swelling subsided. Looking more and more like the man that I loved.

I kissed his forehead, then maneuvered around the bed to get to my purse. My cell was first, and then I grabbed the card that I'd tucked into the side pocket, sure at that time, that I would never use it. As I folded the card over and over in my hand, Hosea's words came back to me:

"If you call him, he'll be down here questioning you."

When Hosea said that, I knew that he was right. I was sure that Detective Green would ask me all kinds of questions that I not only didn't want to answer, but that would really hurt.

It didn't matter, though; I had to do it if I wanted more pieces to this puzzle and only Detective Green could give those to me.

Stepping into the hall, I moved quickly to the Quiet Room and peeked in. Again, my thoughts switched tracks for a moment — I wasn't sure where Nicole had made her call, but when I saw that the room was empty, I stepped inside.

Although it was after nine, I didn't know anything about the working hours of police officers, but every time I'd spoken to Detective Green it had been in the morning. So maybe police worked in the same kinds of shifts.

I tapped in the numbers quickly, dialing against all doubts.

I need to know.

That was what I kept telling myself. It only took one person and about two minutes to get me to Detective Green.

"Mrs. Blake," the detective greeted me. "Good morning." His voice had far more cheer than the two previous times I'd spoken to him. "How did you hear the news already?"

"News?"

"Yes. About the arrest." Then, he paused. "Wait. Let me roll up. Are you calling about the young man who shot your husband?"

"No, not exactly."

"I apologize. I just assumed …." His words trailed off, though his tone remained upbeat. "Well, I'll give you all the details, but first, what were you calling about?"

It felt like I'd been derailed and couldn't get my words together for what I really wanted to know. "The man who shot my husband?" That was all I could get out.

"Yes, we've made an arrest."

"Oh my God." I pressed my hand against my chest and fell back, thankful there was a chair right beneath me. "Who did it? Why?"

"A nineteen-year-old local troublemaker with a long rap sheet. He's actually one of the organizers of these flash robs," the detective said.

"But why would he shoot Jefferson?"

"Well, at some point, we'll need a statement from your husband, but it seems like he made the mistake of getting in their way. Trying to talk to the mob, trying to stop the robbery."

Even though the detective couldn't see me, I nodded. That was so my husband.

"He tried to stop the wrong one," the detective continued. "The leader, the one we have in custody, just fired and everyone dis-persed. Seems like your husband *did* stop most of the robbery, but not the way any of us would've wanted. He was a hero."

A hero. Knowing Jefferson, that was not what he was trying to be. He was just trying to do what was right.

"But the good news," the detective's cheer charged through my thoughts, "is we have the shooter now, and I'm sure that once we pull in a few others, we'll get statements from them since no one will want to catch an attempted murder case. After we get the statements and are able to speak to your husband, the case will be closed."

The case will be closed.

It was those words that brought me out of my stupor, making

me remember the reason for my call.

"That's really good news, Detective, but what about the woman? What about the woman who was with my husband?"

"We only wanted to question her because she was a potential witness," he said. "We're fine now. There's no need to find her."

No! Thankfully, that scream stayed inside my throat. "But don't you still need to talk to her?"

"Getting your husband's statement will be enough. We're no longer looking for her."

"No, you can't stop. You have to keep looking." The words spilled out of me, one after another. I couldn't stop myself. "You have to find her."

There was such a long pause that for a moment, I thought the detective had hung up. Then, "I'm really sorry, Mrs. Blake, but with the witnesses from the flash rob and your husband's statement, there really isn't any reason for us to spend any more resources on her. In fact, I doubt if this will even go to trial. The DA is already working on a plea ...."

"But, I need to find her," I said, praying that I didn't sound as desperate to the detective as I sounded to my ears.

This time, he didn't hesitate to tell me, "I'm sorry, Mrs. Blake, but she is no longer any concern of ours."

That was cop-speak. In plain English, he was telling me that I needed to handle my own business.

"We will want to speak to your husband once he's well enough. We'll be in touch with his doctors."

"Yes. Of course," I said. "Thank you."

I hung up, feeling no further need to embarrass myself. Once again, I was in that place where I wanted to do backflips in celebration, but my stomach was somersaulting with dread. Thank God, they'd found the man who'd shot my husband but closing that left such an opening for me. An opening that I had to know. I needed to know, who was that woman. Was she Lola?

Of course, I could wait until Jefferson could speak, but like Dr. Reid said, what would he remember?

"Oh, God." I covered my face with my hands.

Never finding out was not an option. There had to be a way, but I didn't have any idea what I was going to do.

chapter 31

Jasmine

My feet were like bricks as I dragged behind the children and Mrs. Sloss down the hall, into the foyer and toward the front door.

"Mama, why can't you walk us to the van?" Jacqueline whined. "'Cause we need more time to work out all the songs for the playlist for the Christmas play."

"We finished it last night." I paused to release a yawn. "We don't need ... "

She cut me off like she was the mama, saying, "But I wanted one more review because ...."

Now, I was the one who stopped her. "First of all, Jacqueline, what you're not gonna do is interrupt me when I'm talking and ...."

"I thought you were finished since you were yawning."

Today was not the day, and I was not the one. With all that I'd been through, I had no patience for an obstinate child. "Jacqueline!" The way I said her name made everyone stop, even Mrs. Sloss. The three of them stood by the door, looking at me like I was about to set it off.

My gaze zoomed in on Jacqueline. "Now, like I was saying, we finished the playlist last night, it's done, I'm not walking you to the van, and that's the end of it. Do you understand?"

With poked out lips, she muttered, "Yes," and then she glared at me with a look that made me wonder if she was trying to figure out how she could beat me down. Then, she opened the door and stomped out.

The moment she did that, Zaya held up his arms. "Mama," he said, welcoming me into a hug. When I embraced him, he held me for a few longer moments, his way of diffusing the situation. "Bye, Mama," he whispered into my ear. "I hope you have a good day."

"Thank you, sweetheart."

I said goodbye to Mrs. Sloss and told her not to rush back. She had a doctor's appointment after she dropped the children off at the van, and my hope was that she'd stay away until Jacqueline and Zaya came home. Because right now, I didn't want to be around anyone, not even the people I loved the most — my husband, my children, my best friend ….

My best friend.

Mae Frances.

The thought of her made me forget how tired I was and now, I was just pissed. She was the reason I hadn't slept well last night.

After closing the door behind the children, I marched back into the kitchen and grabbed the tea kettle. Thoughts of yesterday and Mae Frances and Lola still flipped through my mind. As I sat waiting for the water to boil, I went through it all in my mind once again:

"Oh, my God, Mae Frances. What just happened? Why didn't you tell me? Why did you let me come all the way over here?" Those questions rolled off my tongue before we reached the bot-tom of the steps to the brownstone.

Mae Frances didn't say a word; she just held up her hand and in a few seconds a cab stopped. She opened the door and I waited for her to get in, but she motioned for me to slide across the seat first.

As I did, she gave my address to the driver.

That made me smile. The kids hadn't seen her in a few weeks — they'd be thrilled when they got home from school. But before they got there, Mae Frances and I could have a long talk about what had gone down.

But she didn't get in the cab. She leaned down and said, "Go home, Jasmine. I'll talk to you later."

Before I could get my mind wrapped around her words, my cab sped off. From the back window, I watched her walk away, heading east as my taxi traveled west.

I punched in her number on my phone, pressed the phone to my ear, and waited. But, one ring ... and then it went to voicemail.

Ugh!

Was she doing that again? I called her back, again and again. And the same thing kept happening. I kept dialing, she kept send-ing me to voicemail. By the time I walked through my front door, I was fuming. What in the world was Mae Frances up to?

Even at home, I kept up the insanity of doing the same thing with the same results. We did that dance all through the evening, and finally near midnight, I gave up. But that made it difficult for me to rest. Yes, Mae Frances had saved me from Lola, but why didn't she want to talk to me? Why was she avoiding me? Was there more to this story?

It was now after nine in the morning, and I had the same questions. But today, I wasn't going to do what I did yesterday. I wasn't going to keep calling Mae Frances, trying to track her down like she owed me something. Whatever was wrong with her, if she wanted me out of her life, I was out, I was done, it was over.

The tea kettle whistled just as the doorbell rang and the combination of the sounds, startled me. I turned off the flame under the kettle, then dashed to the door. I hadn't picked up any packages from the concierge over the last week, and I was sure it was one of the doormen making a delivery.

But when I swung the door open, I stared into the face of Mae Frances ... and then, I just slammed the door. I didn't bother to lock it; it wouldn't have mattered if I did because Mae Frances had a key and she wouldn't hesitate to use it — which was exactly what she did.

"Jasmine Larson, I know you don't have an attitude with me."

I didn't bother to answer her. Just marched into the kitchen, grabbed a mug from the cabinet and filled it with the boiling water.

Mae Frances stood under the arch that led to the kitchen,

watching me. And I dipped my teabag in my cup, ignoring her.

"So you're mad at me? Why?"

Finally, I looked up. "Let me count the ways."

She laughed, tossed her purse onto the chair next to where I sat, then went to the cabinet, pulled down a mug and poured her own tea. "Wow, you must be really upset if you're quoting Shakespeare."

I didn't change my expression. "You got a problem with that? What? You knew Shakespeare, too?"

My words were meant to be a jab, but you couldn't jab a moving target. Because all she did was sip her tea, then answer, "No, I didn't know Shakespeare …."

I smirked.

She said, "But his great, great, great, great, great, great, great grandson and I back in the sixties when we were in Stratford-upon-Avon …."

I threw my hands up in the air. "Really? Are you going to come over here and talk to me about another one of your mysterious connections after what you did to me yesterday?"

Her eyes widened with innocence. "What did I do, Jasmine Larson, except for help you?"

"Yes, you did, but then you left me and didn't explain anything."

She took another slow sip. "All right. What do you want to know?"

I folded my arms. "First, where were you last night? Why didn't you answer my calls? Heck, why did you just put me in a cab and not explain anything?"

She nodded as she listened to my questions and kept nodding even after I finished. Finally, she said, "Well, first of all, Jasmine Larson, I wasn't aware that I had to explain anything to you."

I glared at her.

She said, "I choose to share things because I love you, but don't get it twisted. I report to no one."

I pressed my lips together. Had I said all that to her?

"But I asked you what you wanted to know, and I'm choosing to answer your questions. Where was I last night? I was with Bubba."

It was shock that made me drop my arms.

She said, "Remember that text that I got while we were with Lola — or whatever her name is? Well, Bubba was at the airport in Little Rock, waiting to hear from me."

"He's in New York?" I asked, totally forgetting the reason for my fury with my friend.

She nodded. "And that is the answer to your second question of why I didn't answer your calls."

All I could do was shake my head. Bubba — I didn't even know his last name; I assumed it was Jackson — was in New York. With Mae Frances.

Oh, my God!

"So, all I can say is that if you had a romantic night going on with Hosea, I wouldn't begrudge you a thing. So I expect the same from you."

I was still pissed when I said, "Well, you could have told me ...."

"I told you, I don't answer to you."

"Dang it, Mae Frances, when you love people, you let them know what's going on. Supposed something had happened to you."

She shook her head. "You know that ain't the reason why you're all up in my business. Ain't nothing going to happen to me. So, let's get to the real reason why you're mad."

I paused.

She said, "Let's talk about Lola."

She was right. I was totally pissed about that. "Yeah, 'cause you had all of this information on her and didn't tell me."

My friend raised an eyebrow like my words surprised her. "I didn't tell you? Or maybe it was that you didn't give me a chance. You had already handled it."

"But you let me go to the bank ...."

"I didn't know you were going to do that."

"Okay, but then you let me go over to her place and give her the money."

She nodded. "Well, it was the best way to teach both of you a lesson. She won't ever mess with my friends again, and you learned that you better listen to your friend." Mae Frances shrugged. "I don't want to be spending all of my time fixing your situations now that Bubba is in my life. I got other things to do."

Mae Frances's tone softened. "Look, Jasmine Larson, you knew when you came to me that I was going to handle it. I've helped you handle every single situation you've ever gotten yourself into and you need to understand that instead of moving ahead of me. You really could have messed this up by not waiting until I was ready." She lowered her head and her voice. "It made me feel bad that you didn't trust me enough."

Her shoulders slumped, the ends of her lips drooped — and it was all an act. I knew that, Mae Frances knew that, but still, I did what she wanted me to do — I apologized. "I promise, it won't happen again." And, I meant that because Mae Frances was right. I could have saved myself a bunch of heartache if I had just waited for her.

She was grinning by the time she raised her head. "Great," she said. Then, after a pause, she added, "But we got her good, didn't we?"

Now, I was smiling too. "Oh, my God," I pressed my hand to my chest, "was all of that stuff that you said true?"

She nodded. "Every bit of it. She's made quite a good living hanging out at conventions picking up married men. At twenty-five thousand a pop, she makes decent money … probably about a quarter mil each year."

I blew out a breath and thought about that for a moment. "I still can't believe I was part of her set up."

"That's the way it goes. When a scammer finds their mark, they don't walk away after they've put in all the work. They're gonna get their money, somehow, someway."

I gave my friend a side-eye glance. "You sure seem to know a lot about this."

"What else is new, Jasmine Larson? You should know by now that I know a lot about everything."

Well, that was true. I said, "She's lucky you didn't have the police waiting outside for her."

Mae Frances shook her head. "Oh no. I'm not trying to mess with her gig." Her tone changed a bit. She almost sounded like she had some sympathy for Lola when she added, "That girl is lost and she's just out there trying to make it. I get that because I've been there."

It was during moments like this, when Mae Frances was reflective that I was reminded of how little I knew about my friend. If I'd had to guess, she'd had a rollercoaster of a life, filled with lots of lows, but I suspected, just as many highs. Last year, she'd considered writing an autobiography and although, at the time, I thought it was the dumbest idea because my friend never told any secrets about her life, now I wondered if I should encourage her — just so I could answer that universal question ... how in the world did Mae Frances know everybody?

Reaching over, I covered her hand with mine. "You're a good person, Mae Frances."

She smiled at me for a moment, before her face contorted into her signature glower. "No need for sentimentality, I just do what I have to do."

Standing, I kissed her cheek anyway. "I don't care what you say, you're good and I love you." But then, I straightened up and sighed. "The only thing — I don't know if what we did with Lola really solves everything."

"What do you mean?"

"Well," I began, pacing behind her, "Lola may be gone, but she's left a lot of questions — for Kyla. I can imagine all that's going on in Kyla's head about this woman."

Mae Frances frowned and tilted her head as if she were trying to remember something. "I thought you made up a story for her about Lola."

"I did, but the police keep bringing her up to Kyla and no matter what Kyla says about how she believes in and trusts her husband, I know her and she has questions. So when Jefferson wakes up, he better have answers."

"Well, he'll tell her the truth."

"But if he was going to pay her money, then, Jefferson thinks he had sex with Lola. And if he thinks that ... and if he tells Kyla that ...." I sighed. "It's not going to be a pretty picture. Maybe I should go to Kyla and tell her what I know."

"No!" Her tone was so emphatic, that I backed up a little. She added, "Jasmine Larson, stay out of it from this point."

"Why? I know the truth."

"But the truth looks different to different people." She shook her head. "The truth looks different depending on the messenger and like it or not, you're not the best messenger. I just have a feeling that you need to let those two handle this situation. You already did your part."

I took in Mae Frances's words and I knew she was right. I had started this because I wanted to prove myself to Kyla. But very quickly it had changed — I really wanted to help the Blake's who'd once been the dearest of friends. So, if my goal was to help, then how would telling Kyla do that?

This was handled. And anything Jefferson wanted to tell Kyla when he woke up, he would. I'd done my part — I'd taken away the blackmail threat.

She said, "And anyway, I doubt if your friend will remember anything when he wakes up. You know bullet injuries to the brain almost always affect memory at some level."

I leaned back and gave Mae Frances a what-do-you-know-about-that look.

"What?" she said. "One thing you do know about me, Jasmine Larson is that I was married to a doctor."

"Yeah, but I never knew if he was a medical doctor or a PhD."

"Oh, he was a medical doctor." She waved her hand, though, as if it were no big deal. "A neurosurgeon. One of the most prominent in the state of New York."

Hmmmm … that was the most Mae Frances had ever told me. Maybe she was beginning to open up. Maybe it was because of Bubba. Maybe I would talk to him and together, we could get her to write that book.

But before I could ask her another question, I heard the beep of the front door alarm and I smiled. It was too soon for Mrs. Sloss, so that meant only one thing.

Leaving Mae Frances right there in the kitchen, I dashed down the hall and into the foyer. And my grin got wider.

"Baby," I jumped into Hosea's arms before he could blink. "You're home."

With my legs wrapped around his waist, he didn't even struggle to hold me up.

After a long kiss, he said, "I should go away more often."

"No, you shouldn't. Because I can't sleep if you're not in the bed with me and I miss you too much." Planting my legs on the floor, I took his hand. "Come on. You'll never guess who's here." I pulled him into the kitchen.

He grinned when he saw her. "Nama!"

She stood so that he could pull her into a hug. When he stepped back, she held his shoulders. "Good to see you, Preacher Man."

"I know, it's been a while and I want to catch up with all that's been going on in Smackover."

Mae Frances beamed.

Hosea said, "But I'm glad to have both of you here." He looked from me to Mae Frances, and then, his smile faded away. He folded his arms. "So which one of you is going to tell me … what the hell is going on?"

***

I guess there was no such thing as client-banker privilege. I knew that Felix Winsome was a tattler, worse than my children, and the next time I saw him, I was going to call him that right to his face.

But right now, all I could do was watch Hosea as he paced back and forth in front of me and Mae Frances as we sat on the living room couch. It felt like we were in the courtroom, both of us defendants, sitting before the judge and the jury.

Hosea stopped moving just to ask, "So, that's everything?"

I nodded and Mae Frances did, too. We'd just told Hosea the whole story of Lola Lewis, picking up from the lie I'd told him about her and Dr. Reid to Mae Frances finding out about Lola and us confronting her yesterday. It was the complete truth that I had never planned to tell — before Felix Winsome had turned me in.

"That's every single thing, Preacher Man."

But while Hosea was focused on Lola, my mind was still on my turncoat banker. "I still can't believe Felix called you."

There was exasperation in Hosea's tone when he said, "Jasmine, the poor man thought you'd been kidnapped or something just as horrible. He knew you were in trouble coming into the bank asking for all of that money … in cash. What else was he supposed to do?"

"He should have asked me."

"He did. And you wouldn't tell him the truth. He knew you were lying. You think you're so good at that, but you're not anymore. Just like I knew that was a bogus story you told me about Lola and Doctor Reid."

Dang! I thought I'd passed his lie-detector test.

Hosea continued, "But I didn't say anything. I was waiting to see what you were doing, waiting for you to come to me." He shook his head. "And the other night when you asked me to trust you — I had no idea you were going to run to the bank or I wouldn't have trusted a thing." He paused. "Where's the money now?"

"In our bedroom. I was going to take it back today."

Hosea shook his head. "Wait for me. We'll do it together, later."

I nodded, then said, "I'm sorry but the only reason I didn't tell you is because I knew you would stop me."

"Isn't that why you never tell me?"

"I just wanted to help Kyla."

He gave me a long stare and then after a longer sigh, he pulled me up from the sofa and into his arms. From the corner of my eyes, I saw Mae Frances dab at the corner of her eye. Like there was a tear about to fall.

That made me smile. I remembered the days when Mae Frances and I first met. When she didn't trust men nor God (because He was a man, too.) But she'd come so far in the years of our friendship. And I suspected this crying episode had something to do with Bubba. That man, my uncle, had made her soft.

Hosea leaned back and my thoughts shifted away from Mae

Frances and Bubba. He said, "Darlin', I completely understand you wanting to help Kyla, but you still should have told me."

"Would you have tried to stop me?"

"I wouldn't have done it just to be stopping you. What you did was good because we needed to find out what happened to Jefferson, what that woman had done. We just would have done it differently."

"And 'differently' would have slowed us down. How long did this take me?"

"And me." Mae Frances held up her hand.

He chuckled as his glance moved between us. "You do know that we're all getting too old for this."

"Who you calling old?" I asked him with a grin. But then, I got serious. "I'm sorry, Hosea, I really thought we were doing the right thing."

He nodded. "Because you're still trying to prove to Kyla which is something that I told you that you can't do."

"I was trying to *help* Kyla."

"Well if that's the truth, there's one last thing you have to do." He turned to Mae Frances. "The both of you, we have to go to the police."

"No! Preacher Man," Mae Frances said. "I'm no fan of this woman, but if we report her to the police ...."

"She'll go to jail," Hosea finished for her. Releasing my hand, Hosea sat down next to Mae Frances. Now, he took her hand. "I get why you want to forgive this woman. From what you told me, she's had a hard life. But if you really want to help her, she has to change her ways."

"Oh, don't worry Preacher Man, she'll be different now. I bet you she won't mess with another one of my friends."

Hosea gave Mae Frances a long sideward glance. "Is that good enough for you? Just your friends? What about everyone else she's out there blackmailing?"

"Well ...." Mae Frances began, but stopped there.

"Don't you see you're not really helping her? There will never be any real redemption for her if she doesn't have to face all that she's done. She's hurt so many people and she'll never stop. She'll never have a chance to heal from whatever put her in this place. She'll never have a chance to be better if no one asks her to become better." He paused as if he wanted to give us a moment to think about this. "That's what you'll be doing by going to the police."

Mae Frances lowered her head and nodded. "I get that, Preacher Man, but there's a lot that you don't know about me ...."

"Whatever happened in the past, Mae Frances, doesn't matter."

"Yes, it does. I wasn't that different from Lola in my earlier days, and at any point, someone could have turned me in, but they didn't."

"But you met Jasmine, and in a way, she demanded that you be better when she made that bet with you to go to church."

Mae Frances leaned back. "You knew about that? You knew about that bet Jasmine Larson forced on me?"

Both Hosea and I smirked and I was glad that I could look back at that time now without complete heartbreak. It was in 2006, right after Hosea and I were married when he left me because he found out that Jacqueline wasn't his biological daughter. I had prayed and prayed that he would come back. And Mae Frances had laughed and laughed because she said my faith was stupid.

But I believed that Hosea and I would reconcile and I bet Mae Frances a Bible and a year of going to church with me. And I'd won — or rather Mae Frances did. Because just a couple of good Sundays of the Word from Hosea's father and she'd thrown herself on the altar.

Hosea said, "Yeah, you're not the only one who knows things. I know a little about who you used to be, but what I know best is who you are now. You were given another chance and I want the same for Lola."

After a moment, Mae Frances shook her head. "I just don't think I can do it, Preacher Man."

"Don't worry, I'll be right there with you." He stood and looked at me and Mae Frances. It no longer felt like he was the judge and jury. Now, he was just the judge and he'd pronounced the verdict.

He glanced at his watch. "I'm gonna head to the church for

about an hour and I'll call Detective Green while I'm there. Then, I'll pick you two up and we'll head to the police station."

This was the sentencing.

He said nothing else, just kissed my cheek and leaned over to hug Mae Frances before he left us alone.

Even though I sat back down next to Mae Frances, I didn't say a word until I heard the beep of the alarm, signaling that Hosea had left.

Still I waited for a moment before I asked, "So, what do you think?"

Her eyes were on the windows. We were too high up to see the park without standing, but still, we had a phenomenal view of uptown Manhattan.

She sighed. "The man of God has spoken, and I ain't never been one to fight the Lord above."

I smiled. There was no reason to remind her that her words weren't true 'cause she hadn't always been saved. And there was no reason for me to feel bad about this either. Now that I knew Jefferson hadn't had an affair, it was fine that Kyla found out. I just wouldn't be the one to tell her.

The only thing, though — I prayed she never saw those pictures. Because even though it was all staged, it looked too much like the truth. It would be hard for Kyla to get those images out of her mind.

Maybe the detective would have good sense not to show them to her. Or maybe I wouldn't take the chance. If I had to go talk to this man, I was going to tell him a few things about married women.

chapter 32

Kyla

"If I work this out right, I'll be back with our lunches before Dad wakes up and we can eat with him." Nicole clapped her hands and I laughed, though I tried to keep it low.

Both of us glanced at Jefferson, sleeping once again.

"Okay, sweetheart," I said. "He'll be out for a while, so don't rush."

"Oh, no. I have to get back. That restaurant that Auntie Jasmine took us to," she kissed the tips of her fingers, "manifique."

"What? Now, you're speaking French?"

"Well, magnificent is not as sexy in Mandarin." She leaned over and kissed my cheek, then did the same with her father before she scurried out of the room.

I glanced down at my tablet. "Do not let your hearts be troubled ...." I whispered the first words to my favorite chapter in the Bible as I read the scripture.

But then, my eyes rose and I glanced out the window. There wasn't much to see from this view in Jefferson's room, just the backs of nondescript gray and brown brick buildings that surrounded the hospital.

It didn't matter, though. It was a glorious Saturday, my second weekend in the city. But unlike last week, my heart was far from troubled and my smiles were wide with hope. Because every day,

Jefferson was so much stronger. That was the blessing for him. And the blessing for me: he'd stopped saying Lola. He hadn't uttered that name for the last two days.

What he said most now was, 'I love you,' words that for a while, I wasn't sure I'd ever hear him say again. And words that made me almost forget about Lola … and that woman … or if Lola was that woman.

Almost.

Twisting in the chair, I turned to look at my husband. He still slept more than he was awake, but the key was that he awakened on his own, to eat, for therapy, and to say, 'I love you' to me and Nicole. That was an accomplishment. To this point that was the longest sentence he'd uttered.

The thought of that made me stand, lay my tablet on the chair, and then I tiptoed to Jefferson's bedside. Leaning against the rail, I stared down at my husband.

There was no doubt — thoughts of that woman were still heavy on my mind, but looking down at Jefferson now, I knew I couldn't keep my focus on her. It might be that I would never find the answer, never figure out the connection.

And that was going to have to be okay. Right now, I needed to keep my focus one hundred percent on my husband because what I knew for sure was that Jefferson loved me. That, he remembered. And so would I.

As soon as I had that thought, Jefferson's eyes fluttered open. He blinked a couple of times, then focused his gaze on me.

"I love you," he whispered through dry lips.

Leaning over, I kissed him, lightly running my tongue over his lips. Then, I raised the back of his bed and held the cup as he sipped water. When he nodded, I pulled the straw away.

"How are you feeling?"

He nodded. "Good. Tired."

I took his hand into mine and lifted his fingers to my chest. "I love you, too."

The knock on the door made me stand up straighter and my eyes widened when Detective Green entered.

"Detective?" I knew it was him, but my confusion with seeing him here made his name come out as a question.

"Mrs. Blake." He nodded at me, then he glanced at my husband. "Doctor Blake."

Jefferson just stared.

I said, "What are you doing here?"

"Well, there was a new development and I wanted to talk to you ... and Doctor Blake."

"Oh." I glanced at Jefferson, not sure that he was ready for this ... and not sure that I was ready for Jefferson to hear anything that the detective would have to say.

The detective said, "I spoke to Doctor Reid and he said that it was fine." His eyes were on Jefferson now. "The doctor told me that you're recovering and I'm glad about that."

"Detective Green, I'm not sure this is a good idea." My glance volleyed between my husband and the detective. "I don't mind speaking with you, but I'd rather wait for Jefferson ...."

"No." Jefferson's protest was husky, but strong and clear. "I. Want. Talk."

"Thank you, Doctor Blake." Detective Green stepped forward as if Jefferson's words were a good enough invitation for him. "I promise, this won't take long."

Still, I shook my head, but Jefferson nodded his and I guessed the guy coming out of a coma trumped his conscious wife.

Before the detective could say anything else, I said, "Detective, we haven't talked to my husband about ...."

"I. Was. Shot."

The detective stepped closer. "Do you remember that, Doctor Blake?"

There was no time for a proper introduction. It seemed that Jefferson really did want to talk about this. I kept my eyes on Jefferson because at the first sign of any challenges for him, I was going to chase this cop right out of here.

Jefferson nodded at the detective and repeated, "Shot. Gun."

"Yes. Well, we have the man who shot you."

He nodded again and I wasn't quite sure that Jefferson really understood; I would have expected more of a reaction.

Detective Green said, "When you're feeling better, we'll get a complete statement from you about the shooting."

Another nod.

"But I came here today to talk to you about Lola Lewis."

Lola!

My eyes shot from my husband to the detective. "Lola Lewis?"

For the first time, the detective was the one to nod.

"So that's her name? The woman?"

"Yes, it seems like it."

"I thought you stopped looking for her." He was the detective, but I was the one with all the questions.

"Well, a witness came in and told us quite a story." Turning back to my husband, he went back into detective-mode. "Doctor Blake, do you know Lola Lewis?"

Jefferson frowned, but shook his head.

"Are you sure? Lola Lewis?"

Again, he shook his head and the detective and I sighed, though I was sure it was for different reasons. Mine was filled with relief. Jefferson didn't know that woman. Just like the doctor said, he was just uttering that word. There was no connection.

And then, Jefferson said, "Lola. Blackmail."

My heart returned to my throat.

Detective Green was so close to Jefferson's bed, I thought he was going to crawl in with him. It sounded like there was a little excitement in his tone when he repeated what Jefferson said. "Blackmail? What can you tell me about that?"

Jefferson opened his mouth, but once again, said only, "Lola. Blackmail." He shifted in the bed, moving from side-to-side as if he wanted to tell us more.

"Sweetheart," I said, hoping that would calm him down.

He took a deep breath and repeated the word, shifting once again.

"Detective," I said. "I don't think my husband is ready …."

"No." It was almost a shout, the loudest that Jefferson had spoken. Then, he motioned with his hand and the detective and I stared at him.

It was Detective Green who figured it out. "You want to write?" This time, his nod was emphatic.

"Okay." The detective had come prepared with a small notebook and pen. He flipped the pages in the spiral book, past the ones he'd written on. When he got to the first blank page, he handed the book and pen to Jefferson and my husband sat up straight.

I leaned over, watching him form the letters. He moved slowly, like a child, and like a child, he was determined.

The paper was small, and Jefferson's letters were big, so he had to use several pieces. That didn't deter him. He wrote and turned the pages. He wrote and I read the words, disconnected as they were.

He wrote until he'd told his story and then, he gave the book to me. Our fingers touched, and he held me, as if he were trying to tell me more.

I passed the book to the detective and as he glanced through the pages, I stared at Jefferson. What had my husband been through?

After about a minute, the detective was ready to put together the pieces of the puzzle that I'd never been able to work out. "So, Lola tried to blackmail you."

"Yes," Jefferson breathed.

Detective Green glanced down at the notebook once again. "She asked you for twenty-five thousand dollars?"

"Yes."

He read through Jefferson's words more. "You were going to give her the money?"

"Yes."

"And this last word," Detective Green pointed to what Jefferson had written, "evidence. You were trying to get evidence?"

Jefferson nodded. "Evidence. For police."

"Okay," Detective Green said, "I think I got it. So like your friend, you were trying to play cop."

"What do you mean?" I asked.

He shook his head and waved his hand. "Nothing." Looking down at Jefferson, the detective said, "I wish you had come to us first. As soon as she approached you, you should have come to us. You didn't have to give her any money for her to be charged. You didn't need that as evidence." The detective sighed and shook his head. "Well, at least you're going to be all right."

This time, I nodded with Jefferson.

"Thank you, Doctor Blake. We'll be talking to you again, when you're stronger. And, we're really glad you're doing well."

Jefferson smiled and leaned his head back, closing his eyes. Just that bit of exertion exhausted him.

When the detective turned to leave, I glanced at Jefferson before I followed the detective out.

In the hallway, I simply said, "So … ," because what else could I say? There was so much for me to absorb. I wasn't sure where to start, I didn't know what to ask.

He nodded. "We found her. And she had something to do with your husband's case. She, and the guy she was taking your husband to meet at that bodega in Washington Heights, are both facing charges."

"What guy?"

"Apparently, Ms. Lewis has been doing this for a while, with a partner, who gives her marks advances on their credit cards. It's a pretty elaborate scheme, but one they've been working for a couple of years."

"Wow!" And then, I paused because I couldn't decide — did I want to know why she was blackmailing Jefferson? Did I want to know what she had on my husband?

The detective peered at me while I battled those questions in my head. After a moment, he said, "Mrs. Blake, there was one thing I forgot to say. From what I've been able to put together so far, Lola Lewis has made her living blackmailing innocent men. "

I released the breath that I didn't even realize I'd been holding.

"Innocent men, Mrs. Blake. Your husband was innocent, he knew it, but I guess he thought that he had to pay her the money before he could come to us. I guess he thought that exchange would be the evidence." The detective shook his head. "This is the second time I've had to give this advice about this case, but when your husband gets well, please tell him to stick to his day job." And then, Detective Green did something he hadn't done in all of my face-to-face interactions with him — he smiled.

"Thank you, Detective."

He nodded. "When your husband is able to communicate better, the DA will want to speak to him, but right now," he held up the small pad, "this will do." With a final nod that was accompanied by another smile, he turned and strolled down the hall.

I pressed my hand against my chest and felt the pounding of my heart. I wondered if it had been slamming against my chest the whole time. I didn't know.

But what I did know was this felt like it was over. I still didn't know what this woman had done with Jefferson, but I was pretty sure I knew all that I needed to know — that my husband was innocent. And the only three words he could put together was 'I love you.'

There was so much thanks that I wanted to give to God and for a moment, I wondered if I should call Hosea. I hadn't seen him since Wednesday, which had been surprising, and now, I had this good news to share.

But then, I thought for a moment. I thought back to the last time I saw Hosea. And right then, I knew there was a reason why he hadn't been back. With the tips of my fingers, I touched my lips — I'd forgotten about that kiss.

I didn't know it then, but that was our goodbye. Now that Jefferson was awake, Hosea knew that Jefferson was the only man I needed.

I smiled at the wisdom of Pastor Hosea Samuel Bush. I would always be so grateful for how he'd helped me to keep it together and keep my faith.

But now, my husband was back.

Right as I was ready to push open the door to Jefferson's room, behind me, I heard, "Lunch is served." Nicole laughed when I faced her. "Are you ready to get your grub on?"

I nodded. "I'm ready. Ready to do anything with you and your father. Ready to live our lives out loud."

"That's what I'm talking about," Nicole said, not even aware of what she'd just missed. "My mom and dad. Together forever. No matter what."

I pushed the door open and let Nicole step inside first. She had no idea how true her words would always be.

chapter 33

Kyla

Epilogue — Two Weeks Later …

I wasn't sure how many times the word miracle had been used for my husband, but as Nurse Debra rolled Jefferson out of the room and the staff began to clap, I knew they were looking at my husband as the miracle that he was. I was sure of it because the tears in their eyes matched mine.

My husband was going home.

Dr. Reid stood in the center of the group, leading the applause.

Jefferson squeezed my hand and I glanced down at him. Then, he turned to the other side and looked up at our daughter.

To the team who'd taken such good care of him, he said, "Thank you. Thank you. Everyone."

His words were so crisp and clear, still short sentences. But the speech therapist said that he would be fine. As did the physical therapists he'd worked with daily since he'd awakened.

Dr. Reid handed me a folder. "These are all of his discharge papers. I've faxed them to Cedar Sinai, but these are your copies for the nurses who will come to your home. And, all of your prescriptions are in there as well."

I nodded and then, gave my own thanks to Dr. Reid, hugging him tightly. There was no doubt in my mind that he was God's vessel, used to save Jefferson's life. After the doctor, I went to each of the nurses who'd cared for Jefferson as if he were a member of their own family. It had been twenty-four seven for a month and we'd had not a single issue. All we'd received from each one here at Harlem Hospital was love.

It was like a receiving line as Nicole followed me, and then, each one on the staff gave their personal goodbye and best wishes to Jefferson.

The most difficult thing was when Nurse Debra began to roll Jefferson toward the elevators. Nicole and I waved at the nurses and doctor until we couldn't see them anymore. The air was charged with all of our emotions and inside the elevator, Nicole wiped a tear away.

"I don't know of another time when I've had such mixed feelings," my daughter said. "I'm so glad to be leaving here, but it's sad too. This had become like home."

I squeezed her into one of those side-body hugs and at this moment, I was so grateful that I didn't have to say goodbye to her, too — at least not right away. She was traveling back to Los Angeles with us and would be there for the next week before she returned to Beijing.

When we stepped off the elevator, Nurse Debra gave us the last instructions. "Now, the medical transport knows that he has to stop by the Plaza to get your luggage and then, he'll take you straight to LaGuardia."

"Okay," I said as we stepped out onto the street. It hit me that this was Jefferson's first time outside in over a month and I wondered what it was like for him. The squint of his eyes from the sun's brightness and the smile on his face from the sun's warmth, told me that he was just fine. He loved this city and I couldn't wait until we came back. Maybe this would be our first trip once he was well, to visit the staff here at the hospital and to make that trip that I so wanted to take back to the Empire State Building.

Nurse Debra pointed to a van at the corner. "There's the medical transport."

We'd taken a couple of steps when I heard, "Kyla!"

All of us faced the voice.

Nicole spoke first. "Auntie Jasmine," she exclaimed as Jasmine and Hosea trotted toward us. "And Pastor Hosea." She hugged them as soon as they were in front of her. "Oh, my goodness, we've missed seeing you."

"I'm just glad we got here in time," Hosea huffed, out of breath. "We were coming from the church and got caught in a bit of traffic in the Uber, so we jumped out …."

"And ran the rest of the way," Jasmine finished for her husband. "We didn't want to miss you." She looked down at Jefferson and smiled with the warmth that was reserved for the dearest of friends. "Jefferson," she said his name softly. "It's good to see you. It's good to see you well."

He smiled at her. "You too. Kyla," he looked up at me, "you helped. Supported. So grateful. Your husband."

"Oh, my husband." Jasmine turned and Hosea stepped forward. "You two haven't met."

Hosea reached out and Jefferson took his hand. "Well, we've kind of met," Hosea said. "You and I spent quite a bit of time praying together."

Jefferson chuckled. "Grateful. Thank you. My wife. My daughter."

Hosea nodded, understanding Jefferson's message. He glanced at Nicole, but then, his eyes rested on me. "It was my pleasure to be here, to support them. The two of them, Nicole and Kyla, they love you very much."

I nodded, understanding Hosea's message, his way of letting me know that he understood me.

Jefferson turned to Jasmine. "Wow. So long."

"I know. Twenty years, can you believe it?"

Jefferson shook his head. "Doing well?"

She glanced at her husband. "I am. I really am, Jefferson."

"Pastor's wife?"

The way he said that, we all laughed.

Jasmine said, "I know it's hard to believe, but I'm the First Lady of a church here in New York."

"Wow."

Jefferson added a couple of syllables to that word and we laughed again.

Then, "I really hate to break this up, but we've got to get them in the van. They have a stop to make before they head to the airport."

I had forgotten that Nurse Debra was even with us.

"Oh, I'm sorry," Jasmine said.

"No, don't be." I shook my head. "I'm glad to see you. And I'm glad you had a chance to see Jefferson ... awake."

The medic driver jumped out of the van and Hosea said, "I'll help you."

As the nurse rolled Jefferson to the curb, Hosea followed them and Nicole turned to Jasmine.

She took her hand. "Auntie Jasmine, please don't let it be another twenty years."

It was because of me that all Jasmine did was smile. She made no commitment, just pulled Nicole into an embrace. "It was so good to see you." Stepping back, she added, "You've grown into the beautiful woman that I knew you would be. And I'm so proud to know you." She hugged her again and then Nicole kissed her cheek before she turned to the van.

That left just me and Jasmine. Alone. In the middle of what felt like hundreds of people passing by. Standing on this corner, my fourth Saturday in New York.

I spoke first. "You stayed away, why?"

She shrugged a little. "Once Jefferson woke up and we knew he was going to be all right, you didn't need us and we didn't want to intrude."

"You were here from the beginning, you wouldn't have been intruding."

She tilted her head. "That's what I said to you when I asked you to stay with us."

"Touché."

"Hosea did call every day," Jasmine said.

"I know. Nurse Debra asked if it were all right to give him information. I told her it was."

"He called every day and ... "

"He prayed every day," I finished for her.

And then, we laughed. No, we giggled. The way we used to when we finished each other's sentences.

"Okay, well, your husband is securely inside. You better get going," Nurse Debra said as she rolled the wheelchair up to me. She hugged me before she returned to the hospital.

Turning back to Jasmine, I let a silent moment pass.

"It was you, wasn't it?"

She squinted. "What?"

"You tracked down that woman, Lola Lewis. You tracked her down for me."

She bit the corner of her lip. "Who told you that?"

"Nobody. I just know you ... now."

She glanced down at the ground, saying nothing. And that right there, let me know for sure that Jasmine Cox Larson had changed. Detective Green hadn't said a word about who had given him the information. But I knew it was Jasmine. It had to be. That was why she'd been with that woman. She was trying to figure it out.

But she wasn't going to tell me that. She wasn't going to take the credit.

Her eyes were still on the ground but when she looked up, we spoke at the same time.

She said: "I'm really sorry."

I said: "I forgive you."

Then, we blinked together, neither one of us wanting to cry.

She said, "If I could take back anything in my life ...."

I nodded. "I believe you now, that's why I can forgive you."

She took in a couple of deep breaths. "Well, I don't know what this means."

I shrugged. "Maybe it means that we can talk a couple of times a year — at least on holidays, maybe birthdays."

"Okay." I could tell she was trying not to sound too eager.

Stepping toward her, I held out my arms. And we embraced.

She spoke as she held me. "It was good to see you, Kyla." There were tears in her voice.

"It was good to see you, too." When I stepped away, I wiped the sweat from my own eyes. Taking her hand, I said, "When you go home, tell Jacquie and Zaya that ... Auntie Kyla will see them soon."

She pressed her fingers against her lips as if she were trying to push back sobs and I turned toward the van where Hosea waited at the open door.

Stopping in front of him, I paused, I smiled, and I let him pull me into a hug.

"You are such a good man," I whispered.

He stepped back and I noticed the way he made sure that his head didn't turn toward mine until we were a bit away from each other. "Well, if I'm a good man, it takes one to know one. And there's one waiting for you in there." He opened the door wider for me to slide inside the van.

I said, "Take care, my friend."

"You do the same."

Once I was in my seat, Hosea closed the door on this trip to New York. As the driver pulled away from the curb, I only had to reach a little behind me to hold Jefferson's hand.

"Are you safe in there?" I said, knowing that he was well secured in the wheelchair that we'd bought and would take home.

"Yup," he said.

"All right then." I looked across to Nicole who was beaming at me. As if I'd just done something right. I shook my head, but that didn't stop my own smile.

I did feel pretty good. My husband was alive and would be fine. My daughter was happy and would be spending a week at home.

And then, there was me — I'd learned so much over these weeks through the wisdom of Hosea and Nicole. So many lessons, but the greatest one came from God. What the Lord said was true and always would be ... forgiveness indeed, would set you free.

*If you liked **Temptation:
The Aftermath**, check out
It Should've Been Me*

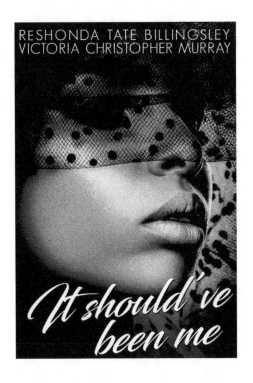

Enjoy this excerpt …

Chapter 1

Tamara Collins

In my last film, I'd played a psychotic woman who stabbed her husband in the stomach thirty-two times with a Swiss Army knife. Now, looking at the man who'd just stepped into this huge conference room made me curl my hand into a fist as if I were holding that knife again.

"This cannot be happening," I mumbled, as I stepped to the other side of the room that had been set up in the Renaissance Hotel for our first rehearsal. I pivoted, so that he wouldn't see me and I could get my face together in a few seconds.

I was already upset because this jacked-up, twenty-degrees warmer than normal Atlanta temperature had turned my Brazilian Blowout into a Philippine Poof. Now I had to deal with this, too?

Clearly, I was being punished for something I had done, maybe in a previous life. I didn't believe in reincarnation, but that was the only way I could explain why I hadn't had a movie role in two years. Or maybe it wasn't punishment. Maybe it was because my name wasn't Cameron Diaz or Jennifer Anniston or that my skin wasn't the color of mashed potatoes.

Yes! That was it. That was the reason why I was in this room, an A actor (okay, maybe an A minus or at worst, a B plus) on the play circuit.

Now, don't get me wrong, I loved theater, always had, always would. Some of the greats — James Earl Jones, Cicely Tyson, Vanessa Williams, even Denzel Washington — had all slayed the stage. And August Wilson's "Fences" — now that Pulitzer Prize winning play was one of my all-time favorites. Having a role in "Fences," on the Great White Way, in the magnificent city of New York, would have been as much of a coup as just about any big screen movie.

But this wasn't "Fences" nor was it "Aida" or "Fela." And this wasn't Broadway. This wasn't even off-Broadway, it wasn't two blocks over from Broadway. This was down the street, around the corner, across the river, and almost nine hundred miles away from Broadway.

And once we began touring, we'd leave Atlanta and go deep into the 'Chitlin Circuit,' probably visiting cities I'd never heard of and towns that sounded like the butt end of jokes.

I did have a little secret, though. One that I would deny if anyone ever asked me – I liked these off, off, off, off, off Broadway plays. Over the years, I'd attended quite a few if I happened to be in the city where one was playing. Of course, I made sure I was unrecognizable, always wearing huge sunglasses, always wearing a hat *and* a scarf, always keeping my head low so that no one would know that, I, Tamara Collins, the classically trained actor, laughed at all the off-center jokes, swayed to all the off-key songs, then stood with the audience at the end, giving all a standing ovation.

So while the title and some of the scenes ruffled my classical Yale University School of Drama sensibilities, I couldn't knock the thousands and thousands of fans who enjoyed these plays and the thousands and thousands of dollars that I was being paid to bring my talents to the stage.

Glancing over my shoulder, I checked to see if I'd been spotted yet. But *he* was still talking to Gwen Tanner, the creator, writer, director and producer of this play. After taking another moment and a deep breath, I sat in one of the chairs lined up against the wall. When I was ready, I raised my eyes and stared. Because him seeing me, and our having to speak to each other, was inevitable.

This made me once again ask myself what was I doing here? It had started just about a month ago. My agent, Maury had received the script from Gwen. I already knew her name. She was new on the play circuit and she was the first female to have massive success. Two plays, two NAACP Image Awards, and lots of buzz for the uplifting messages that followed the slapstick comedy. After I'd read the script, I was even more impressed. Yeah, it had the typical female-on-female hatin', female-on-male drama, but at the end, there was a powerful message of never allowing anyone's voice to be louder than God's.

So with Gwen's reputation, the ten thousand dollars per week they were paying me for the ten-week run, plus two weeks for rehearsals, and the sad fact that I had no other offers, I'd signed on, knowing it was the right thing to do.

That was what I believed when I signed the contract two weeks ago. Heck, that was what I believed yesterday, this morning, five minutes ago. That was what I believed until Donovan had walked into this room.

Donovan Dobbs, the hot R&B singer and a heartthrob who'd been commanding the stage and stealing hearts for twenty years, ever since he was sixteen years old. He could even act a little, but his major talent – he was fine. It was like God decided to toss Michael Ealy, Blair Underwood and Idris Elba into a blender, hit start, and see what came out. Yep. Donovan was the personification of brown and beautiful.

And he was a low down dirty dog.

"Well, well, well …."

My plan had been to keep my eyes on him. But I guess as I'd taken that little jaunt down that lane filled with bad memories, Donovan had spotted me.

"If it isn't the love of my life." His tone sounded like he wasn't surprised to see me.

He was still several feet away when he'd said those words, and I could feel the others in the room pause, then stop and watch as Donovan walked my way with his signature strut; he had swagger before the word had even been invented. He had swagger and that smile. The whole time he kept that smile that I loved. That smile that I hated.

"So, when did you get in?" he asked when he stopped in front of me. He opened his arms, then reached for me as if he was crazy enough to expect some kind of hug.

I wanted to hug him all right. And if I'd had that knife from my last movie, I would have – hugged him and stabbed him straight in his back. Instead, I glared and hoped that my stare was filled with the heat that I felt. I hoped my stare set him on fire, and I swear, if I saw a single flame, I wouldn't even spit on him to save him.

Standing, I didn't part my lips as I moved away. I heard his chuckles as I stomped by, but though I wanted to stop and swing on him, I kept marching until I was right in front of Gwen.

It didn't matter that she was chatting with one of the other actors. We hadn't all been introduced yet, so I had no idea what role the tall, svelte, with a tan that made her one-degree above white, woman was playing. I didn't care. There was only one piece of business on my mind and Gwen needed to handle this now. "I need to speak with you." It was a demand, not a request.

"Yeah, what's up?" Gwen replied, giving me just a quick glance.

"Privately," I said.

The actor, who I pegged as a newcomer since I didn't recognize her, gave me a smirk with a little attitude. But before I could roll my neck back at her, Gwen said, "Camille, give us a minute," and the woman did a moonwalk away from us.

As soon as she was out of earshot, I hissed, "What is he doing here?" I jabbed a finger in Donovan's direction.

When Gwen and I looked his way, Donovan winked.

Gwen grinned and I wanted to puke.

By the time she turned back to me, her expression was stiff with seriousness. "Who? Donovan?" She gave a little shrug, and then with a wave of her hand that made the dozen of wooden bangles on her arm jingle, she announced, "He's in the play."

My glance took in the woman who was really quite striking in the floor-length West African print duster that she wore. Her sister locs were swept up on top of her head and wrapped in a matching band. But right now, I didn't care that she stood in front of me like she was some kind of African Queen. I was the star of this play, and she needed to address the problem I had with this.

"I assumed that he was here because he was in the play," I snapped. "What role is he playing?"

I guess that was the question she was waiting for me to ask and the one she wanted to answer. Her grin was back when she said, "He's playing your love interest."

My nostrils flared and my fingers began that search again for that knife. But I stayed calm, remained professional, though not even my Yale training could hide the fury in my voice. "I thought Jamal was my leading man."

Jamal Brown was the R & B singer turned reality star, who didn't have the voice or the looks of Donovan. But what he did have was my approval. Seriously, my contract said that I had approval of the man who would be starring opposite me.

"Oh, yeah. Well, he had to drop out at the last minute," she said as if that fact were not a big deal. "He got a movie deal."

Wait! Stop! What? My thoughts did a little rewind. A movie deal? For a moment, I wanted to keep the button pressed on pause and ask, 'What movie deal?' because this was the problem. This was why actors, like me, couldn't get roles. Singers and reality stars and everyone who couldn't act were landing contracts and taking parts that rightfully belonged to those of us who'd been trained.

But I had to come down from that mental soapbox and stay focused on what was in front of me.

"So, Jamal left and you're telling me that you couldn't find anyone else?"

Gwen tilted her head a little, frowned and stared at me as if my words had put her into a state of confusion.

Clearly, she had no acting training. Or maybe it was just that no matter what she said or did, I knew what this was all about. Everyone in these United States of America knew about my drama with Donovan – it had been covered by every gossip blog, played out in every major tabloid, and dissected on every entertainment show. So Gwen casting Donovan in this role was no mistake. She was trying to take my drama and my pain all the way to her bank.

"Tamara, I'm sorry if you have a problem with Donovan, but the show opens in two weeks." Her tone was saccharine sweet, leaving a bad aftertaste in my ears. "I'm grateful that Donovan was even available on such short notice."

"Well, I'm not about to be in this play with him." I folded my arms and raised an eyebrow. She needed to know I was serious about this.

There was no way Gwen would ever be able to convince me that this was a coincidence. First of all, my mother had always told me there was no such thing as a coincidence. And secondly, I was just supposed to believe that she'd written a script about a woman who'd been left at the altar and now I was to play opposite the man who'd left me right there?

Oh no! I wasn't about to become fodder for the tabloids and the blogs and the shows again.

"Now, Tam," Gwen said, her sweet tone still in place.

"It's Tamara." I snuggled my arms tighter across my chest.

"*Tamara.*" All of that sweetness was gone when she said, "I know you're upset, and I'm sorry I didn't realize this before …."

Yeah, right. She must think I'm BooBoo the fool.

"But I know you wouldn't want Entertainment Tonight, Access Hollywood, Black Voices and every other entertainment outlet to know that your ex ran you off from a professional production, would you?"

I was not impressed because whatever they said about me leaving wouldn't be nearly as bad as what they'd say if I stayed.

I kept my stance and that made Gwen add, "And, if that isn't important to you, just remember, you have a contract."

"And?" I smirked.

"And, you know contracts are binding."

That made me stand up straight, lower my arms, and stare at her as if her brain had just fallen out of her head. Was this heffa threatening to sue me? Over a freakin' stageplay? A Chitlin' Circuit stageplay?

"Look," Gwen said, taking a deep breath before returning to a more natural smile. "I don't want any disgruntled actors, but I have a show to put on and I know you're a professional. You're one of the few talented black actresses out there," she added, I guess believing that flattery never hurt. "I have all the confidence in the world that you'll be able to handle this." Then, she leaned in and lowered her voice as if she were about to share something with me like we were just girls. "Don't let him get to you."

I wanted to tell her first, that true thespians of the female persuasion preferred to be called actors. And then, *don't let him get to me?* How would she handle this situation?

I knew I was trapped, but while I would never admit it, I wanted her to admit one thing. "You did this on purpose, right?"

"Oh, you give me too much credit," Gwen said, making her bangles jingle again.

Yup, she'd never taken an acting lesson a day in her life.

"Look, while this play bears *some* resemblance to your life, trust me, it wasn't done on purpose. Besides if you think about it, it's not really that close to your story. You never made it to the altar, remember?"

My fingers began that clutching thing again.

"Is there a problem, ladies?" Donovan asked over my shoulder. I didn't even turn to face him, not acknowledging him in any manner. Well, at least not on the outside. Inside, I felt a little flutter, and I cursed that right out of me.

But while I tried to do nothing, Gwen flashed a smile. "And why in the world would there be any problem?" she said, her glance settling over my right shoulder. "I was just going over some last minute script changes with Tamara."

"I'm looking forward to working with you, Tammie-Poo," Donovan said.

I whipped around. No, this fool didn't call me by the pet name he'd given me when we'd first met.

"Whatever," I said, shoving my way past him.

He scurried after me. "Hey, hey, hey, I've been looking forward to this, baby. What's the problem?" he asked, taking my hand and stopping me.

I looked down to where he still held me, then my gaze inched up until I met his eyes. I snatched my hand away and hissed, "You're my problem."

Stepping closer to me, he said, "Please don't be like that. There's a lot you don't know. So much that we have to talk about."

I blinked. Inside his voice, I heard something – like truth, like love.

He moved in what felt like the slowest of motions: His hand

raised, he reached toward me, his fingertips grazed my cheek.

And a wave rolled through my center.

Inside, I cursed again. This time I cursed my libido and Donovan. Squeezing my legs together, I wondered why my own body would betray me like this? I hated him and I needed every part of my body to remember that.

His hand lingered on my cheek for too long, and I slapped him away. "Look, Donovan." My tone was as sharp as the edge of steel. "We're both here now, so we'll do our jobs and get this over with."

"Great." He exhaled as if somehow my words had given him relief. As if he'd been concerned that I'd walk out the door. "I was hoping you would stay and now, I hope this means that we can hook up …."

"What?" I exclaimed.

"For a drink. Tonight. I just want to talk."

Hook up? A drink? To talk? After I let the gall of his request settle in my mind, I said, "Donovan, you want to talk?"

He grinned and bobbed his head up and down like a puppy.

This time, I was the one who leaned in closer. "Then go home and talk to your wife."

He blinked.

I added, "Your wife, remember? The woman you left me for."

I did one of those moves that I'd learned in freshman drama – a half-turn pivot, before my arm swooped down into the chair where I grabbed my hobo, swung it over my shoulder, and then I did a slow, hip swaying strut right out the door.

Want more? *Order your copy today …*

www.BrownGirlsBooks.com

CPSIA information can be obtained
at www.ICGtesting.com
Printed in the USA
LVHW031803300821
696476LV00014B/284